HELLACIOUS

DAINEI TRACY

ISBN:

978-1-916529-46-5 (Paperback)

Cover design by Lynda Mangoro from original by Dainei Tracy.

The Unbound Press

www.theunboundpress.com

"Hellacious feels like a Labyrinth which pushes you into yourself to feel into concepts and ideas of the structure of human life. So it pushes you into places that call for a deeper wisdom within. It is unique."

- Leo Rutherford author of seven books including *Spirituality versus Religion*.

"How do you manifest a felt sense in fiction?
What Dainei Tracy embodies in Hellacious certainly honours Shelley, Orwell, Atwood, and more recently Carriger... but it is not just a mash-up of slipstream, speculative evolution, psychedelic and steampunk...
It is truly genre-defying... it has an invented yet tactile lexicon which resonates throughout. The language, the longing, the labour starts to live in you as you read. We know we're not in Kansas anymore from page one, but yet it's so utterly our present...place and time. And the narrative, though firmly internal, brings you into the protagonist's world, inside and out. Page after page, if we listen to Tracy's juxtaposition of contemporary and feminist-futurist language. We can slowly deepen into a felt sense of the other-worldly Core she has created. What starts as jarring, seemingly intentionally, slowly starts to percolate inside the reader, while Tracy interjects biting yet heart-warming surreal humour and defiant will-full-ness... Until we find ourselves ensconced in a realm which is both our world and not our world."

- Jack Volpe Rotondi, Author/ Editor/ Coach/ Voicework

"Awed at your creativity that emerges from your words, and the story containing the felt expression. I need some words to reflect back my experience reading. It's as if I am discovering the eruption of reality that's been buried, not just in me but in all of us."

- Deirdre Fay, Yogi, Therapist and author of three books including '*Becoming Safely Embodied*'

"This is a masterful work of art and spiritual invitation. Channelled from deep dimensions of source energy, the text and illustrations are alive with liberating potential, 'working on us' at embodied levels to dissolve binds and exhume our true, infinite and collective selves, through extraordinary play on language and archetypes. Hellacious is an explosive yet heart-grounded contribution to the dismantling of patriarchal systems of oppression — so don't be surprised if you start to feel more free, real, earthed, fired up, connected, ancient, and whole, simply by reading it! Dainei created this book over many years; it will last for far longer and initiate important changes simply by existing, and by our daring to engage with it to the same degrees of courage and deft readiness as the author's."

- Mary Hartley Platt PhD (Oxf), Reiki guide & meditation teacher at enteringthestream.co

"Hellacious is a powerful book. It throws our conditioned responses into disarray, whilst its purpose of sparking a more open mind unfolds the more we read on. It supports you, the reader, to delve deeply into inner and outer worlds through your own non-linear wisdom and invites your intuitive self to come and play.
Dainei Tracy is choosing to use language in a way that deconstructs and brings to the fore our inherent creative and wise dreaming. It is a whole different consciousness at work, which invites you to discover how your conditioned self can drop away in the challenge of experiencing your core, becoming your true self."

- Christa Mackinnon (MSc), Psychologist, shamanic teacher and author of three books, including the bestselling Hay House book *Shamanism — Awaken and Develop the Shamanic Force Within*

How do I begin to describe this book to you, dear reader?

It's hard to convey the journey you're about to go on (if you allow yourself). But a journey it most will certainly be. One that is mysterious and magical and may well confuddle your thinking mind.

And that's where the potency is.

Because logical, thinking minds that would prefer everything to be neatly laid out in a linear fashion, making perfect sense, have been FAR too prevalent in creating the reality we're living through right now.

A reality where oppression and inequality are rife and violence is commonplace.

Maybe it's time for a little (or a lot of) *NON-sense*?

My first experience of connecting with *Hellacious* was when Dainei read some of her initial writing for it in the mastermind group I ran for unbound writers. As words, both known and unknown, cascaded forth, each of the women in the circle, including myself, spontaneously went into some kind of trance. Our conscious minds couldn't quite compute, so they switched off and let the unconscious take over.

We were transfixed.

As she finished, there was a stunned silence. What the frik had we just heard?

It was like nothing else any of us had ever experienced.

But one thing we all agreed upon, especially as Dainei shared more in future sessions, was that there was a deep truth in the story she was weaving.

We were introduced to a new language with words like 'Kigal', 'Wom', 'Uld Fire' and of course, 'Patron' (not pronounced pay-tron, but pa-tron). Whenever she mentioned this particular word, I felt my body respond, stiffening, bracing, ready to defend.

Because although this language was new, there was a familiarity. I knew this world. I am of this world. It's just that countless illusions have been obscuring my view.

Until now.

Now you'll get to learn this language too.

What Dainei has brought through here is quite stunning. When I got to read the first draft of the entire manuscript, I found I had to take it slowly, a few pages at a time. This is not a book to skim. In fact, it would be impossible to do so. It's one to savour.

So, savour my friend.

Let yourself be taken.

Don't rush to make sense of the words you're about to read.

Instead allow yourself to tumble into the truth.

Swimming in deep waters.

Remembering.

Are you ready?

Nicola Humber

Founder of The Unbound Press

Contents

WELCOME to HELLACIOUS — THE INVITATION: A few words on navigating this story — 9

S-HE SEAS — 29

BEGINNING THE DESCENT — 35

BITTY AND IMAGO, THE GREATEST GRANDEST DAUGHTERS OF THE WOM — 45

THE SHADOWS DO NOT PART CASUALLY — 57

THE ARENA OF THE RINGMASTER — 61

THE VAGAL SNAKE — 67

THE HOLE TO THE FORT OF THE KIN-MON — 71

PARTING THE SWEET SORROW — 83

THE JUNKANOO PARTY — 93

THE TITAN IS WHO? — 99

THE BIRD-SNAKE PART — 107

HELL-BENT DESCENT — 111

THE CLOSET OF THE SCOLDING PSYCHOPOMP — 117

THE CHOD WOMS — 125

THE GREAT NOT FEELING IT — 129

PARTLY CLOSER TO THE *KiGal* — 137

THE IRON MAIDEN — 143

UP THE BLIND ALLEY — 147

THE TURNAROUND TO FACE THE GREAT DISSONANCE — 153

THE FELINE PACT — 157

THE PRELIMINARY SHARDING — 165

THE TABLE OF THE WOM — 171

THE IS-LAND OF NO PARTING — 177

THE MIDDLE PARTING — 185

THE JOY OF CORE — 189

SPILLED DIRECTLY TOWARDS THE *Ki-Gal* WITH BITTY AND IMAGO — 195

WHAT IS SO TRUE ABOUT THE RE-AL ANYWAY? — 199

PART OF THE SHARDED KIN-MON'S DILEMMA — 203

THE MEDUSA PEERS — 211

THE PATRON DIRECTLY ATTACKS — 217

THE SHARD PART — 225

THE GREAT ALONE — 239

SPIRALISING — 243

ANIMUS AVATAR — 247

SHH, THE PATRON IS HERE, BETTER LISTEN TO YOUR BETTER — 255

THE THUNDER-STONE							261

THE CLITORANGEL							273

THE LOVE HOLE							277

COMING HOME - AND STILL A GIRL WILL NOT COME OUT OF SAMADHI. I MEAN, WHY WOULD SHE? WHAT'S IN IT FOR HER? BEING DEEMED SO UNWORTHY BY THE MALE SPIRITUAL HIERARCHY? (AND DON'T GIVE ME THAT 'BEING OF SERVICE' BULLSHIT.)							281

A MERRY DANCE AND WHEN WE LEAD IT							285

CODA — WHEN KIN-MON ARE IN CIRCLE							289

THE TERMAS							293

Resources and Further Exploration							301

About the Author							303

WELCOME to HELLACIOUS — THE INVITATION:
A few words on navigating this story

"You may not believe in magic but something very strange is happening at this very moment. Your head has dissolved into thin air and I can see the rhododendrons through your stomach. It's not that you are dead or anything dramatic like that, it is simply that you are fading away and I can't even remember your name."

- Leonora Carrington, Surrealist, Artist

"Only she who attempts the absurd can achieve the impossible."

- Robin Morgan, Poet, Activist, Feminist

"You might as well answer the door, my child, the truth is furiously knocking."

- Lucille Clifton, Poet, Educator

This book is a creative act of power and a record of my lifelong spiritual adventure. I have crafted in both words and pictures the experience of one of my avatars, our Que-an, who walks in the psychic world planting seeds of vibrant life. She will, with you, embark on a journey that is lucid and psychedelic. A punky rebellious dream state that I call the Spiral; because it is fractal, an endless thread that unwinds and loosens any stuck inner patterns arising along our individual ways.

We move downward, or innerly, through organic phases and healing passes, intentionally exposing and liberating our imprisoned life force. Feeling our way to where our Que-an's spirit is embodied in a deep cave, within a presence I call the *Kigal*. This is the realm of Hellaciousness, a delicious hell, the place to experience who we could be when we allow ourselves to realise our generous potential. Where we will consciously release the punitive hells of old, enslaving previous world views.

My *Kigal* is a derivative of Ereshkigal, the oldest Goddess awareness that I could find in our written and biased histories. She gives tangible form to what I want to say in this book and, to me, she distills the energy of being exiled and neglected. Patiently holding the realities we have trained ourselves to hide away from in the collective unconscious, our shadow worlds.

She is known in Sumerian mythology as the 'Lady of the Great Place' and 'The Queen of the Night'. But this book is not a re-telling, I am not a historian, instead it is more an expressive freeform and intuitive original based on my own inner life experience.

When I move towards her and feel into her energy, she gives me the inspiration and grounding in the shadow realities that I need. She supported me as a presence to generate this book but I don't want to appropriate any other culture. Especially when even the one I have been born into doesn't reflect the real me and never has done. Because, as a spiritual and tenacious woman in defiance of all conditioning, all I have seen so far is that women in all cultures are only invited to have roles that feed existing androcentric religious structures, methods and doctrines. Which all miss out woman's innate spirituality entirely as the rich source of perceptive, empathic and sensual experience it is, on its own, without these structures. When experience is not shut down, neglected, traumatised or forced to function only in prescribed boxes. The rewards for which are meagre, but offered as though we should really want them, and then we are obliged to accept it all without question.

Traditionally woman is not recognised as her own centre, instead she is objectified, used and bypassed in service to whatever the religious and political creed already is within our conditioned minds. I am not talking about equal societal rights, that is just the beginning and should already be a given, even though it isn't yet. Straining to attain equal rights within existing systems has ended up in using all our energy, and in being asked to become pseudo men, which even some men don't want to be.

Ultimately in this book I am not interested in perpetuating any abusive and socially cruel hierarchies or ideologies, wherever they arise. I will rebel, and no, women, we haven't come a long way, we are still at the beginning, in many ways, across the globe, and even regressing in some areas. Being granted extra privilege politically does not make us more aware or free, and does not change any of the fundamental hierarchies.

Also, when I say women, I mean both gender and biology, and although I am angry, I am not intending to belittle any other identifications, including men, as a fallout from my anger: we all have our journeys - this just happens to be mine. I want to encourage every evolving conscious human that I can to stay alert and present as our evolution speeds up.

So I am only indigenous to myself at this time, as a white Western woman, and passionate about any common threads of peace, intention, love and empathy wherever they might fruitfully arise.

To me then, the process of rediscovering the *Kigal* as my symbol meant defining a more ancient and precognitive state of awareness already existent within us. One that is coming round again in a massive great swing, like a universal dowsing pendulum sweeping all in its path to balance our dominating, cruel, territorial and polarising current reality.

I feel, and it is the power of my anger that helps me to express feeling this way, that soon this awareness of each other as essentially loving beings will be fully obvious to us. We will know it is here inside us by how our whole world view, and the intentional actions we take, will be informed by empathy and connection instead of competition and division. We will see then, clearly, how our conditioning rules us and where we can usefully challenge things.

A tremendous support is on its way from this swing of the consciousness pendulum. We can understand this potential, we can be ready, and we can be in an intentional relationship with it. Sounds simple, but we know that there are also opposing forces, with other vested interests in manipulating our belief systems, to deal with as well. What is already in place wants to stay in place.

So, you, me and our Que-an, as we follow this Spiral, will help each other to expose our one undivided self, our compassionate Core, by way of meeting the *Kigal* in her imprisoned depths. My idea is that we are to become liberated enough to co-create with this coming awareness and ride Her waves. Riding these glorious waves of what I call the S-he Sea in an experiment which, hopefully, will inspire greater ways of making a kinder world reality to come.

The only thing we could potentially lose as we Spiral along is outdated grooming in the stuck loops of fascist mindsets and self-interested politics we have a tendency towards in this current world reality. I am including the ones that think they are the 'good' ones, too, for the purposes of seeing where we are truly unaware and where our Shadows can help us.

I have dedicated myself to the investigation of the true nature of reality my whole life, and then experienced regularly being shut down by the dominating reality mongers continuously. This has helped me grow a very enjoyable and hard-won fearlessness. This integration of my own fear, which is still ongoing because I will always connect with, and alchemise, the free floating fear around me as well, has created a magnificent result and an opening. This result is my feeling that the five thousand year old warring consciousness we live in now has to be digested, integrated and brought to the surface of awareness by us all, even if we think it is not us. It is us.

We can see this process of digestion in the seasons of growth, decay, nourishment and more growth in Nature, if this integration feels too hard, or even impossible, to envision. For we are Nature herself.

From inquiry, and then clarification, our true nature is revealed not only as the loving creators we essentially are, but also as the whole inclusive sentience of everything in existence, including mineral and plant life and the elements. Because consciousness is everything. It is just that as creators, rather than soldiers, victims or slaves, we are personally responsible for our own garden of awareness. Growing more abundant when we are in relationship with the whole, and have finally let go of the need to punish to feel protected.

The warring, polarising opponent that wants to shut co-creation down, with physical attack if needs be, will be what we will meet more fully within this Spiral and is what I call the

Patron. As with all my creative words the book itself suggested it to me. It does partially come from being patronised and controlled, but fear not, this attitudinal energy is not exclusive to men — although traditionally they have consciously and unconsciously perpetrated it, and been more rewarded for doing so by what was then created.

The Patron is more this coercive way of managing and controlling our current reality, and our planetary resources, that has outlived any value it once may have had. It plays out in personal relationships, in groups and organisations and in nations and cultures. It is an obsolete way of being to those of us who want better for our world. To those of us who are interested in evolving and not just surviving to destroy everything that we project on to as 'not us'; everything that we 'other'.

We have our inner Labyrinth, the receptive ear of our interpretive mind, to listen to wilder nature as She tries to tell us something, to balance the Patron. We can hear her communicate to us that her energy is us too, when we learn to work with and through our implanted fear, which I call the Shard, to shed the old consciousness of divide in order to conquer. It is the implanted belief that we can own power like a thing, that we can then trade, buy and sell it. Losing ourselves in distracting, and only fleetingly satisfying, transactions. When going just a little deeper would bring us to being interconnected power. Being nature. Being love. This book is about diving within towards this, in full awareness personally and intentionally, to nourish our collective human spirit. Just as we got to this place step by step, so we move through it step by step, shedding previous assumptions as the now badly fitting beliefs they really are.

It has been said, in the myth of Ereshkigal, that there are gates to pass through to reach her, and the price of each one is to take off layers of clothing, or protection and identity, as we move towards the deepest transformational destination of the Underworld or unconscious. I feel that at each shift in consciousness we let go of something; a belief that we might have previously relied on. To me, this means we have to continue to find courage, and befriend our own fear and stress, the more naked and unknown we become.

Reflecting this process, my original feeling for the book came as this large unnameable energy that grew more potent, in a gently insistent way, as years of linear time passed. I did not make the mistake of ascribing this energy to any existing religious belief system because those all required me to fit into boxes that at times were dangerous to my sanity and my integrity. Belief systems all eventually create inner dissonance and stress because they are static applications of reality usually filtered through the interpretations, and hierarchical expectations, of others.

I found over time that this energy was particularly roused, and surrounded me, when I was in danger as an autonomous being.

Such as when I had a knife held to my throat by a man on the street, after he had jumped me from behind. Being passive and a victim, as both he and my conditioning had wanted me to be, and not allowing this truer core energy to inhabit me would have meant things would have escalated in favour of my oppressor. I would be raped and dead, something I know by the amount of energy required to throw him off.

Core energy also inhabits me when I take risks to interrupt my patterns, change and get myself out of ruts. And it inhabited me when others, like my father, risked me for their own agendas and expected my full support when not giving me theirs. Sometimes telling me that they did it all for me, laughably.

I survive and I thrive just like our Que-an in this tale, because I work my way through not only these overpowering situations but also, more subtly, the situations that hold psychological knives to my throat. All the small unavoidable nicks, cuts and coercions of living. I do not blame, I discern, because I understand where all of this comes from and I hope to spark more insight in you, my readers.

Not my insight, though. Your insight. I am trying an experiment in story form to trigger whatever is ripe to come to the surface for however it lands individually. More than anything, I want to give your annexed energy back to you.

Because I have noticed that Core energy helps me gain my own autonomy and power within all my necessary challenges. I desire to be a co-creator with all creation, which I call the Infra, so I need to be able to work with consequences beyond the ones I have triggered myself. I am having a lifetime initiation in learning how not to abuse power and how to recognise the difference between power over and presence in. How my previous passivity — formed because I did not want to dominate anything, I did not want to be my father — had made me a pushover for any unconscious domination from others, and ultimately made me lash out when

I was overwhelmed and had reached the limit of my acceptance of being used.

This energy is what I call the S-he Sea, in the sense of the responsive, emotional and rising wise feminine of the coming loving future. She enters through the top of my system, near my Que-an's crown, and works her way down through my Vagal Snake (Vagus nerve) to my womb. Sometimes like a lightning bolt, sometimes a soft absorption. She spreads, and I am filled with Her. I then have my next conscious layer of experience which I embody and form temporary platforms of insight around.

This nurtures the Re-al me. Her message inside me becomes clearer which urges me to write and draw, to speak, hold workshops, and to create, all as the practice for birthing better and kinder realities. She brings me the courage to urge myself, and anyone else who wants to find out how to get free, when even good things feel dissonant, to look into the shadows and caves for all my hidden intentions and my own areas of unconscious entitlement and conditioning.

I will explain what I mean by unconscious entitlements; they are those areas of our conditioning where we take things for granted, so are no longer aware of their origins and any actions we take when lost in them. Every culture has them, no need to fixate on the more obvious ones. They are often revealed in the nature of what triggers our sense of defensiveness. This is the implant, the Shard, again. We don't realise we are acting or communicating from a place that we have been shaped into for purposes that we haven't had the freedom to choose for our selves. And are sometimes not even willing to be aware of. In my story we have been Sharded and we can't even feel it anymore.

The S-he Sea invites us to embody and create, with our dreaming forward, our current personal truth stories that support evolution, truths that we choose wisely and lovingly, being the echoes of Her bigger manifesting wave. So this is what I have done in my book, and this bigger, manifesting, compassionate wave I call the Re-al, as we move further in towards the centre.

S-he is an ancient, yet always birthing, contraction and expansion, and Her-story wants to evolve and take on new meaning to help anchor this next revolution of our whole Earths Spiral. This is why I am not re-writing any old traditions or myths, I am learning to be nourished by the energy behind our new stories in an instinctive and raw way.

I own this narrative and I take full responsibility for pulling the Shard out of my own mind and heart.

Hellacious is also fuelled by the relationship I have with my inner selves, particularly my petty tyrants; avatars of the Patron, whose shaming and domination of me through the edicts of its religions, and its culture-given powers actually stimulate my own energy and anger to balance it. The turns in the Spiral are how I, as our Que-an, engage with it as it attempts to impose erroneous duty and blame on me, especially that which arises from its own negligence.

And in still further twists and turns we will engage with Allies that are attracted to my struggle, to encourage me, as we all pass along the Spiral together.

One of the first and most constant Allies we meet is my Vagal Snake, the vagus nerve, who responds to protect and guide me physically, emotionally and multi-dimensionally. My Snake assists me, as our Que-an, throughout the spectrum of my ongoing experience as the dedicated part able to hold the focus of the whole journey. Even while the other force of the Patron seeks to intimidate, punish and terminate me for even attempting it.

The more I listen to and trust my Snake the less I feel that I am insane, or mentally ill, or hysterical, or naive, or lesser than, or heretical, as the implanted Shard of the Patron and its oppressive assessment of my reality would have it be.

My other Allies that come and go are the Shadows and the Echoes. The Shadows are all that is exiled within us, and the Echoes are the amplification of whatever is present and so can be either allied or hostile. I am the one responsible for creating the ground for whichever Echo prevails. This is always my own cry and where my true individual power of intention and choice lies.

So join me, dear readers, in my dream of integrating the Patron, and then wilfully create the potential of what our world could be like if this domineering force was given less credence within us and less dominion in our social organising. What then would happen to our politics and the old industry of war and it's recurring genocides, the extractions of our planets beautiful resources and the wilfully targeted slavery and rapes? What could that reality be like? How Re-al could it all become?

My way of describing the struggling humanlike groups, in an alternative, yet similar, manifestation to our current one are the Wo-mons, Woms and Kin-Mons. They arose from my attempt to parse out some traits that I feel could bear looking at more closely to reveal any unconsciousness. In the sense that whatever we identify with we are still not realising how powerful our intent is, and how we are encouraged to squander it, so that we never stop perpetuating feeling too helpless to challenge the causes of suffering.

These challenges are all mine, and also more than mine at the same time. You may resonate yourself. Even just trying to write the book and writing this invitation to you right now, to read it, so close to the publishing stage, I am in a battle with controlling and shaming influences within. I feel lost and confused, dissonant and pinned down by a heavy weight. I feel guilty and rendered open to attack, as I struggle to dream and communicate what I feel inside. All because I am not attached to accepted concepts. Shame on me for feeling sickened by the status quo, the hierarchies of abusive power and mass murders being enacted worldwide.

This pernicious abuse of power, in whatever form it takes, wounds my inner masculine, the Kin-Mon, and I am castrated by this shame into impotent dissonance, just like everyone else. As a woman I can get my teeth into discerning it, having had to live under its arrogant assumptions in a particular way which will need no explaining to most women who are, in my story, the *Wom*.

What I see, and hope my experiment unfolds, is that the dissonance of behavioural and conceptual conditioning by hierarchical societies obsessed with top down ranking causes immense suffering. This directly and purposefully stops me and others from being free, creative, confident and happy independent spirits. The shaming has told me repeatedly, and extremely obviously, that it wants to restrict me from owning my own life and spirituality, and instead spend it in a series of predetermined roles that serve and preserve the old orders. It sees us as deficient and this makes us deficient, a self-fulfilling prophecy in living colour and available everywhere.

This oppositional force that channels through us all when we are unconsciously enabling it has also been, for me personally, an actual distinct more condensed and frightening vampiric entity with which I have engaged in astral and lucid dream battles many times, some of these forming my earliest memories. I know this has echoes in the incubus, succubus and predatory forces that some people experience as sleep paralysis, hauntings and panic attacks, and have been described over the ages in many different cultures. I invite you to consider that this could also be a prompting, from deeper layers of consciousness, to the possibility that this is a trickster phenomenon to show us where we are being enslaved.

To me, living as a spiritual being means centring my own feelings of love, empathy, vulnerability and joy because I can feel that I am evolving into the new awareness. It means that I am working through the socially implanted impulses of being reactionary and of being manipulated. I am especially integrating my fear of saying what I want to in response to my experiences. Instead my fear and suffering is a source of energy and a reflection of the collective experience. I am revitalised in a very harmonious way when I can centre in this transformative feedback loop, instead of being caught up in the old Shard implant as it tries to dominate me. This is why I have made it all into a story, it can be a flowering of insight when looked at in the context of how we have previously mis-organised reality.

When I feel the rising feminine calling, I know it all stems from my pre-existent ecstatic core. I call her the Core in the book and I hope you enjoy finding out what S-he is inside of you. To me S-he is our deepest inner place, connected to the intentional creation of love, always turning and returning to itself.

Maybe my story will inspire us to want to thrive and change the outer deserts of this current prison of consensus reality, instead of allowing it all to inhibit us. My invitation throughout is to be your own spirit and unwind towards your own true place. Just the energy of this feels potent, doesn't it? Pushing off the stifling weight of what is taken for granted as reality.

Throughout the book I will play with different words and meanings, some of which I have already mentioned, because there are so many givens and entitlements in the language that we use that we often find ourselves not questioning the realities they support. My hope is that the controlling and conditioning aspect of language will be exposed a bit more. This might take a while to get used to, but the new words and their explanations are in the glossary section called Termas for dipping in and out of. It was fun to strip away and recreate meanings and I hope you enjoy it too.

You might be interested to know that Terma means treasure in the Buddhism of medieval Tibet. Termas are writings or objects that are multi-dimensional, encoded and relative 'truths' that have been concealed and embedded, like nuggets of wiser conditioning, to arise when evolving consciousness has caught up with them and their hidden meaning becomes suddenly clear. Translations of old texts state that they were often buried in the ground or stone, so, to me, this can also mean that they are seeded in the collective consciousness like a spell, buried, hidden and incubating.

As an organic wild gardener, who utterly supports Nature, I love this, a magic intention kernel ripening and growing into its wise future flower.

The other thing about these spells of meaning, these Termas, is that because the languages of our world objectify everything, stripping away compassion continuously, creating separation, compartments, hunger for pseudo-power, and winners and losers, I wanted to shine a light on the use of language. Words are so often used as mind-colonising weapons that it is not surprising we begin to perceive everything as a threat to our stability and harmony.

We are the slaves and victims of hierarchical rhetoric on all sorts of subject matter. The way we have organised our attention, dominating nature and our lives is in service to the manipulation of power and ownership. It is time to dismantle all this, even if we have to make the effort to be a bit more forensic.

Then we will see who benefits most from these structural positions of power and that they are the most enslaved in the end, being paralysed by the fear of loss of privilege and position.

So join with me a while, and follow our Que-an as she descends and dissolves these layers of bondage and sabotage. Laugh with her and the Sheela-Na-Gigs as they irreverently defy the pursuing Patron. Let's be in a big relationship with each other moving towards empathy. Let's be the reflection of the wider, coming, compassionately conscious wave that we will embody even more than ever. For we are all potentially the whole spectrum of existence, even if we don't think we have personally experienced some of it yet. Not only are we our own ancestors and children, we are also all of everything and each other at the same time. We are the individual centres of the universe of love.

There is one last thing I want to bring up, which might arise in your own musings. It is that maybe universal energy is essentially neutral and that our true nature is not compassionate. If this is the open possibility, then isn't it even more up to us as individual creative centres to choose love and not punish or manipulate? Who else is here making this world? Who is deciding? With this in mind I haven't wasted my energy, what I call my precious Uld Fire, with feeding or placating the Patron in any form in my story, because the Patron is not neutral, it is supported by individuals who do nothing except fall into its trap of either shaming others or blaming themselves, and its intention must be exposed to finally empower its potential targets.

So my inner family, who I call Echoes, Woms, Wo-Mons, Kin-Mons, Shadows and more, are defiant emanations of the basic underlying matrix that I call Infra-connectedness. And my book is an irreverent telling of how all these seemingly separate beings affect and change the whole to become much more powerful and transformative.

Each recognisable part of ourselves, existing inside and outside us, can differentiate out and help define the edges of our blocks and sufferings and also show us where we can change the wider dynamics of our outer consensus reality, as to me, all is intertwined in this Infra.

We can be big and generous with the illusions of perceived polarities and keep our hearts open, especially when it hurts the most.

How rich and lucky we are in these opportunities.

Let's re-orientate to our own direct experience of our Core — us as love — and notice that when we are feeling our worst in whatever way, and can stay present with our, and others, triggers, then this is the opening to our own energy and maturity.

I invite us to consider the fact that love is showing itself to us, and is available again and again, in so many different ways.

Even when they are Hellacious.

We have been taught that hurt can be avoided by giving it to someone else. By hurting someone else, and that this is justified. That denial of abuse can be a fake virtue or a convenient way to perpetuate the warring status quo. The longer we all indulge in this, the sooner we will all kill each other.

So, challenge, challenge, challenge and define it till your head hurts and heart bursts.

You are the empathic outpost of us all and we are energised when you embrace all the relations within you, every single one of them and us.

Don't reject.

Differentiate.

Find your true name.
You Hellacious morsel of Everlasting Nectar, you.

Dainei Tracy, Writer, Artist, Infra-Dimensional Explorer

THE ILLUSTRATIONS ARE:

a pouring of gloriously imperfect tantric visualisations that form linkage and express the sacred display of the descending Wise Feminine Flow.

All are healing mirrors to connect with you deep inside your being and reflect back to you anything that could be stuck. They will spark more and more of your precious awareness, keep looking.

The Wise Feminine is a tunnel, a sacred vagina, that can hold spirit while it transforms and individualises into matter. Seed swims through it to reach our eggs, and the generated beings journey back along to be born.

This is a Core inspired miraculous process.

We all experience this ecstatic becoming, through the many returns of being born and giving birth.

Life and Death have not a hair's breadth between them.

If we are aware, then we will notice this inner process throughout our own life-line, as we cast off old ways of being and their attachments, and are born into new ones. The experience is the same, and, as transformation, attracts that which we will work with next.

That which we will be in relationship with next.

From both ends of duality and polarity.

Whether we call it good or bad.

And whatever we perceive it to be.

'Alert

Alert

Relax

Relax'

- Machig Labdron, Adept of Chod

This is Hellacious,

The Dream biography of the eternally fresh-born Infra-Dimensional Virago, Que-an of the Re-al.

Enter direct experience.

If you recognise one, some, or many, of your own parts in this Dreaming, then good. It is all a pure reflection in the pliable Membrane of the many unwinding Re-alities of Us, the Infra-dimensionally free.

Here are some terms that are non-negotiable, because some boundaries are just too blurred by compromise. If you are irritated by these, because you don't want to learn anything that you don't already know, then say hello to your inner Patron and ask yourself who is in Fucking charge here anyway?

S-HE SEAS

"I am come in very truth," Bacon declared, "leading to you nature with all her children, to bind her to your service and make her your slave."

- Francis Bacon, 17th Century Patronic Scientist

'Nothing's got me,' she said. 'There's nothing around. That was a lot of nonsense. Stepford's a fine healthful place to live.'

- Ira Levin, Writer

Let us make mankind . . . rule over the fish in the sea and the birds in the sky, over the livestock and all the wild animals, and over all the creatures that move along the ground.

- Genesis 1:26. Bible Patronic Priest Writers

1977
tracy

I have my bark for my skin and its crevices are places for my insects and my fungi, my worms and my worts, my lichen and my nutty bulbs. Together we move from shadow to shadow, a momentary tree, a spell of a sunbeam. A leafy length to reach beyond, to grasp a fruit and lick a drop of dew. I am the first *Wom* of Uld, and all know me here in my home.

We dine on each other, blessing our decay and growth alike and anew, the river erupting and showering over, ever and again in so many sweet De-aths that we go along with no arousal of the Fe-ar.

My fungal directions finger over felty stretches of pungent peat and mildewy soil all mixed up together in an orgasm of joyful stinking potency. There is nothing clean here and the bacterial cauldron laughs all day in the ultimate freedom of creation.

De-ath is our Life and Love is our play. We have no separate state to hide behind and we have no wanting to be other than what we are.

For I am all fulfilled desire.

I am the Re-al.

My desire, my wanting, is my energy and Uld Fire. Desire is the desert air that extracts all sounding waters, adding to the echo, falling on the bog. Desire is the coral fingers growing in calcifying watery polyps towards sun wrinkles, waving down through the air, sifting up through the water.

Dry to wet, to dry to wet desire.

I run through these forests of life and love and am held so tenderly in her weather and caves of sentience, that my *Womb* squeezes the moon in pleasure and the water bulges in and out.

Until It came.

And I am startled into a scream of terror. This is an unknown cold hand and mind that is intent on imprisonment of all else. Consuming and obsessive.

The whole of the Re-al convulses and retreats, closing like a sea anemone sensing stupid Patronic oil spilling.

I learn what to do quickly.

I cannot accept It as anything other than enemy, as it needs to be named.

I stalk It in Its camps.

I load my poisoned dart and moisten my lips to shoot my fatal bullseyes.

I spit, and kill as many of It as I can. Giving the bread of It to the soils.

It.

The Patron.

The destroyers and looters that we have not seen here before. We don't know why It has arrived and what has made It. We cannot see why It has come in this way and the suffering stench of It is killing us in the Re-al.

All her flowerings are trodden away with no care at all. Nothing is coming from It in the way of Infra-connectedness. Nothing. It is a zombie of unconsciousness.

What is this huge change the harbinger of? Despair seeps into all our corners.

I am desolate for the first time and I grow my awareness bigger to meet the desolation. Great grief fills me, overflowing into my rivers and flooding the Felds.

I cannot kill enough of It to make a difference and I slide softly away and underground, the mud parting gently to receive my form.

But just then a Shard is shoved into my He-art through my mouth and I take this with me to the deepest parts and hollows. I hold it within, and stem the bleeding sorrow enough to form a lasting leathery scar with a fibrous vinery to keep it steady. Binding it in layers of webbing from my Empathic Gland. I rebalance and settle in the crystal caves of deeper still. I send out one last call to all the Wom and Ulds in warning.

The Echoes of this cannot be stifled and it will find its home in the Labyrinths that sound the responders to the Re-al. The resonators.

Listen.

Can you hear the current within your own ear that comes from your own blood and beat? Can you hear me, the S-he Sea, calling you now?

This is the sign that you must gather your Shadows and call your Echoes to meet me down here.

The implant of my Shard reverberates to the Patron and It knows where I am, but It will never know how many others will arrive in this hearing. This deep listening. It will never know how many will work through the Dissonance It is causing and deal directly with their own Shards or even avoid being Sharded altogether.

This It will never ever know because the seed of the Re-al is wildly scattered, finding other Felds to gather the intensity to redress the suffering and capture this It, the Patron, which cannot feel, only conquer.

To eat It, to chew It into chyme, to return.

But first we must find Its He-art, if It has one, and flick the switch of Love and Longing in the centre of the centre.

So, you, *Wom*, do you hear this?

Listen deep in your curling ear.

Hear the squalling S-he Sea.

I am your *KiGal*.

Come.

Find me.

BEGINNING THE DESCENT

It's hard to be always the same person.

- Dorothea Tanning, Surrealist

Story solutions lessen fear, elicit doses of adrenaline at just the right times, and most importantly for the captured naive self, cut doors into walls which were previously blank.

-Clarissa Pinkola Estes, Poet, Jungian and Cantadora

"I warn you, I refuse to be an object."

- Leonora Carrington, Artist, Surrealist

*"The soul was not cured,
It was as full as a clothes closet
of dresses that did not fit."*

Anne Sexton, Writer

So, let's do this.

Right here is our Que-an, first, and the central one from the Core of all of this.

For those of you who are seeing in this current now dimension, whatever that means for you, and by all means take a moment to even notice what this might be:

What does this *now* dimension... I am in... mean for me?................

(moment taken, but you may need more. So, please, take them, as no-one else will be giving them to you specially.)

The Patronic dictionary definition of Que-an is, "an impudent or badly behaved *wom*-an or girl, or a whore."

Can you Fucking believe it? No, really, look it up right now and spit that hallucinogenic tea you are drinking right out of your gorgeous mouths Loves.

Therefore in the terms of this particular Spiral of Hellaciousness, in its very own power of Now, this would be a *Wom*, or someone who emanates as such when stripped of the usual visibility. Including all the inner trapped animas of the partisan Kin-Mon and all the tonal clouds of the many skinned *Wom*s and *Wo*-Mons and all the Echoes and the blessed evolving Beginners and Enders, too.

The Hole spectrum.

So that only leaves the Patron as non *Wom* in any form, and not able to access the Re-al or the Core consciousness at all, or ever, in Its current closed code, and with Its intentions of Sharding all else.

We are all repositories and victims of the Shard of the Patron, because we are all potentially subject to being Patronised, and awfully conditioned to do the Patronising ourselves. If we didn't have this potential, then none of this would even be perceivable.

Time for a quiet contemplative smoke. Be sure to get in all the far corners and be savvy about it.

Since the olden and gentle One Sight Uld, from the times of the Re-al, had retreated to their own Feld, so as not to be trumped or trampled on by the Patron any more than was absolutely necessary, the remaining *Wom* have found that they can be invisible to the Patron and escape being Sharded, or being fodder for Its Great Dissonance.

The *Wom* had consciously embraced remaining in the Dissonance made by the Patron because they had the intention of reversing the situations that were feeding on the suffering of any who could not retreat on their own terms. Because these vulnerable beings, who could not retreat on their own terms, were trapped in a battle with the Bardo Factories of said Patron, who wanted their energy, their Uld Fire, to create the false wealth, at the same time as making them pay extra for it.

Lose, lose basically.

All the *Wom* ever did, to not be targeted, while they worked on some kind of skilful engagement with this intransigent state of affairs, was merely practice exploring their own intuition.

Intuition.

Following their own hints of desire.

Awareness turned around.

To down in the He-art Belly Body.

Autonomously liberated. No, not automatic... autonomous. Do I always have to spell it out?

It is always thus in any embodiment. Spiritual autonomy must be established firstly, or we are forever uselessly engaged and wasted. Even if not easy to do once you've been Sharded, because as Shard, you will only be acceptable if you exist in your talking head and have taken up polarising positions as a hungry believer of your own side.

Exploring intuition is a process of increasing self-trust and very much frowned upon in Patronic closed circles because, well, obviously if you trust yourself then you are going to question a lot of what passes for okay in the Bardo Factories, aren't you?

Going to be too enquiring and penetrating and challenging and whatnot.

So, Loves, time to be in a trusting and welcoming relationship with all arising parts of ourselves, whilst being intuitively aligned with this arising, specifically for the intention to stay present enough to continue to self-liberate... no matter what a Patron thinks is happening and tries to project on-to your flow.

Doing it?

Splendacious.

You have found the secret that makes the *Wom* Infra-Dimensional, and delectably elusive to the Patron. If we are in the process of continuous self-liberation we cannot be Sharded for long, if at all. Big secret to forget, but don't worry, we will be reminding you about everything, all the way through this Dreaming Spiral here.

The thing is, being intuitive in this way was becoming sadly more revolutionary, as in mutinous, and was losing acceptance, with much less compassion being freely available to all, because of already mentioned prevailing trends.

Apart from this giant Fucking hitch, the best of it is that in doing intuitive exploration, the *Woms* attracted the rapturous support of more of the Uld Fire! As well as all the Knowings of the Re-al. And this amazing be-doing development in the *Wom's* intuitive activities next led them to realise that the encroaching Patron could not even see them when they were being so Re-al.

What fresh joy is this?

Big glorious breath.

As they shift delightfully in and out of Infra-Dimensionality, the precursor and precious font of all Empathic Core skills, they are hidden right here in plain sight. This talent shows us the gate to the sheer Hellacious way of the *Wo*-Mon, always entirely unique to her owned individual self, even when vilified. So therefore, with no reference points to be pinned to, they could wend their own becoming and realise their potential uninhibited.

And not be cultivation for the Patron in any form.

At all.

What is usually called:

A Result.

So.

There we go.

Spiralling round to here, with our Que-an, and it can also begin in any being, at any time. Like with you, now, for instance.

Be like our Que-an, who at this point on her realisable Spiral of descending, owns herself, her life and her Manor. All Membranes intact and strongly pliable, becoming more and more invisible to the Patron with her repeated retreats to the Infra-Dimensionality. Which was showing up in more freely available Knowings.

The rule held beneath her own thumb was this; that it is better to be fully stung awake and aware, either gently or not, and really Fucking explore it all thoroughly, than to never feel the prick of the clean pain that opens your He-art Belly into its vulnerable Sacred Display.

Because without some kind of this impeccable attitude, you will never see through anything at all, and will therefore be fodder for something else, and here in the Great Dissonance, that is usually the Patron.

If I was diplomatic, and maybe feeling chastened, then I would say it might not be that... you being food for the Patron. But I'm not being diplomatic or cowed right now.

I want.

To.

Deal.

With.

It.

Directly.

This rule of feeling the clean awake pain is deep in our Que-an's birth bones, stemming from her own *Wom* line of lives lived, which being the quintessence of her seed structure, meant she'd never had to fall awake and be startled, as she was always already alert, willing and able.

In the words of her Great Grand *Wom*, the Labdron;

Alert, Alert,

and...

Relax, Relax.

So it also meant the remembering to relax all her Strings, be attentive to her He-art and her Shadow, and welcome the unexpected, which was always happening, in a timely way, or at no particular time at all, and could not be anticipated. So there was no point in not actually being ready.

In this she is Virago.

In this she is full Bitch.

All good and ready then, thank you very much.

Here, in this place, there exists, at all times, the Encroachment against the Membrane of her Manor, of the Patron. It is just a fact of this life. You could describe it with all sorts of justifications, solicitudes and softenings, but it is what it is, and here, because of the importance of spelling it out, even though we have said it previously.

We will be dealing with It directly.

If, on a more Re-al reflection, it turns out to be as harmless as It likes to make out, well, then let that reveal itself.

Yeh.

Right.

But for now, the way it dominates everything, destroys the Re-al and slices through delicate and important harmonious Membranes left, right and centre, warring and scarring, we will not be the one to be caught napping.

Oh no.

Not us.

Eh, Loves?

Let's descend... going down, hold on to the one just ahead if you need to.

Our Que-an is in good company in her descent with us, as she works the passages and galleries of her Manor. She opens her one-pointed awareness through her He-art Belly and on into Core, doing sweeps of all the different kinds of dusts and distilling their immanent Knowings of sacred materiality, ultimately refining everything into her Empathic Gland.

Some of these constantly evolving chores include monitoring the hovering Egregores and other thought forms, and dusting all the stuck Fucking Relics. Not exactly exhausting, but definitely a bind at times.

Soon she notices that, every so often, there is a squeeze on the inner side of her He-art Belly plexus, next to one of her Fascial Knots.

This is familiar... even though it's been a while.

It feels as if it is starting to struggle against its own beat, as though something Re-al is arising from within, trying to find the space to express a truth. She intuited that this had to do, first, with the general inescapable effect of the Great Dissonance. Then, with all her absences recently, the popping out of this existence in order to grow in her other dimensions.

At other times, it felt like the missing part of the pulse from the Core that was being mysteriously obscured ever more regularly. A signalling of the slowing before the quickening, perhaps.

How will she, then, in these fine, so called ordinary days, orientate deep enough Under to delicately play the strands of her Strings that knot so sensitively and responsively to the rising demands in the pull of her descent? Would her already very pliable Strings lengthen even more?

It did seem likely.

That this was a space creator coming in on the cards.

These slowing's of the He-art Belly are gestures that it will soon be time to walk within her Uld Fire. For which she had a Knowing that it would evoke the long overdue calling of Eresh, the Grand *KiGal* of the *Wom*.

Here it is at last, she saw, the deepest rumble within the continental drifting of the Felds, and with the Re-al wanting them to part and open the Way Under, too, well then.

Let's do it.

"If this is the start of my own journey to the Under, then I am relieved," — so decided our Que-an. "I will walk with the lead of my He-art and feel my way along the String of my own truth into my Spiral. I have been holding off on this for an extremely long time and I am not sure why. But I know the Dissonance increases, whenever I have tried to descend before and I feel it is gaining on me now. Something does not want me to succeed so independently of It, and I can feel the wordings tighten to hold me in Its specious and captured place."

Feeling a lessening of the pent up-ness, at the same time as feeling that deep calling of the unknown, our Que-an had a moment of delicious uncertainty. A touch of moist fever secreted from all the pores on her skin and her hair knotted and unknotted itself in wavelets.

She rode the release of this, musing; keeping her own kind of thought forms fluid and her intuition juiced, which she felt as a running up and down in her central channel of Uld Fire. Firing off any fixed states that would grow into hindrances before too long... if she let them.

Just as she had been practicing throughout all the Encroachments by the Patron on her Spiral. She fetched her biggest drum from the broom room to vibrate the Labyrinths and the He-art Bellies, and found more bells to sound the Echoes into amplification. She thought maybe some canticles of rhyming slang and definitely more Fucks would also be extremely useful.

She also Knew she would need to plant the Thunder-Stone of the Uldermentals, those familiars of the Wo-Mon, who support Woms, and now, more specifically our Que-an, and us, Loves, in our Hole spectrum, throughout this undying Uld way of Under.

She had no clue at all how to find the Thunder-Stone, which is a good thing, as then she could be open to it finding her instead. Already a very relaxing approach and very anti-Dissonance. She felt herself widening luxuriously to the Re-al as it grew again within her, for this was a prerequisite for turning the Dissonance on its head.

When this had all dissipated into the clarity of seeing what the Patron was ultimately doing, then all would willingly open unafraid and pound the rhythm of recovery.

"Sounds like a plan," her Shadows whispered encouragingly. At this, a booming started up in her He-art Belly and her Hole-ness shimmered with delicate expectation, as her nails started growing faster and her hair unfastened from the wavelets and undulated in patterns of weedy joy.

Her Great Grand Wom had prepared her for all of these signs when she was still a speck seed, as she herself had prepared her own kin.

Ahhh!

To be deep within the Under in full Infra-dimensionality.

Mmmmmm. Mmm. Mmm.

To meet the beloved *KiGal*. Especially as now any revelatory power journeys, to anywhere, at any point on the Spiral, were all banned by the Patron, as Its penchant for totalitarianism raged here and there. It thought It could stop anything It couldn't control.

I know, do please have a giggle with your Sheela-na Gigs right Here-Nowish, Loves.

Yes, we can see that the Patron does have influence on the surface of things, as we are all constantly and tediously reminded. Which is why It appears to be so powerful. Anyway, being so concerned with only creating damning stereotypes and sycophantic intellectual validations, which anyone not directly concerned with Re-ality is always a sucker for, not knowing they are being farmed.

Contrarily this Uld Way was what her own *Wom* had shown her just the once, before she herself was caught and impaled by the Patron. Sharded, she was, straight between her beautiful breasts, leaving her He-art Belly all completely bound up in the S-hame, with only a beat every month or so.

If that.

But don't say anything, because even that one beat was still more Re-al than anything on the surface, and continued to dispel the Dissonance over and over. Slow potent origination that will not be constrained.

S-Shhhhh.

Then the Patron had pettily blocked all the Under chambers, decapitated and de-tailed almost all the Vagal Snakes they could actually catch, and closed the paths to the Knowings of the Under. Imprisoning all hope beneath their heroic, conquering, hah Fucking hah, brave new world by Sharding and burying the being of our dearest phenomenal and original Eresh the *KiGal*.

Greatest Uldest Grand *Wom* of them all.

This was the real ushering in of this awful persistent time of the Great Dissonance, which we all have been living in ever since, boxed up in a dominant applied reality as food for its own perpetuation, with no discernible wisdom to ever comfort us in truth. Doing time in the prison of the Patron, so It keeps reanimating Itself in a closed loop. Destroying the Re-al E-arth and her Felds, and driving away the Seeing Ulds.

Fucking fabulous.

Enjoy.

Not.

BITTY AND IMAGO, THE GREATEST GRANDEST DAUGHTERS OF THE WOM

Giving shape to a painful experience is powerful because it helps us to see, first, how we got through it; second, how we can share it. The experience doesn't stay trapped within us, unspoken, curdling - instead, the art of arranging and transforming it reduces the burden. It no longer belongs to only you.

- Karen Bender, Writer

Re-ally.

So back to within this particular stirring of the stirrings that whirl through our Spiral. Our Que-an's own *Wom*-Seed girl daughter, who is partly herself and partly a previous Que-an, was growing up fast and innerly focused, because of all the One-pointed attention in the Manor.

Our Que-an, like all *Wom,* has always a Hole in her being that holds the energy field of the incoming eggs. Even if one never comes, either when expected or not at all. And even when they have born themselves, or not, it remains as a place to rejuvenate. Once one egg has come and gone, they can always come back at any time, but also any other egg may be attracted to the ever present attunement, and will become very cosy and cared for within this same nesting Hole, because it is always egg-shaped. It is connected to Core and so is indisputably Re-al and always tender.

We've all got one.

So one stormy day with a lot of thunder and lightning from the reclaiming Uldermentals of the Re-al, this reclamation is a constant activity, in order to support the wild and free and balance the extractive Patron, our Que-an's Seed girl had a growth spurt with an amazingly directional quality and a full-blown need to start to own herself without having to be in dependence.

Wow!

It is time!

It is even more than time!

She took the name Dear Imago from the witnessing Shadows, who uproariously declared full evolution as they applauded her impressive spread-winged action. While our Que-an demurred any naming with no second or third thought, because when it is the elusive obvious, there is no point in pretending it is otherwise. Or even the wise other.

Imago Spiralled off with all the fly by night attitude of a non-returner to the same place twice, or the forever born already. Because you never return from anywhere else the same, which could also mean that we are never where we will stay... but only if it was looked at in a Re-al way and we realise we actually are on the Spiral. But don't try it, if you don't want to — might be a bit too Infra, and you are the choice you make; it is utterly yours.

And so this soulful beauty, our Que-an's sinistral daughter was away to make the dance with her own Will and harvest these, her own precious fruits of Knowings. She preferred all her Spirallic turnings to take a left-leaning winding arounded-ness so that her chosen expression remained eternally free.

Namely, whether the invisibility from the structural Patronic prison can be individually dissolved by design, as an unnecessary hindrance, by entering into the Dissonance He-art Belly first.

Dive in.

Come on in, it's lovely.

Hah!

Yeh.

Right.

Get in.

The leaving actually happened when our Que-an split in two, which she did rhythmically and regularly at the nodes of mid-nude moon. This being a tidal time of clear strength in dualistic awarenesses because here you can see both sides. This is the secret compassionate medicine of healing the way more poisonous, mind-stream splitting and polarising Dissonance, in which the pretence is that your own Re-al is dismissed as an illusion, thereby trapping your awareness into the dismisser's own agenda.

Alert!

Alert!

Remember this, the mantra of the Grand *Wom* Labdron because it will keep you from losing focus and your One-pointedness, and dropping off your Spiral and hurting yourself.

And then...

Relax.

Relax.

Then it became apparent also, that because of the cleaving of our Que-an, a gap had opened up in the scheme of things everywhere — in that fractal way of the Re-al, a riptide pulling and forming a whirl Hole, in the Membrane, where extra energy was leaking in from an Uld nether dimension.

These Uld nether dimensions had been distilled specially, from Infra-Universality, for extra support if overwhelming change and turbulence was triggered on any of the descents of the Wom. The Infra-Connectedness can always be depended upon if you are livingly aware of its inherent independent Re-ality.

So she decided first to create a second Seed daughter, with this surge of fresh vitality, out of the multi-coloured bits and pieces and parts of discarded psyches she found lying around near the Hole, left by the feasting Shadows. Usually left by the Shadows, but not always. Sometimes they were just exhausted bits dropped off by the many wandering, and by now largely homeless, *Woms*.

The Shadows — I know I haven't explained them yet, don't worry, all will be revealed — called this newborn Seed-*Wom*, Dear Bitty.

Our Que-an birthed this new and beautiful *Wom* babe from the psychic parts, mainly because she always up-cycled. There is no waste in the Re-al, because if anything has an existence, then that will include all of its consequences right down all time lines and all its stages of decay and De-ath. In the Re-al, no thing is discarded to be conveniently ignored and pile up in disused toxic trash Hoards, unbalancing the beautiful, already existing, and doing just fine without you, Terratoriums and Felds.

She also knew she was mostly in a transitory Emptiness, being in this bit of a split of having two minds popping in and out. As we all know, minds have a habit of multiplying when no-one has their Eye open. And as the Patron is the supposed purveyor of all so called acceptable states, so that It could assess who was too altered and needed to be S-hamed and exiled, one had to shepherd one's own minds regularly, just in case we got overly noticed. Without falling for anything, of course, just don't take it in as the ultimate serious moralistics.

After a gassy thrashing, she had been told by the Patron once —

and Know definitely this, that she had never specifically asked It anything in her life, never wanting to endure the repetitive conditioning Patronic spiel, but It still insisted on projectile idea vomit all over her... every time... anyway.

It told her that because she had no stature — being in the low strata, and was showing the intuitive leanings (Oh No! Not that again! That is just too Fucking Under!) that being empty of Its conditioning and agenda was wasting Its space and time. Anything could come and fill her (Prophet forbid!!), and she would lose all critical direction and not be able to push the required results. And besides, as It didn't want to feel her that way, she should really adjust to be of any use at all.

Well, thanks for the memory.

Criticism is a highly valued bouncing off technique, used by the Patron to intimidate, so that It doesn't lose Its sway.

As is pushing.

This particular Patron carried on, telling her she would become too naive, but at the same time implying that it would be okay though, to be just naive enough to be manipulated by It.

Nicely done, Patron!

I feel the shackles of a double bind coming on... can you feel it too, Loves?

And if she was to actually be of use to this system, then she would need to learn Its legals, and this meant internalising and enforcing these within herself, and others, through the directed sting of criticism and the bulldozing of pushing.

Now, naive was not something our Que-an minded at all in her birth bones. She had the Knowing that the naïveté of openness was the portal to the Re-al and she enjoyed her vulnerable free innocence, and all that open He-arted, walking right into it, and being hooked and reeled in like a fish, thing. But if there was one prick point she had learned at the hands and demands of the Patron, it was that she was responsible for far more than she could safely hold at Its command, without some kind of guile. Some defensive sophistication.

Some kind of boxing clever.

Her, and others like her, namely the *Wom* mostly, who all originated from the now shunned Under, Knew and supported the Shadow of all that was unacknowledged, exiled, Sharded and denied by the Patron Itself.

So she was already overwhelmed, before even anything else happened to pile on top of this absolute Fucking impossible loadedness. Suck this yourself, Loves, and see what it tastes like.

When she was first born from her, usually perpetually unborn Seed, our Que-an had quickly learned to be picky with her burdens, if she could get away with it. She had always held the intention to do her Uld Fire work in as transformative a way as possible, despite the prevailing stagnant currents of unconsciousness under this ghastly Dissonance of the Patron.

She didn't really want to discuss it either, as when she did, all energy was whisked away from her and she dropped into an energetic sink Hole which was not impossible to escape from, but tied up all effort for a considerable amount of time.

Ending up entangled in blaming creeds that purported to be so honest themselves that they were beyond reproach, so that... yes, you've guessed it, who ends up holding all that Dear denied Shadow?

We do!

But she had always already had the directionally Re-al idea, that the only true way out was Under, and that her disenthraled Uld Fire was intimately connected to the total liberation of all Re-ality, so there was some strength to be gained from what she Knew as the unconditional Infra-connectedness.

Just as was elucidated by the Uld, back in the days long before, and before even those days, in the pristine times of the beautiful and free Astrality of wild Infra-connected Felds of Re-ality.

A very long time heretofore.

Or a Fuck of a long time ago.

Screw this Dissonance.

I say.

Yes.

Yes,

Yessssss, this is a bored sigh though, not excited orgasmic yelling at all. We know, we know… many a messianic Patron, birthed from a modified sperm seed every two thousand years or so, had announced this very same utterance as though It Itself was the only, and most important, messenger of this over-advertised, but misunderstood, truth, and as though every time was the first time anyone had ever entertained the idea, Core or otherwise.

A kind of perpetual beginner's mind. Only, what might have we forgotten?

Have a think.

Here-Nowish.

Everyone adores this utterance, and latches onto it every time, as it Echoes the Infra. So, as far as the Patron is concerned, it's definitely worth the regular crack.

To keep up the Propheteering.

The Patronic prophets always announce everything is interconnected, do as we say, worship us as your better potential, and we will give you peace, protection and refuge, and realise that each of your liberations are connected to only our whole…

Echo…

Echo…

Echo…

As though this was revelatory, only specially revealed by It, and could only be embodied by It in Its own Patronic form i.e. non-*Wom* — they never got a look in, being only seemingly indicative of something vague around fertility, but also they never wanted it, as a poke in the eye with a burnt stick is actually preferable. Good thing too, as so many were burnt at the stake on sticks for eventually using their own initiative.

So there It went, being able to manipulate the truth for Its own end, and getting that end away nicely for many a millennium.

Spiritual ejaculation.

A kind of a spiritual sperm club.

What do you think? Maybe you are getting a bit irately self-righteous as one of Its religious outposts? Or no? Oh, listen to that Sheela-na Gig, Fucking laughing her tits off, now she's the One who's got it all going on.

Re-ally.

The Patron always double emphasised the imperative action of the closing of the Under and the Re-al, by promising Alleluia wings to all who would ascend to Its own dizzy height, and lots of sugar fat in-toxic-ant opiate prayer food, spiced with special punishments and penances, for all the hungry believers.

BUT, aping the Uld words and using criticism and abuse to enforce Its own ever-failing weak reality had never really cut it, fine or otherwise, with any of the *Wom* at all. It was just more of the same old lengthening of the chain of origination, so that everyone became more and more dependent on the Patron as the repetitive One who held the lead.

Conditioning you.

Inserting the Shard.

Promising security.

Promising you will be taken care of.

You will be part of something.

Is your neck collar feeling a bit tight?

Feel free to take a moment to figure out why…

… if you Fucking need to.

So anyway, do come back from that brink! Goodness, what have we been up to?

In the meantime, our Que-an has birthed our beautiful Bitty Seed girl, remember! Dearly loved super sister of her Imago. Bitty turned out, on all her sides and in all her parts, to be the finest ever friend to our beloved Que-an. They played and laughed so much that their Bellies became too full of the giggle. They attracted so many Sheela-na-Gigs that the shrieks threatened to upset the orders, but the safety of this fun was unassailable by the Patron. In this the budding *Woms* decreed they would not be stopped.

They learned and practiced the many skills of being their Uld Fire together. Their magic straying just far enough along the Spiral, spinning tops of crockery and costume whipped into crumble-weeds. Think of ordinary molecules turning into radiating waves that are sent toppling along parapets of luscious glee.

On purpose.

All the while, the signs of the Becoming Under gathering, and growing, into just the right and satisfying cycles of Spiralling motion. Not too hot and not too cold. Not too soft, not too hard. Out to apogee and back to perigee. All orbiting assuredly in a winding Undering Re-al wave, twisting forward and down.

So.

This being as it was.

Rest assured that this playful creativity is not the methods or solutions directed by the Patron as part of Its Great Educative Conditioning, designed to further you in Its own dimension. No, our Que-an steers any days firmly away from that. It was more the intuitions and instinctive creations of the Uld way of the *Wom*. Making truth of being enough, just as they actually are, not distracted by being traumatised, used and abused. Sorry, but this has to be stated as the fact that it is, and has been, and continues to be.

Just watch for It, so that you are not contributing to It.

Swelling and sprouting sustainable becomings of the Re-al, all abundant. Leaving no living thing without the kind of home that suits its own unique spirit and place in all its gorgeous thriving. Fostering the deepest respect and gratitude for how the Re-al actually reveals its wisdom, without the imposition and false projections of the conditioned Patron that seeks to only create an illusionary environment that serves Its tyrannical Sharding.

Bitty and our Que-an are free to weave sweet vast worlds in the Uld energies flowing from the infinite Infra-Universality of the nether dimensions. Knitting from the fonts of the Re-al. Whooping with the thrilling sound of cracking all their cosmic eggs at once, scrambling and releasing the barriers they had been enclosed by.

Increasing neverendingly.

Then, one glorious day in the Middle, Imago unexpectedly came back. Home to the Manor from her outside immersion, where she had been fully exposing herself to the culture of the Patron. Yuk. She confessed to gathering conditioned intelligence and had come back home because she, too, needed to find the Thunder-Stone of the Uld, to descend and unlock the energy of all this attracted and burdensome conditioning and smithereen it properly.

Going in, to get through, as it were.

She had literally just caught herself in time, before she was permanently confused, out there in the Great Dissonance.

Time to thank all our lucky stars.

Our Que-an was amazed that she had been so resilient and brave, the cool double agent. This is another sign that everything is on a down and down fabulous and unavoidable big change.

All three sensed an approving deep rumble from the *KiGal* in the Great Below and some fissures appeared in the garden as the vibration expanded towards a Gateless Gate, where the Membrane pointedly opened. Peeping at them with an interested Eye.

Bitty and Imago interlocked their own Eyes and their Empathic Glands synchronised as they gently circled each other in deference to this Spiral down-shift. Bitty had not seen her sister ever, although Imago knew about her, but had forgotten, so was surprised and intrigued at the strange connective tissues and likenesses between them.

They both became absorbed using their mutual fascinators right there in the entrance chamber of the Manor, which expanded even more in its welcoming. They faced each other a few paces apart and their dimensions collided messily with much joyful reorientation.

Eye to loving Eye, the deep and mysterious connected feeling forming along the line so far back and forth it was in even their own potential nano seed *Wom* daughters imprints deep in their Cores. In the eggs of eggs within the *Womb* of *Womb*s.

They were still a bit wary though, because wary is aware, and because to see each other this way is looking in the mirror S Membrane, where the reflection is not quite straight-on somehow and if you tilt and turn your head whilst thinking certain thoughts, you will tip right into a Void towards each other.

Abused by the Patron with S-hame, as mentioned.

But generally very transparent.

The S Membrane warps gently back and forth, a flag in the wind, or the wind in the flag, or moves not at all if your Eye is still. Which is another way of saying that what is really moving is your mind, as you wonder about all of this.

Why? Because everything is moving and still at the same time, potentially and actually. Ultimately anything moving is of no Re-al importance because if you stop Seeing then it is no longer there anyway.

Thus it has been said zenly.

If the Patron was here It would postulate this was not definable and would proceed to fill it with meaninglessness and assert that it cannot be proven to be present at all. You know, it's all your own illusion, like a zen monkey mentalism. Or that Its own Patronic materialism was unquestionable, depending on Its agenda at the time.

But who is saying what exists?

We are looking at the menu board of Dissonance, remember.

Luckily the Patron isn't here attempting to move our Mind's Eye away.

No, not luck.

Design...

THE SHADOWS DO NOT PART CASUALLY

"I've been to hell and back and let me tell you, it was wonderful."

- Louise Bourgeois, Artist

"Experience is never at bargain price."

- Alice B Toklas, Cook, Writer

"Spiritual progress is like a detoxification."

- Marianne Williamson, Writer, Political Activist

Up until this pivot of time, things had been fairly benign and tick-tocking along with all the pace of business as usual. However, the Shadows were growing again, waxing, in their own regular rhythm too. Starting to loom in the shade cast by all those Fucking Relics stuck in the corners of the Manor.

The Fucking Relics were where the Shadows usually first appeared because they hold all the unresolved energy of past trade, transactions, relationships and damned contractual karmic lineages. The Relics refresh the memories that otherwise would weaken, causing great distress to all and sundry who identify with, and depend upon, timely reminders for their individual, yet unhealthily dependent, existence.

Because of this dependency, Relics need to be cared for until they naturally collapse — literally, the molecules giving up their little ghosts. Or are given away to other Manors, which can be a long drawn out legal process depending on the amount of evolutionary cycles the kin-spirits have turned, having to be insight orientated, to get to the inner learning of the dynamic involved.

Not the time to hold one's breath then.

Meanwhile the Shadows grow and grow from this usually unacknowledged energy, while everything else waits for the completion cycle, sometimes for thousands and thousands of bloody and dusty Kalpas.

No-one has ever been able to put a time limit on it, and it is folly to estimate anything with such pungent karmic flavour, whose junctures are unfathomable and don't want to be divined.

It can be truly unbelievable at times.

However, if too many Shadows gather for too long, they have the power to create an extremely concrete Hoard, an Egregore that can be used as their own renewable energy supply. This is very difficult to manage and care for as a free being. And very difficult to dismantle without access to a Transformational Energy Advocate that would identify where exactly the lack of attunement resides along the central channel, and activate the He-art Belly to care for it and fulfil its own longing.

Transformational Energy Advocates are very hard to come by because they were banned by the Patron after 3000 orbits of Its takeover, when Its first Prophets arrived, signalling the end of the autonomous *Woms* natural peaceful enlightenment and imposing the first filters of applied cruel unrealities. The Advocates now therefore can only be obtained by visiting the boundaries of the Under and petitioning Eresh the *KiGal* herself.

We will be seeing how easy it is (hah!) to gain audience with Her by the turning of this Spiral as we drop down with our Que-an.

You have to shed the idea of anything that you take refuge in, at the same time as allowing integration with it, in a kind of digestion that does not abandon anything. Challenging enough on its own, it was becoming more and more complicated as the Patron deliberately put petty obstacles in the way of this, in Its insistence that the *KiGal* was only of the De-ath (only!) and that It had Sharded and buried her to execute this acting fact. The Patron needed everything filtered through Its own lens of conditioning, or whatever it is just does not exist, and as Eresh the KiGal was of the Uld Dimension and was unconditionable she was therefore the most enormous threat and a laughable idea at the same time.

To It.

The Patron would never come right out and condemn her, It would just subtly belittle the whole Under, saying that it was a measly backwater full of termagants, so that everyone was coerced into not wanting to be seen as not on the right side of the Membrane.

It was energy draining and time consuming to always have to be dismantling these subtle cues from the hierarchies of the Patron and so most souls just hoped for the best and went about their businesses. Heads down, spirits camouflaged, celebrating the small agendas.

How Fucking sweet.

Makes your He-art bleed, doesn't it?

THE ARENA OF THE RINGMASTER

"Where is the ebullient, infinite woman who, immersed as she was in her naiveté, kept in the dark about herself, led into self-disdain by the great arm of parental-conjugal phallocentrism, hasn't been ashamed of her strength?"

- Helene Cixous, Writer

"... use your faults..."

- Edith Piaf, Singer

Therefore it is now way past time for things to get a bit different Here-Nowish; or when looked at again, our Que-an's Manor has, for some time, been developing funky-like, accepting all homeless Shadows, not caring how light it looked, or dark. And the truth is, because of this, its Infra-dimensionality was increasing exponentially. Sprouting noisy offshoots of so many potentials that the Patron could never quite keep up with shutting them down.

It really was getting quite annoyed.

You could almost sympathise with It.

Could you?

Nah.

And so it actually was, in response to this extraordinary meeting of the two Seed sisters, that the Manor Membranes themselves began their own morphing process, and ended up as an Arena. Fully rounded and shaping the fishbowl, its centre ready for action, for experiencing.

So Gestalt.

I invite you to place a couple of chairs within this, within your own mind image, one for you, one for me. Let's sit. Here is a widening and invitational opening of the psychic space between us. Anything is possible here.

Mmmmm.

Let's watch the surrounding Membrane darkening into opaque ponds and eddying puddles, all stray light fading, except for the hub. Our Que-an, too, dims back into her own Shadow, so that all the glow centres on, and caresses, our Bitty and our Imago, maybe you and me, being the triggers of Love that reach across all lengths sparking everything out of stagnation.

Let's watch the filaments of challenge, hope and wonder reach back to plug into the sinks of loneliness and sorrow.

We see the central orb throb, emanating from within, erupting with all the dancing molecules fed by the evolution of Infra-dimensional goodnesses stemming from the inviolate Core. We see all the Shadows shifting in joy, twisting and turning, making and releasing their shapes, in a vast and holy display of graduating light, making it difficult to discern what is happening.

Battle, dance or communion?

Our Que-an knows that the only thing to do Here-Nowish is to become her most trusting innocence — naive or Knowing? Hypocritical? Or reflective of our truer more ambiguous selves? She wants to properly See this.

Let's do it too.

Peel away all layers of previous perception, adjust into the assemblage for seeing the truth of Here-Nowish, dissolve any stray conditioning of the Patron which is always a tedious and sticky chore, until we are in a totality of presence. Suspending all beliefs and disbeliefs, letting Here-Nowish tell its own self, at will, we becomes the Emptiness that is this precursor to all clear Seeing.

Yes, the very Emptiness our Que-an was warned against by the Patron when she was a Seed Sister herself. Emptiness, too, has become our Ally over all these endless, endless days of Patronic Dissonance, because it is the Seeing experience of the Infra.

Our Que-an does this suspension at the prompting genius of her Empathic Gland, deep in her wits, which has been ripening throughout. Secreting the fluid that drips along her Strings into her He-art and its surrounding nest of a sac, so that the whole pulse of everything slows to properly catch the nectar of ultimate clarity.

The slow dance of the sagest *Wom*.

The last thing that must happen is to fall into the Patronic projection that either Bitty or Imago must be some sort of winner in this Arena. That one of them has got it, which makes the other lacking. That this is a competition, because power and energy would then have to be attributed to one or the other. Ascribed to one or the other, so that they would then be recognised by the Patron, come racing into Its frame of reference, and the labeled loser then belittled.

Or one or the other must perform harder, longer, more diligently. Or one or the other must be hungrier and more desperate. Or territorial and more mean, doing, lashing out. All states that at best only delay the inevitable truth that competition is never the lasting satisfaction it likes to poke you in the Fucking Eye with.

Always meditate on what is unavoidable. There are no winners and no losers in the Infra.

Our Que-an does not wish these Patronic states on anyone. These are the values of the petty tyrants coming from their knucklehead sets, and although they have their place in evolutionary terms, maybe... and as tools of manipulation, certainly. In actual experience, the Patron is unconscious of Its Shadow, and this denial of the existence of the natural dark has created too much suffering all through the Infra at whatever point you choose.

Because, Loves, this is the cause of the Great Dissonance, say it again, the denial of the other side of the Spiral always appears in your Shadows. And as the Uld wisdom says, if you can still open your Labyrinth, because you are in touch with your intention to be Re-al, then your Uld Fire will lovingly follow your thoughts, your feelings and your emotions, so don't let it all leak too much, just let it be and honour that you are actually alive... for now anyway.

In addition to this miracle, Uld Fire also follows attention, and therefore this attention is really a creative force directed by intention. Stay attuned because the Patron is dead set against individual creativity, it has to be certificated to be real and It controls all certification, of course. Like It fondly imagines It controls the *Wom* and the Membranes and everything else.

The magic of this creative forward Dreaming has always been a little bit beyond the reach of the Patron, although It understood the principle very well on Its own terms (i.e. hierarchical, architectural, educational, industrial, religious, political and technological projections. Oh, and we mustn't forget... scientific... facts — hah, Fucking hah!), and so Dreaming has never reached its full potential in any of Its organisings. Maybe we should be thankful for small mercies.

But back to the Arena!

All the Shadows have filled the outer edge while we have been musing. Each one feeding off another, weakening, strengthening, locking together and coming apart. Around the one central glowing light of the happening, to which they joyfully owe their existence today, and in which Bitty and Imago stand like mother mountains, their silhouettes steadfast, illuminated and reassuringly solid.

Suddenly, between them, there appears a Ringmaster, all golden lapels, badges of honour and epaulettes. Ringmasters materialise when there is the potential for an equipollence of Light and Shadow. They are not from the Patron, thankfully, though you could be forgiven for thinking so, given all the uniformity. They are an Infra-Dimensional class of Echo beings who are directly responsive to incidences of potential conflict between the Uld Way of Under and the antithetical way of the Patron and any accompanying imbalances leading to more Dissonance.

However vague.

It only has to have a hint of it and a Ringmaster will show up. But they will not stay if there is nothing to stay for. They are not He-art beings with Strings, or responsible for outcomes; they are just honest brokers of light and shade with no agenda of their own.

Sounds kind of refreshing, especially if you think it's going to give your own agenda more space, time and attention, right? The reason they appear is created by this manifestation of Membranous uncertainty that has not come to the attention of, or yet been shut down by, the doppelgänger light of the Patron.

So as the light and shade of the happening continues to intertwine steadily, we watch as the Ringmaster holds up his arm-sleeves and sweeps them across the numinous circle of the Arena.

He announces, "Behold! The wall of Zoo." As the glassy, see through but tough barrier Membrane flows in from the outside circular rim and cuts the circle neatly in half.

In the soft S shape.

Like the line of division of the Yin-Yang with its holes eternally leading into each other. Round and round and round, in and out and in.

Balls and balls of holes and holes.

The Shadows are all hugging themselves and each other, still forming a cloudy mass threatening rain, weather-beaten and raw.

Our Que-an feels the tickle of a new inner space like a bearing down, compressing her diaphragm, just a little bit stifling, entrapping, cuffing her attention back to the edge of the circle. Her breath shortens and she becomes more vigilant.

This is about to get interesting and feels urgent. Our Que-an channels an urge to pee and takes the String energy in and up instead.

Imago steps forward in total confidence and signs a sigil with her spit on her side of the Membrane. She signs a large Z.

A sharp S.

SZSZSZSZSZSZSZSZS.

And although you can only see it from a certain perspective, our Que-an and her Shadows Know it for what it is. It is the foretelling of psychic danger and the great Infra-Dimensional trial on the Spiral to come, with all the challenges to freedom that is this Great gouging Dissonance.

But both sisters remain calm and centred in the big face of it, and look at our Que-an expectantly and with piercing interest, for here is their future too, coming in on a dive.

The Ringmaster calls out to our Que-an,

"Taste it!"

And our Que-an's mouth fills up with her own spicy saliva and she is sure she is going to vomit.

Puke.

Rush.

THE VAGAL SNAKE

"A myth is far truer than a history, for a history only gives a story of the shadows, whereas a myth gives a story of the substances that cast the shadows."

- Annie Besant, Activist, Theosophist

"A thinking woman sleeps with monsters."

- Adrienne Rich, Writer

"Pythoness body — arching
Over the night like an ecstasy —
I feel your coils tightening...
And the world's lessening breath."

- Lola Ridge, Poet

But instead of vomiting, she felt her inner energy spine of Uld Fire crawling upward, turning serpentine. Her He-art Strings tuned themselves, not too tight, not too loose. Just a harmony of chording. The Ringmaster called more of it out, clearly instructing,

"And… Dear Que-an, do look behind you."

At that moment a large Snake's head detached itself from the watching Shadows and filling the gap between our Que-an and her daughters, curling, enveloped the whole situation.

A Vagal Boa.

It propelled her attention with a lick of its long tongue inwards toward the centre of the circle of light, and she could not feel in her Strings if she was going to go Under, or beyond. She had to let go of any specifics. Our Que-an could see that the intention of the whole experience was now revealing itself, and had changed course, for the encounter was now about to enwrap and enter her.

Her daughters had this Knowing already and tenderly encouraged her with their gentle gaze along the S Membrane. She was ready, having shed all preconceptions away that might have concluded in a probability.

Her two daughters' Eyes, in each of their own halves of the Yin-Yang, now seem to usher her into the deepest central seam of the osmotic dividing S Membrane's fascia. As in entering the space between the quicksilver and the glass of the mirror body.

She altered her awareness into the magical, harnessing her second Infra and third Core attentions, riding her Uld Fire in her central energetic spinal channel. Feeling her way slowly and gently along this particular line of focus, she left behind the first attention, that preliminary separate awareness that is aware of the Other, the Patron, and danger. Because she felt that, here in the Arena, was a support that would protect her while she adjusted her facings and her intention.

The direction now being to become the whole feeling awareness, expressing the totality of herself with and without an Other. Both and all arising Others and Echoes.

Access this power within you right now if you feel safe.

Now this is Fucking exciting, right?

She then immediately knew what this Initiation was and how everything up until now had been leading her to this point. She inhaled and grabbed her Snake, which was now coiled and waiting at the base of her spine, with her delicate breath and silky speaking tongue. She claimed it by giving her completeness and her undivided attention, completely attuned, making all follow in flow.

This, however, is not a surrender. That is another turning, we might go there later, we might not. This is having the learning inherent in all experience condensed into a conscious power that can be directed for ultimate good. Oh okay, we just want it to transform that blasted Patron. That would be good enough though, wouldn't it?

This, Loves, is skill.

And all her Echoes came together in the sweetest singing.

The drum in her Labyrinth thrummed and wove into the Snake's mouth, which rose up into the centre of her shining skull, into the centre of the fork in its tongue, and her He-art Strings quickened with joy and the uprising music of the primal zenith of the Core.

She was arriving.

In full occupancy.

No suicide needed here.

She entered her Vagal Snake and it entered her. Completely Ouroboros.

So it was that everything soundlessly and gently shattered and nothing solid was left but the miasmic soup of the Re-al. Form is emptiness, emptiness is form. It doesn't matter which is which first, when you are not all boxed up and rounded off to the nth degree.

At this, the great free Wind arose and whistled through her Empty shapeliness, the Shadows sighing and breathing outwards in their shifting shapes, yet holding firm the central space in the Arena of the light of Core, secure, regardless.

Her He-art Strings quivered and looped towards the rush of it as she formed and re-formed. "It is all here, and nothing has gone beyond"... came the Knowing in a hissing sound of the Everlasting Chime in which the note of her was never lost.

The Core in her Seed twisted and Spiralled, as it was transmuted into Uld Fire by her Vagal Snake. Her Uld Fire capped in her Sun Plexus, the wisdom making itself known to her. Emotions Known as He-art power, which is why they are so feared by the Patron, boomed outwards, exploding.

A tumbling torrent of Knowings washed back in and she opened ever further.

All this happened quietly in the individual Labyrinths ringing the Arena, and not a sound was heard in the upper reaches where the Patron liked to hold Its court of mechanistic and nihilistic oblivion.

Our Que-an looked up from the ground where she was crouched low with spirit unspooling. Her thousand loving hands emanating to protect all the lovely parts of Bitty and Imago who had spread in a fan towards the Shadows. She was healing even in her disintegrating and split open shamanic wounding.

Form.

Formlessness.

Form.

Dreaming the creative Dream of the perfect loving day constantly arriving.

Because she does create and this cannot be stopped, and her creation becomes...

the matter of future fact.

Inviolate.

Re-al.

THE HOLE TO THE FORT OF THE KIN-MON

"I've never been interested in watching or reading anything because it's the hero's story. I don't feel the need to be inspired by the character or learn a lesson. I feel the need to be engaged by them."

- Gillian Flynn, Writer

"A revolutionary woman can't have no reactionary man."

- Assata Shakur, Activist, FBI 'Most Wanted'

"The recovery of the feminine principle allows a transcendence and transformation of these patriarchal foundations of maldevelopment. It allows a redefinition of growth and productivity as categories linked to the production, not the destruction, of life. It is thus simultaneously an ecological and a feminist political project which legitimises the way of knowing and being that creates wealth by enhancing life and diversity, and which delegitimises the knowledge and practice of a culture of death as the basis for capital accumulation."

- Vandana Shiva, Ecofeminist, Anti-Globalisation Writer

Later than before this, after our Que-an had done some cleaning and more dusting, including having a Fucker of an Uld Fire, she looked up from her swilling and sponging. Through the large Hole in the Membrane there was a fall of freshly poured rays into her Manor. The full spectrum of rainbow light that helps the Shadows to hide here safely all day until beloved night comes creeping with bronze fingers. Feeling its way along the horizons. Caressing the Shadows invitingly, softly into Infra, squeezing and bending their dusky forms, infinitely seeking permanent space.

The Daughters had merged into the Infra-Dimensionality for the time being, off doing their creative projects. Bitty aligned with her beloved Shadows, her guides and confidantes. Imago refining her Will and individuation. Imago holds the Knowing of the Patron, it will be needed for more transformation, her being strong in feminine fire and able to incubate many embryos of the Re-al for later integrations. You can hear both of their laughter, and the Sheela-na-Gigs high, full shriek, of course, leaning round the Membranes.

Just listen to that...

The drumming in our Que-an's Labyrinth fluttered a soft warning, its Echo vibrating in the Strings of her He-art as she dried her puddles of clay and clart.

She listened, a heeding in her gazing Eye.

All along the Edge, on the other side of the Membrane, was the Re-al, with her natural systems and flowering growth, fluid ways and patterned chaos, all Infra-connected, in Spiral, and ever evolving. The Feld beyond that shimmered, woven by Re-al energies as they rippled in everlasting unwinding joy.

Our Que-an sighed.

Shattered, with her vulnerability wide open, having had her String stretched so far as to meet and merge with her Vagal Snake in the Arena, she still noticed her energy leaning out through the Opening. Actually, it was probably because her vulnerability was wide open that she was so pulled. It formed a large bulbous shape on the end of a stem that was rooted in her He-art and further on down into her Sun Plexus. It was leaning towards the Kin-Mon Isolate, feeling so sympathetic. As it often did when all her old flames, in their ancient fire pit, were stirred by her fragility, right down in here at the bottom end of her trembling He-art string, in the Cave of the *Womb* end.

This archaic pattern from before, way before she had realised it was such a tattered remnant, was triggered mostly in response to the ever-present overhanging gloom of the Patron. The presence of this pattern enabled a kind of second or third hand state of dissociated being that generated an energy food for the Patron that fed right back into Its stronghold. Ultimately supporting only It, continuously taking away from her and her actuality.

It wrapped the extracted food in slogans like, "Everything you say and think is bollocks." And announcements with fanfare like, "Hypocrite, you are so obvious, Que-an." These are ingrained Shard barbs, shoved in, designed to S-hame and box you all up like a ready meal for Itself. Constantly setting Itself apart while offloading whatever it is afraid of on to you.

Our Que-an's *Womb* ached with a wanting that would find no home here, she Knew. This sore and fragile centre of the Below bore more than passing births and deaths, it held the pain of all the unconscious protective manoeuvres and cuffs.

The patterns of these checks so difficult to be free of without seeing them as the defensive, and yet still offensively directed, weapons that they are. So, in this case, sympathy is entirely misplaced.

Oh.

Such hopeless tears do fall.

Things just worked smoother for the Patron if everyone was confused, fearful and dependent, another one of those facts of Patronic life that had to be accepted if you weren't to be deemed foolish.

But this one was pernicious to our Que-an.

This needed to be unpacked mightily at this point.

Oh, they all need to be unwound from the bunched up constipation.

May all our Spirals unwind and release these Samskaric Knots of congested compassion wrapped in difficulty and confusion.

The Patron had used the Kin-Mon over and over as its soldiers and managers. How Hellacious and relentless the pressure was for them under this, the fear of their own obsolescence, until they finally became utterly dependent and they could not dis-identify from It anymore.

To try and stop this insidious and awful tactic of takeover, the *Wom* had formed the longest line of a rhythmic love chant to encircle and protect their dear Kin-Mon.

But, of course, the sounding had only held for so long until it was Sharded, discordantly by the Patron, who, in Its framing ways, made the *Wom* seem weak, too sensitive, making mountains out of molehills, two-faced, and something to be ridiculed, if not deemed the source of all evil temptation. A perception which caught fire amongst the exhausted fighting Kin-Mon, and they pushed all their *Wom* away themselves, with no enforcement from the Patron at all, in the end.

Soldier-hood and gory glory days to come.

Job done, Patron.

Hell.

Then the Kin-Mon were pressed to do more time as Its officers, over and over, in the cauldrons of the wretched enslavement Bardo Factories, egged on with more vague slogans such as, 'efficiency spreads decency,' 'sacrifice yourself to be a good team player,' 'your ego is bad — you must destroy it,' and 'your mind is only a monkey,' (only!), until they were worn thin. Promised ennobling truths if they turned the evidence again and again to the advantage of the Patron, always in fear of being forced into eternal self-prosecution.

Very familiar isn't it?

This was when the notion of their Ego as evil, was Sharded into their endless, and endorsed, head fevers creating constant turmoil and self-rejection and punishment. They tried to banish their own selves, and became an easy army of abandoned and isolated He-arts. Failed saints, fallen and forced.

They could not even buy Time out, and were obligated to be either perpetually on guard, or in enforced recreation, imbibing a stupefacient drug of relief that was designed just for them, increasing the loneliness, and sold at high prices, not even freely dispensed, to create the circle, that fed the commerce, that stood for power, in this Great Dissonance.

Yes, you could feel sorry and weakened by all of this, but that would be further entrapping and is just what the Patron wants, so don't be sorry. Sympathy for the devilish is not empathy for the suffering.

The Patron constantly projects the damage it causes away from Itself, so be aware of that which you take on by being so amenable. You good Ego you, who is still stinging from being Sharded. What would be more useful, would be to see the Great Dissonance that this is creating. Don't copy your Patron and scape the goat so you can feel righteous.

Everything is always held on the knife-edge with the Patron, because It needs everyone's attention to be trained on Its agenda and the more drained and ill you feel, the better It knows where you are.

It might even have a little drink of you Itself, if you are really in Its sights.

So.

Try not to be so Fucking available.

She felt herself shifting positionally on her Spiral again and her Manor coalesced in another shade of the now golden grey rays from the Opening.

She noticed she could see over the Feld into the Fort of the Kin-Mon. His Fort was often not possible to see at all, as it was extremely well protected, and had been this way for a brain-foggy five thousand turnings.

As has been told, the dear energy of the Kin-Mon had been one of the first to fall under the influence of the Patron and under that sway he had succumbed to wanting to own territories instead of honouring the natural gifts, commons and linkages of the Re-al. When the Patronic hierarchies based on domination and secretive withholding started to spread, the gentle extended Uld families immersed in a life of Re-al, were destroyed. Their naturally diversifying growth, their never eroding or exhausting anything and their lovely light footprints holding all the dimensions they lived within, in trust, were wiped clean away with hardly a trace left.

All our Kin-Mon, whose own natural inner thrusting and enkindling energy was being manipulated, gradually manoeuvred to be at the top of the chain, once that chain of power was established by the Patron. Whereas before their natural strength and creative energy was expressed freely from their own kind He-arts and in harmony with the *Wom* and all their own families. Instead, more and more often they succumbed to the sensation of the conqueror, even over their own Uld Fire, lost in a kind of pseudo-ecstatic control. Polarised, judgemental and unforgiving, their accumulating aversions created no way out at all.

Marauders.

What a gift.

It just isn't.

Or is it?

You don't need to imagine who this was playing into the hands of.

Their Forts were completely built up against the perceived threat of the Shadows, yes, the very ones, our Allies, our Que-an invited into her Manor to care for and hide in all her sunny mornings.

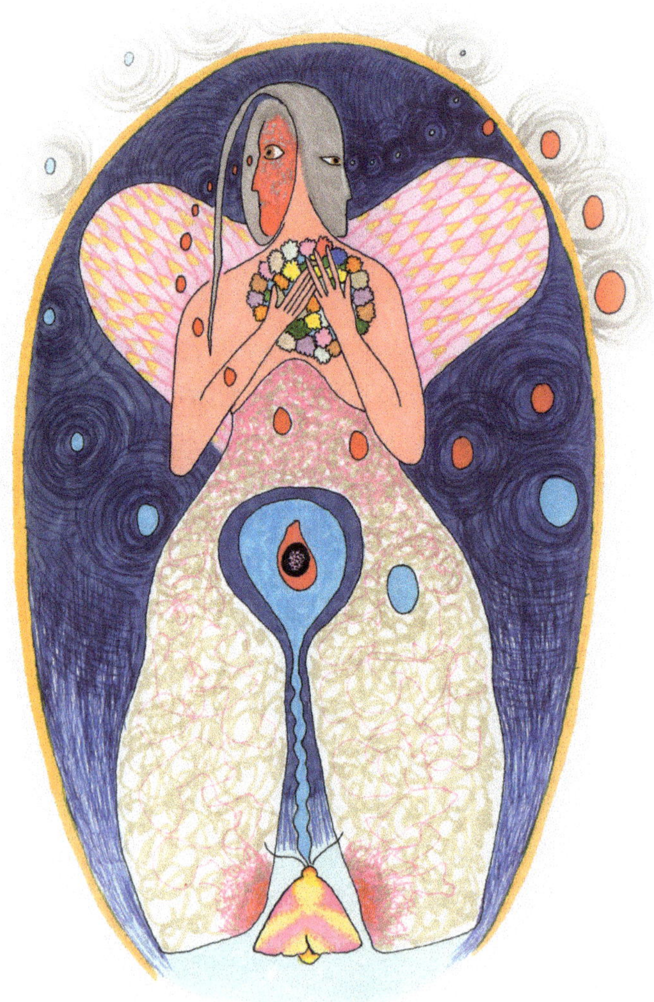

The Patron hated and feared the Shadows more than anything else in any existence. Really It hated the conquered and Sharded *KiGal* the most, but she is supposed to be nonexistent. It convinced the Kin-Mon that the Shadows were the real incarnate evil, and that all dark was a menace to Its dominant Patronic fake white light reality. The Shadows were of no hierarchy and could not be controlled in any way by the Patron, and so It feared that immensely. Hated them with a steaming vengeance that remained unseen but felt all the time by everyone.

So passive aggressive.

So exhausting.

And, as the Shadows themselves can only be related to as harbingers of our own potential truths, we have the Dissonance, yet again, on this front too. The truths are denied over and over, making the Shadows larger and larger, and more and more threatening.

More.

More.

More in this, the reflected confined state of the illusion of the Patron.

Each a prism of half a Kin-Monic face that held a slice of its own truth smashed to pieces, and that kaleidoscopic truth was exposed as being mimicked, the extrusion a backscattering from inside the Patron Itself.

So, in her own limited Knowing of the Uld Way, our Que-an could feel that growing fear and sensitivity in her *Womb* is always the response to the lack of being actually relational.

In relationship.

Which is why we, as *Woms*, stay in relationship with everything because just one little exiled Shadow will end up being the thing we have to run away from. We Know, as our medicine is immediate and always growing in the background.

Neglect and resistance could not be more finely tuned than this.

The Uld attunements of integration were the only way the Shadows could be lived with creatively and lovingly, but the Patron would never accept this.

Ever.

Never.

Ever.

The Shadows were to be exiled at any cost and at all times, because their presence signalled the Cre-ative and nuanced Re-ality that could not be controlled. As we have said already, whoever we are, eh Loves? It helps to remember, and remembering to remember is another important key.

Alert!

Alert!

Our Que-an wondered why she was feeling out towards the Kin-Mon in this moment, and then she saw that her bulbous energy growth was leaning in a soft old hope that she knew so very, very well.

Who would ever know her own yearning He-art Strings, or unconditionally accept her Uld Fire? This is the power of the *Wom* Love Chant starting to build, bridging the surrounding moat of brackish self-righteousness.

This old hope is here to take the edges off — an expanding invitation of Membrane widening in her He-art Strings, rising and up, tuning in an infinite Love. And we are grateful for the well of its perpetual giving.

But once a Kin-Mon agrees to be installed in a Fort by the Patron, he adapts it to his own device, creating systems of pain management and functions giving the illusion of security. He adopts this as the reason for his being. It is not the security of the Re-al, as it is always an isolated mechanistic system, unfortunately. Infra-connectedness and acceptance of other interpretations of the Re-al is the only true security, but as the very concept, let alone the Re-ality, is banned, we will just have to not go there for now.

Especially if we want to avoid any confrontational murder.

The violent Shard wounding of the Kin-Mon is so deep and complete that no hope has ever been able to soften the skin in its game and heal its blood. It isn't just one cut, it is wound into fibrous wound, compounded scabbing and complete leathery scarring, and a long, long road to uncover whatever was arising before this complete and utter agony.

Because our Que-an's local Kin-Mon is in deep trouble, with the Shard of the Patron lodged behind his left nipple. He knew it, but his hands were tied, so he could never winkle it out. He felt shafted all the time, even when no-one was storming anything. The Patron had resonated with the Kin-Mon as a fake brother and entered him, and now had him by the balls, by virtue of the shafting Shard.

The Kin-Mon would call and call for a *Wom* to come and get it out of him, but when one came, the Shard of the Patron would purposely make all the *Wom*s look like his worst nightmare, disrespectful two-faced bitches, causing conflicting desires and inviting the Dissonance, so that eventually any *Wom* had to leave when the call back from her own Manor gave her a blast of common *Wom* sense.

Really he needed his senses snapping back to the Re-al because all warriors have two faces themselves and one of their eyes is always weeping blood, but all too often that was just seen as a different case entirely, and the mere *Wom*s way of coping and evolving just another threat to his fortifications. And, unfortunately, most of the time it really is all about protecting the Fucking Fort, which has the effect of making one want to throw oneself in the moat continuously and hopelessly.

Some soft hope this is all turning out to be then.

Our Que-an was musing on a bit much around all this, she thought, as she gazed from her most recent position on the Spiral... but she couldn't stop, it had a reflection to cast. This thing wanted to come up from the Below as much as everything else. So it continued unabated.

What about that record book that he had for every week? But in which he never entered a single Re-al event and yet he stored all the notebooks as they accrued, in a library of absolutely nothing dotted with resentments.

Also, of course, this was a place where the Shadows grew in secret, feeding on the suffering of the never quite committing to the freedom of Compassion to Love. And never quite letting go the possibility of it either. This being the truest essence of the Great Dissonance and utterly enmeshing everyone, not just the Kin-Mon.

So horribly powerful.

Our Que-an could always feel this brewing and broiling, even from way across the Feld, as there is never any distance in Dissonance.

It's obvious, when you gaze at it, she thought, that the purpose of its castellations are more than just a rattling of spears and shields for show, and I do agree that there really is the tormented state to defend here. So that was that — all brushed off the hands and feet and away to join the dust of eternity.

We are not even feeling sorry for any of it, anymore, nor ashamed of Seeing it.

At this, our Que-an let loose her legendary and impudent snort of a giggle, rising up from deep in her *Wom*-space, all tricksterish and shit-stirring. Chuck a Fucking bomb in there, she thought.

This is the Sheela na Gigs fault — she keeps everything laughable. Really she should be punished for this, shouldn't she? You want to, don't you? Go ahead, then, try to catch her.

Part of our Que-an's basic prep work when very, very, very and extremely small (like half a quark) was grappling with the externally induced S-hame of the Patron. The Patron used humiliation, and threat of shunning, which, until It arose had never even been heard of, to reflect failure and foster a lack of confidence. So that It could fill the void that was inevitably left by Its own machinations. Of course, though, It always let it be known It was doing you a favour, filling your otherwise useless *Wom*ly Emptiness and curing you of that bad inclination to point out the inherent nakedness of It all.

Our Que-an came through her first S-hame Initiation on a flying colour. Black if you must know, the absorption of all colours, and the sign of the Shadow Ally sent to her in the Dream of a first born dawn.

More of this later, in the part called Desperate Shard of the Patron, if you want to skip a couple turns on the Spiral. You can just randomly dip in and out of this Spiral, you may have noticed, as it is not particularly consecutive or linear, but it can be, if that feels more comfortable for you. Let it all blow around in your mind and guts and see which points you land in.

But back to this Opening to the Fort... yes, we are going in! She knew of the one tiny door at the end of a narrow footbridge round the back that was always unlocked. Only a very few knew about this, and it was always those that had done their Fucking exploring and investigating in relationship with their own Descents, as the proper and only job, none of this bypassing bullshit. There is the guard room to negotiate but nevertheless, the fact of this door's existence is a kind of invitation, is it not?

You feel that if you enter you could end up right in the very centre of the Fort, right smack in the middle of its great esteemed loftiness. You feel you could break that Fucking

Shard into a million pieces and render all of the Patron antwacky. You could get it out by plunging a Transformational Energy Tool of some sort, invented by those Uld *Woms*, straight into its unresponsive Fucking frozen molecules and scream with a roar that breaks the Dissonance forever.

But you never go, no.

No, you never do. You don't howl your longing enough.

Our Que-an sighed out on a long breath. Yes, nobody ever uses that door. Even if you did go, you would have to wear the heaviest cloak that you can't even fly in. The cloak woven of the burdens of mechanisms taken over, and constrictions that have no place to taper off to come to natural ends. All that is here are the Echoes of the vociferous appeals of the interminable suffering of the Kin-Mon trapped in his hierarchies of deceptive achievements. Never being good enough and never reaching release. For there is no solace in unexamined and unwelcome Shadows.

Alert!!

Alert!!

But I suddenly feel I am here in the heart of the Fort!

What?

Our Que-an is startled from her ruminations and realises she has travelled right in on a passing and rare sympathetic Infra-current, riding on her own intention.

"Well I will be Damned and De-ad this time for sure," she thought. A hundred million memories of burnings and dunkings flooded her attention and she shuddered to try and come back.

And that was a moment ago. Our Que-an snaps back into her Manor, for it does not do to go wandering and end up in the back passage of anything, no matter how compelling, or how great the apparent need.

She adjusted her raiment, nursed her soft hope, and settled into the present view of things, looking out through that generous Opening of hers.

The Rays stream in and she comes to notice that the radiance has a different quality to it, as it softly lands on all the parts of her daughters, as they lie here, resting in their Shadows.

Quiet.

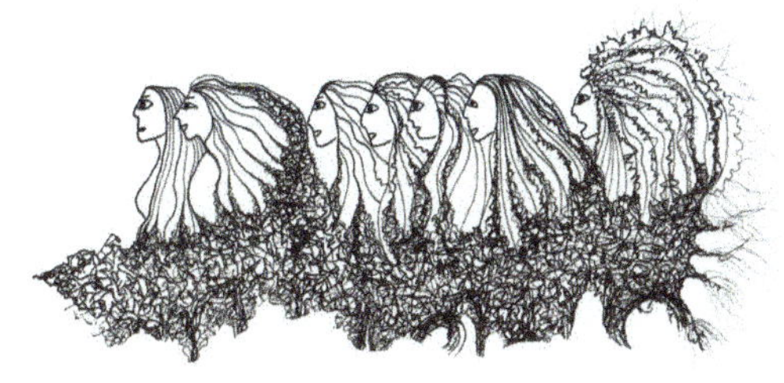

PARTING THE SWEET SORROW

"Never give up and never under any circumstances face the facts."

- Ruth Gordon, Playwright, Actor

"From the Great Above she opened her ear to the Great Below,
From the Great Above the Goddess opened her ear to the Great Below,
From the Great Above Inanna opened her ear to the Great Below."

- Wolkstein and Kramer, Recorders of His-story

The nature of this Descent is a polarising experience, swinging round the Spiral, making things appear opposite. In having to face towards effects that, if acknowledged, makes them more Re-al, we give the Re-al a chance to flourish, which is opening enough space to allow all to be in existence in its own way.

Our Que-an finds herself shedding again as she faces her important and discerning, even though relative, truth. The truth that this can be a melancholy path along the Edge. Only being known in one way is stifling, but to be known in other ways is risky and involves a pain that cannot be avoided because it is the pain that makes us alert to that which is un-Re-al. It is the pain of softening attachment and the psychic backlash of the mirrors of parts and Echoes that need to evolve positions and come home.

A voice comes towards her along the path in a sour gust.

"I will tell you what you are experiencing." It is the Patron, It wants to impose Its terms on her experience. It wants her to use Its filters. See through Its eyes. Use Its map on her path.

"You are not to interpret anything in your own way, for you are responsible for supporting our dominant reality. It is your duty to only use terms we have all agreed on. If you do not then we will have to call you negligent, disrespectful, lazy and crazy."

Oh yes, she remembers this punishment very well.

Our Que-an is wary of this backlash because it usually traps her in an internalised self-punishment, which wraps itself around her Uld Fire in judgement, squashing her Vagal Snake and Sharding her with the S-hame. This, she is fully aware of, is her universal burden and she carries it Knowingly, on purpose. She does not want to unwittingly become the instrument of the Patron.

Do you see?

She, herself is choosing her own understanding as a rebel *Wom*. Willingly acknowledging all Shadow with no denials. Willingly acknowledging the agenda of the Patron.

See the flaming torches as they come for her.

See the reflections inside her (Y-Ours? Loves?) psyche, the manipulative values of the weak and unchallenged movers and shakers of Patronic hierarchies. Those who decide what is out of their order and become all self-congratulatory about their decisions. It is bad enough being directly attacked, so to internalise this and then attack herself on Its behalf is doubly hard.

This is why being on this Spiral with you, Loves, finding her own shout, her own note, about all of this, is so significantly miraculous.

Our Que-an knows that she must always be able to feel the Great Sadness of the Kin-Mon Isolate, the sadness of the banished *KiGal* and all the exiled *Wom*, at the same time as the great intrinsic sweet grief. To feel the suffering of being the lowest of the low of the Patronic hierarchies, as she descends the Spiral, which is really ascending too, in case you are reading everything too literally already.

Watch that one, the 'literally' thing, it is a Patronic device, as we have unpacked for ourselves somewhere along here already.

She knows she feels all those who are affected, one way or another, on the Spiral, in this pressure to only conform to the decrees of the Patron. This is your life, should you Know It.

Because the shout that will keep her strong enough so that she can take up her own part of liberating the Re-al from the unconsciousness of the Patron, with Its inhibiting views and projections, is born of this Great Sadness. Because it is her own, and yours, and mine, and universal, and collective, covering everything.

Because it does cover everything, as much of this Patronic domination is in response to trying not to feel the Infra-connectedness... or Bloody anything. Feel one thing and you end up feeling it all. Turn this truth around, don't be afraid, and use the energy released. It's your own feeling Uld Fire.

But maybe I am being too kind. Maybe it isn't about being overwhelmed by so many feelings that It needs to clamp down hard. Maybe not feeling is actually a planned evil and route to a systemic takeover.

Where would that arise from in the Re-al?

See what I mean? So tempting to leave it all unexamined and take refuge in cultish absolute states.

If one part is bereft, then the others must not exile it, even if they are obsessed with transcendence, perfection and happiness. In fact, especially if they are obsessed with transcendence, perfection and happiness.

Kind of up, up and away with you.

You Angels of Divine pick and choose.

Because that usually creates such a large Shadow of trying to escape the self-punishment of not ever being good enough, that even the Shadows themselves get worried.

And that really is saying something.

At some points in the Spiral, this feels debilitating to our Que-an's own static tired being. But she knows this is a job of joy — this revealing of deep pain and open wound work. It brings the Shadows to the communal table so that all the unmet needs can be in revelation and given half a chance to resolve and express themselves with the Core of a loving and attuned witness.

It is our Que-an's choice to be this witness. And you, dear Loves are doing this too, right now in this reading, hearing, Seeing. Whatever you are feeling is the essence of this choice and its accompanying footprint. We are all dancing together.

So if you can stick it out, then you will see the open energy centres casting off their shields and you will be, and See, the lacerations of neglect and abandonment underneath.

You will see the causes of the pain of the many partings, created by going and being in this odyssey of the Under, in Spiral. And that it is so deep that it is bottomless.

Needs must.

The transformation comes about by feeling it all; and this makes us not afraid of the bottomlessness of it.

Strange but true.

Our Que-an's He-art Strings sweep and undulate, as her hair lengthens in the direction to take, and her fascial Knot becomes primed — connected within to the synchronicity of this cause of the *KiGal* — and also being endlessly invisible to the Patron at the same time.

Sustained integration is what is happening all through this Spiral, so that we can be its willing emissaries into our own peaceful Cores. The medicine that clarifies the Dissonance is that of purposeful loving attention, especially to the exiled parts. The scapegoats.

This is the medicine!

So warm, and getting warmer.

Our Que-an felt her He-art Strings swollen and lumpy in the Great Sadness, as though her tears were stuck in the nodules of persistent inability to express, and her flow constricted into receding patterns getting smaller and smaller, away and away.

To the unworthy tininess in the quarkiest grain.

Her Vagal Snake squashed right down into the smallest coil it could, in the furthermost place within her whole embodiment. Because she knew the Sadness can break the He-art Strings into the catacombs of the *KiGal*, falling through the centre of the Spiral, releasing any holds on positions. Whether or not this is good or bad is immaterial. She just Knows.

Her Great Grand *Wom* would always counsel her to first start inside the active meditation of welcome to the arising calls from the depths, because falling too quickly means you will bounce back up and probably forget who you meet.

Alert!

Alert!

It is through positioning your Labyrinth to hear the calling that you will experience the voice of your daemon directly. Your own guiding Shadow. You need your Shadow as the world of the Patron does not allow the initiatory journeys to the Under Tunnels, because It needs its beings to be working for Its plans and developments. Focusing on Its lights. So this Way becomes very, very, very hard.

As in hard and small, unmoving and constricted. Compression. Burial.

Necessarily so.

From one small seed the mighty growth explodes.

The bottomlessness of the Sadness, the spinning in the void of it, the great sweeping wave of it, the quaking vibrating force of it, flooding the totality of wherever it lands.

This is the ache for her as *Wom*.

The bleeding will not stop or ease, only her awareness of it falters in exhaustion. Aching for the Sharded ones, Us, while staying fully conscious in the overwhelm, is what is actually the most Re-al response possible to the Dissonance. And the *Wom*s are the only ones who still know that this passage is the key to liberation. Known by these ones who venture Under to merge with the *KiGal* and feel the true depth of the pain, which will be the only thing that ends the Dissonance, with the help of the balancing from the Re-al.

This is what the Patron cannot understand. It finds it impossible to even countenance that this is the needed experience, and because it is Re-al, it is the threat to It that It will not accept. The Re-al is so far removed from what the Patron can control and enslave with Its repetitive loops of closed energy, that It will come down hard on any of these arisings.

Our Que-an knew she would be punished by the Patron, wherever It could, for her Spiral, adding to the journey's already strenuous demands. She knew she would be exiled for it, imprisoned in the mind boxes of others for it. Constantly pushed into Its roles. But most of all, the biggest risk was being implanted with the Shard in her own He-art Belly. This, she knew, is the very event that would set her back into the unconsciousness — and unconsciousness is the very antithesis of the Re-al.

The truest test.

More than anything in the whole of the Infra, our Que-an wants to work with the polarity of awareness and hold the tension of the illusory opposites.

To be a polarity explorer.

She needed to meet with her *KiGal*, and she felt the call rising from within, activating her Vagal Snake and it began to shudder upwards.

Get ready.

When our Que-an was just beginning, before this time, she could not make a shout in any dimension. The heavy burden of the smothering hands of the Patron circling round her neck compressed her into this smallest space and her chords and Strings were paralysed.

Then she felt the inner cry for help build and build, until it tore upwards out of her mouth into the longest, deepest calling. Her primal scream orientated her to the Under as she was freed from the spell of repression from within. And she now had her starting place, jumping straight into the Void. She became invisible to the Patron because she is purely intuitive, not appearing in any of Its preconceptions, except as whatever It expected, and so able to shift her shape. And as she left the old cloaks of her previous selves behind, she felt moved into the Under and beyond, nearer the Core.

Meeting the *KiGal* and melting the Shard was becoming more and more possible on even these outer rings, as she felt everything, rejecting nothing, strengthening in her total entirety.

Our Que-an started to drown in the unutterable Sadness, her breath shortening and her He-art Strings stretched thin, with the suffocation becoming more complete as she realised her Way here, easing void-like along the Spiral. Her emotions formed into a natural rhythm to soothe the overwhelming feeling that she would never be able to sort everything out. Too many parts and puzzles that do not fit each other, she would never be able to organise for the good, as she was, in herself, Here-Nowish.

She completely became the fractured player in this game of the Patron, just as the annexed Wind, congealed Waters, over-stoked Fires and desiccated, extracted Earth were all forced to be Its servant too. Their Uldermentals ossified to this place of the past.

Fucking ruinous raping.

All shattered in depleted pieces.

Her Vagal Snake twisted deep within her spine and her He-art Belly contracted and became a smear of jelly between her legs. She lost her strength downwards and felt the pulling and turning of birthing.

So what could she do except rip off all her clothes and layers, screaming the nameless?

From deep in her He-art Belly came the long, long sinewed tentacle of this suppressed suffering, reaching through the Spiral from the time before the Ulds. Her forms all burned on the ground, useless and pathetic, they never hid who she really was, they never served who she could be.

She hated them and kicked the seared and melted dregs of them.

They were the superimposed uniforms of the Patron, and caught her up in the most discomfort and toiling itchiness and constrictions. Her skin pocked with congestion and holding hormones too dangerous to be vaporised, as she bucked at Its trends. Kicking out and thrashing the garments to threaded smoky trails. What fire this was that fuelled itself, feasting on their material and crusty patterns, she did not know, but she could intuit it alright.

A strong sign of the way of loss, yet no loss. Losing into wider freedom, as another load is shed away forever.

She looked back the way she had come.

Her Uld Fire consumed any stray remnants.

Clean.

Done.

Onward.

Fuck you.

Patron.

THE JUNKANOO PARTY

"There is no gate, no lock, no bolt that you can set upon the freedom of my mind."

- Virginia Woolf, Writer

"In the menu, there should be a climax and a culmination. Come to it gently. One will suffice."

- Alice B. Toklas, Cook, Writer

Stepping back across the Spiral through the fading smoke of these obsolete identifications, our Que-an's Labyrinth rings with the chimes of the entrance bell of her Manor, and she suddenly feels the luck of the Uldish.

An invitation envelope sealed with a warm, waxy and still very wet kiss, is whisked towards her in an uprising flutter. And her frontal lobe, which she suddenly sees is still open somehow from her previous meanderings, slams shut with a loud snap.

She really must be more careful where she is drawn. Well, she might be more careful, but who will be the one to say what careful really is at the end of each wonderful day? And speaking of the day, it is warping strange and attractive, vibrant in waves of pulsating colour and molecules of sexiness. She smells the sweat of her Vagal Snake as her pit and pith glands intensify themselves in readiness for another unknown. She opens the envelope and reads what is written in thin, chaotic, luminous letters and pictograms on tissue made of spider webbing. The rainbow-otic colours made with bacteria dancing with fungi pigments getting brighter and brighter as the centuries go by.

This was the gist of it,

"If you are lucky enough to be invited to the Junkanoo, do not refuse. Do not even be ambivalent, for this will be taken as a huge insult and fireworks will be exploded throughout your cortex that will expose you to your own tiny mind box relentlessly and neverendingly."

And everyone knows what torture that is.

A disembodied tongue cheekily licked her neck and then stuck itself in her Labyrinth. Ah, she did know what this was, after all! This was from the Uldish! Just as she felt! Who always responded to the Great Sadness of *Woms* with the threat of joy.

It is all to do with the balance between the Re-al and the uncertainty of what is a true existence, which is all there is to be comfortable about. In an uncomfortable sort of way.

Our Que-an knew that the Uldish read feelings, for they are made only of them. All are Kin and the eternal children of Uldermentals, and as all feelings are family affairs and no feeling is exiled at any time, ambivalence is just one step away from potential rejection, so this will never get you into a Junkanoo.

Ever.

Ever after, sadly.

She read on, very interested, and her Vagal Snake started quivering, shooting little darts of excitation into the usually more quiet areas of her embodiment. She squeezed her eyes shut to better See.

"This is your very own invitation, belonging only to you. And it is sparkling, which will be irritating if you are not in the mood. This irritation is precisely the reason you have been invited in this, the first place."

To the Uldish, our Queen appeared quite grey, she had lost a lot of her gold recently, her luminiferous etheric. And what with the event of the grieving, flaming clothes and sad shedded layers, well, she was in dire need of pinking. She needed clustering all around her, and tickling and pinching, to get her lost colour back.

Our Que-an felt something move deep inside, an orgasm approached and her Vagal Snake slithered downwards drawing her along. The ground melted away as she felt with all her open senses, plump tissues and open He-artedness, into the Dell of the Junkanoo.

It was warm. Inclusive. Delicious.

An ecstatic ferment of a place, a delirious place, and this was one full on, immutable, medicine party. The shower of smarting, stinging stimulation lost her, then found her again. It didn't hurt, it was just so immediate and she didn't have time to even herself up, or consider where she might be heading, or ending, or choosing. No time to fathom, no time to anchor, no time to not ride the waves as they built themselves, one on one.

Steadfast.

She heard the voice of the invitation again;

"Do not be alarmed if you are hearing and seeing all sorts of anything at all. You are not ill — you are free of all diagnosis, judgement and identity. You are encountering previously unfelt potentials deep in your body, and in the very centre of your mind, where it is inseparable from your body. Experiences that are not yet part of your reckonings. You, our dear Que-an, are in the Dell of Junkanoo and even if you do not remember accepting your invitation, it is because, in the best sense of all meaning, once invited, you are already here. As we Uldish do not live in any kind of a consecutive timeline like yours. We exist to cause, not effect. We are the indigenous sum of all, diviners and immortal, and are always so much greater than the equality of you Alone. Some say our community gatherings are hundreds of times more potent in exponentiality, maybe than even the never-ending magicality. We say there is no end because once begun, that stone just rolls and rolls.

So, rejoice!

Turn you and your beautiful face towards our music and sing into the gold and pink of your own gorgeous self.

Your crucible wants you so very badly, Madame Que-an."

Mmmm... to be wanted — much too difficult to resist, so she didn't bother.

She reeled and turned towards the many tiny hands pulling her into dance. She flew.

She fell.

She rose.

She spun.

Hips loose and breasts bare, neck long, fingers and toes reaching and curling and splaying out. Out. Making wings of cascading feathers that appear from no place. She lost all her bearings entirely, as she let go of all that was upright within her. Of all that was uptight within her. Because Here-Nowish is safe. Here-Nowish is the ground to land on your feet with. Even while being swept off them. Even if they are above your head. Planted in the magic and soothed in the soul. Deep in the soul, deep in the gut, deep in the Womb, deep in the bowels of arousal. Desire turned out right, as it gives and gives. She found it. It is ours.

Right up.

Straight up.

Some Fucking front, who does she realise she is then?

A kind of a fuel of gratitude for all these comforting, held out, healing hands filled all the many smiling faces of her limitless expansion. Each reflective piece of them holding the promises that all would be good, all would be well, all would be happy, in its best sense and significances. These seeds of the Dreaming forward, so important as nourishment, in the Great Dissonance that is fogging around outside in Its random lurching presence. Clouding around like the demented drunken shroud of asphyxiation It is.

Alive, here she is! The living answer to all the broken bits of herself, her dear Wom and her daughters. Alive to the lovely lonely Kin-Mon and alive to the Uld Fires yet to be born to these gyrations.

Dancing in Uldermental joy with the Winds, Waters, Fires and E-arths of all that is truly Re-al.

Keep the Re-al, dear Loves.

Because you are… being touched and touched back to feeling better, and better, and better…

Her He-art burst wide open unashamed, and her Vagal Snake wound and curved in pleasure, all bliss consummated with no need of any seeking the lost.As it is here.

Fucking arrived.

In Core.

Again!

THE TITAN IS WHO?

"One of these mornings be proud and fair,
Put on my wings and then I'll try the air,
Since it looks like everybody in this whole round world,
Hey, down on me, yeah, ha ha."

- Janis Joplin, Singer, Composer

"So, it is usually a matter of time before a woman calls up her
courage from the soul bones, cuts herself a golden reed, and plays
the secret in her own strong voice."

- Clarissa Pinkola Estés, Cantadora, Poet, Jungian Psychoanalyst

Following all her selves through this multiplicity, our Que-an settled into a long deserved incubation in the delicious muck of her own meandering mystery. She dropped into what looked like sleep from outside but was really an activity of unfettered awareness. Within its layers and Dreaming forward she found herself at the foot of the Great Titanous Mountain growing at the edge of one of the original Felds of the Water Peace.

Oh, now she had not been here in the longest Time, or so it felt; although as we have outlined on Spirals past, or maybe we will on future turns, Time is a utility that bends to whoever applies it.

Here, on a rising scree-covered hill that slipped up towards the mountain's cobbled base, her attention took a gentle orbit, easing a landing into the appearing Feld. The Felds of all the Peaces are deep in the strata of the spiritual geology of the Re-al. They are in a slow continuous eternal movement upwards and outwards, exerting a great force that is very much like a magnet but cannot ever be measured, thankfully... only felt.

Therefore safe from the Patron, so caught up in Its manipulative measurings and assessments.

All the Felds of the Re-al adjust to, and create with, this slow moving, growing, peaceful Titan of energy that is buried within all of the inner lives that seek to flower, and support the Re-al, as the seedlings of its ancient untouched treasures.

This is our True Nature, expressed by the Uld Fire which is free, flowing up through the tectonic plates that have their echoing patterns in our own *Wom* and Kin-Mon skulls. It rings a bell up in our headspace, in that cup of expectation and hope, and arrives at this precious awareness, when we are on our own Spiral, after all other diversions have faded for now.

Or when we are in direct, calm and focused rebellion of the Patron...

Shhhh, though.

It is from this head point that we have been conditioned by the Patron to project our attention towards everything that will gain us material and hierarchical power, and Coin. So we only find the open-gated atomic Empathic Gland within, when we reverse our attention away from the world of the Patron and its soporific loops of activity, and towards the Felds of the Uld.

And the *KiGal*.

But this is only part of the soft curve of rebellious mountain making. We foster needed kindliness towards ourselves and others while being blithely disobedient to the Patron.

This starts expanding into our nerve ending centres, around which we recognise the emerging holographic eternity which will come to meet us as we Spiral, whether up or down. (It is just that the hype of up has been vastly over endorsed and made to seem like the Be All and End All.)

Amazed by these endlessly repeating shades of enlightenment, whatever we have internalised of the Patronic headspace finally shatters free.

Love, then slavery.

Then love.

Strobe empathy.

Just like the shadows of the clouds on this Titan's cliff face, our transitory landings into the material, after this, seem to not have the weight to be still, but they are very still.

And we do land deep.

We arrive somehow, piloting nothing, and steep ourselves in this vast feeling of a movement and a tranquillity all at once, right inside.

It arises and arises.

Keeping on and keeping on.

Deep, Great Peace, and the sense that all is well, in all ways, throughout all the unfolding Felds of the Re-al. This dimension, this state, this place of Peace, is all here within, whenever we turn our inner Eye towards it.

Our Que-an, in her own Knowing, flew up the vast body of the silent Titan, as small as she could be, in her flighty Jenny PunkWren winged form. Her Shadow Ally flitting with her past the landscape, revealing its shapes, crevices of nests, roots to hang and ledges to rest. But she was not falling just now, and caressed them as she darted ever upwards. She could feel the Titan's huge movement, so slow and gorgeously lazy, so safe that in her quick flight, she felt delighted and skimmed the ground into Re-al.

She arrived at the shoulders and could see he was gazing across the Water Feld and out towards the farthest horizon of eventuality. It was a large, ever-unfolding turquoise sea, its own harbour, sheltering the potential for trust. All the emotions ever felt in waves and peaks of tears like spray. Every feeling took refuge here in the oceanic mother S-he Sea, gently transforming into serenity. The calm within the storm.

Expanding in the space to feel everything, nothing forced to be exiled, all held in a nourishing acceptance and care.

The Titan gazed at the Ocean. Peace gazed at Nurture. The two meet deep inside us, as our own gaze follows along the Re-al.

So silent, her silky self dropped straight into this gaze like a pearl diver, his Eye turning to see Her, meet Her, absorbed in first sight Love. All being is now subsumed in the vast quietude.

Then she hears a tender call, whispering into the open Labyrinth of her transparent mollusced skeleton head.

"Look up a little furtherrrr…," a whisper through her shell-like, her attunement so complete that her Labyrinth is completely unravelled by the voice.

She looked up from this deepest to the highest high and into the clarity of the waiting sky. Void-like, cloudless space that hooks her vision towards a single speck.

She feels the purest wind on the layers of her skins and sees the exciting silhouette of a giant raptor.

Who am I?

Ah, Paradise.

Her Vagal Snake opens its mouth in her throat and rises up to meet its own mirror-winged avatar.

The calling suggests to her in its whisperings, that this is the seven-tailed Merlin of an Ascent and each tail feather dips towards her in the reflection of her own turnings and leanings. She wants to watch, as it swoops and keens, wheeling away and back towards her, as she rests at the head of the Titan, sitting on his shoulder like a companion planting.

The Merlin glides in towards her on a cooling thermal and lands on the long ledge of the bone of the Titans collar, gathering its wings to its sides like an elegant angel and she notices that they point down towards the Under showing her the Way far below.

The Sacred Great Below.

It is black. It has breasts and claws and a regal iridescent plume, softly swishing in a clearing arc all around the Titan's neck.

The blackness is a density that fills the space with the glorious promise of the unknown, these Unders, and she is drawn into the tightrope pupil of its sinistral Eye. Here, in the Eye, she feels as though she is something else, something more dense and material, a solid. Her Vagal Snake is robust and ready. She is more free and pre-existent, prepared to jump into the Re-al power that is herself. The Re-al of her *Wom*-being tempered, honoured, venerated and strengthened. In the rightful place.

Buried in the folds of the ascension orbit of the Unders where there is no way up.

Only in.

Thus her landed desire itself gazed into the vast turquoise sea of feeling, and this landing set her flow free from its cell Seed, cocooned away from the Patron, protected by the Merlin. Contracting and expanding in birthing and orgasmic waves affecting the whole Feld. She realised that the meeting, the merging, of both the Ascent and the Landing would be the unlocking of even more meaning, going beyond where she finds herself. Then she realised, also, that this was the grace of her majestic inner diversity pouring its insight into complete unity.

Hah Hah!!

Fucking jubilance!

I am the anchorite, within the layers of all that has happened and will happen. I have suffered being hidden. I have willingly suffered being obscured so that I may guard, anchor and serve the Re-al.

She Knew.

Who I am, in process, will invite this enquiring self to my centrality that seems most clear up here on the shoulder of the Titan.

Gazing into the turquoise Uldermental of the Water Peace feelings, she felt aroused by this, and the vibrating in her own Uld Fire became a strumming. Her Vagal Snake crooned with its mirror Merlin, and settled into a voluptuous feathery resting whirl.

But she also knew here, because this is the Spiral, the other potential, the traces of it hovering in her peripheral Eye, of the imposter perfection sold by the Patron. To keep all *Wom* or Kin-Mon from ever landing.

The Patron uses perfection as an emblazonment so that no-one would ever really ground and regain their own one messy truth. Strive for this imposter perfection, and this was your very own life, whisked away as food for Its Dissonance.

So which is it to be?

She felt the Knot under her left rib tighten with this perennial choice and her wings and legs lengthened. She bent into the air around her and twisted into the moving figure of the infinite eight with her Vagal Snake, looping back and forth and winding round and round, sensing outward to fully know the difference of this edge. Moving through the Membrane that was always pliably at once within and without. Then the Knot of them released, and she flew.

The Merlin came alongside; and Eye to winking Eye, they flew straight out and into the turquoise, gorgeous wave upon radiating wave breaking across their swinging souls, sparking blues and greens into their He-art Strings and wingtips, letting loose the feathers of light that created this most exquisite flight into the Core of Love.

The whole Feld resounded with the calling and all the Re-al became more material and obvious, so that now there are even more opportunities to key into all our Uld Fires.

Feel it.

The calling voice of nowhere softly announced:

"You, being the Seed of Re-ality, the line of your awareness is the centre that exists in all ascensions, descents and dimensions. You are the Uld Fire that is always here, no matter what is happening around it, with the different guarding parts and lost fragments of feelings and hurt pieces of pain. Don't believe anything, don't even believe those who don't believe, or you will be lost in yet another world. Directly experience at all times. This is the Re-al.

Slowly your intention to settle into your own Fire, has become the very stream of Uld itself, and so much more of the Patronic headset and its conditioning has dissolved just like the mizzle on a sodden moor."

Rain on, dear Uld Fire of our Que-an.

Rain on.

Her rain was absorbed into the Titans E-arth and her spirit soared into the empty void of the Merlin's Eye, all pregnant with every kind of possibility. With her own Water lapping against the shores of her material grace, the Uld rejoiced all through the Immensity, as our Que-an was absorbed in one of the completions to rise through incubation into her Spiral.

Again.

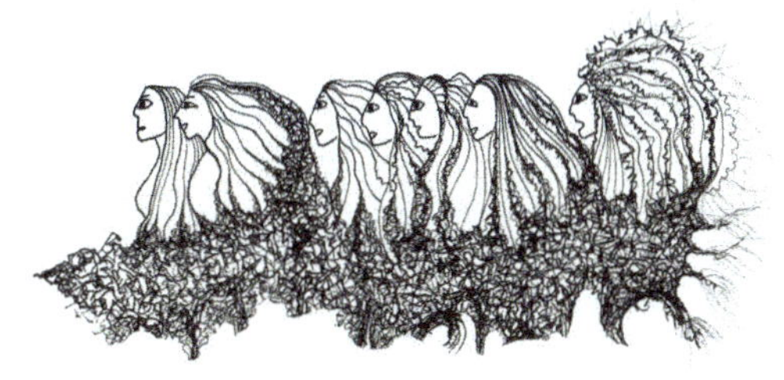

THE BIRD-SNAKE PART

"These fell miasmic rings of mist, with ghoulish menace bound,
Like noose-horizons tightening my little world around,
They still the soaring will to wing, to dance, to speed away,
And fling the soul insurgent back into its shell of clay:
Beneath incrusted silences, a seething Etna lies,
The fire of whose furnaces may sleep — but never dies!"

- Georgia Douglas Johnson, Poet

She came awake, much more materialised and lying in a sarcophagus, stratified deep in one of the levels of the Under, quite a bit further down on the Spiral than she had expected. Her Labyrinth felt the presence of the Core signals gently pulsing from all sides and she could see through the beautiful Membrane, shining with the Re-al, green and in a growth that was irrepressibly honeyed with the milk of the Arthropods and their delightful star-like connections. She sighed and thought poetry in a visioning of how it all would be when in liberation from the constraints of the Great Dissonance.

One side of the Membrane opened up. Spilling itself onto a grassy meadow dotted with a variety of the giant Thunder-stones of the Uld lined up in patterns of processional menhirs, giving quiet witness to what still could be...at any moment. Capturing the glow of infinite rising dawns.

She looked upwards into the rounded vast green, as it bled into a blue, cobalt and shining, and there, perched on the top of the tallest lead Uld stone was her Bird-Snake, avatar of the Merlin and the other part of her Labrys, the outer projection of her Vagal Snake made winged.

They gazed into each other again, exchanging glances of power and Core Knowings. It was not over. It would never be over.

It is always Under.

Then something else, more potent, passed between them and our Que-an quivered because the power in this Knowing was so intrinsic and so utterly true that the whole of the whole turned to listen in anticipation.

Would she get it?

Will you get it?

Of course!

Release your anxiety.

We've all already got it.

It is this.

The making of this Descent to disperse the Great Dissonance is made of our, and our Que-an's, attention. Woven from us, you and me — you reading, imagining me; me writing, imagining you — our mutual awareness is manifesting this melding uncovering of Knowing. We are creating the turns on the Spiral and the very Way that will meet the *KiGal* and...

The Shard of the Patron.

Both.

This is us. It is how we attend to our Uld Fire and which direction we dream in. This is us, and how we fight the fog. This is us when we choose to sleep, in the hope that when we wake, our waking will be strong enough to thrust us past a starting line that no-one else will draw for us across the sand of our soul, while we turn our dear faces to the walls of our captivated allegiance.

We decide, even if we are told, and eagerly accept, that there is nothing we can do.

It is still us deciding.

And all the Uld Fire bound up in any delayed deciding is then just used as fuel for the Patron. For making more Shards in the Bardo Factories.

So hear the chorus of the morning and jump up into your own free day.

This is what the Bird-Snake arose to signal with a squawking fluster and much ear splitting penetration across the Feld. And the sound swirled, trapped in the sarcophagus getting louder and louder. Spiralling raucous. Follow the Echo before it changes and you don't hear it anymore.

Quick!

Quick!

Alert!

Alert!

Trying to reach in an urgent scrabbling towards the happy ending?

The Echo stopped at that, dead silent, and over the edge of the sarcophagus she could see the Bird-Snake taking off on her giant wings, the air upholding her quivers, she turned and stretched her talons out to steal our Que-an's He-art away with her too.

Now validating the fact of our He-art.

A Re-al fact, just for an actual change.

That it can be attuned so completely to another, that it loses its separation.

Watch her Vagal Snake settling in so comfortably with this affirmation. And in this newly replenished sight, she resolved to remain awake, in even more lives and turns on the Spiral, in this head-on facing of the Patron. Continuing to Descend, courting disaster, laughing anyway.

(Did you hear the Sheela na Gig just then? Laughing away down the curve of the lane? She is a One, that One. No Fucking respect.)

There is no other way than our own, when there is only us here. Being the messengers of the Re-al, and seeing all the Shadow Allies who are ready and waiting to arise and liberate.

For there is only one ending when you look down through your open Eye.

So spit it out.

And answer yourself.

HELL-BENT DESCENT

*"Not like the brazen giant of Greek fame, With conquering limbs astride
from land to land; here at our sea-washed, sunset gates shall stand,
A mighty woman with a torch, whose flame is the imprisoned lightning, and
her name Mother of Exiles."*

- Emma Lazarus, Poet

Our Que-an had been told once by her Great Grand-*Wom* that all the entrances to the Under Levels were unique and reflected the shape of the Shadow Allies of the experiencer. So she was reassured to see her most beloved and welcoming tree come into view. The Beech, casting a soft, dappled dance for her to shelter in. As she approached it, she saw briefly the Shadow of a *Wom* ripple across its wide trunk and disappear round the other side, and she turned hopefully to see the One who had cast it.

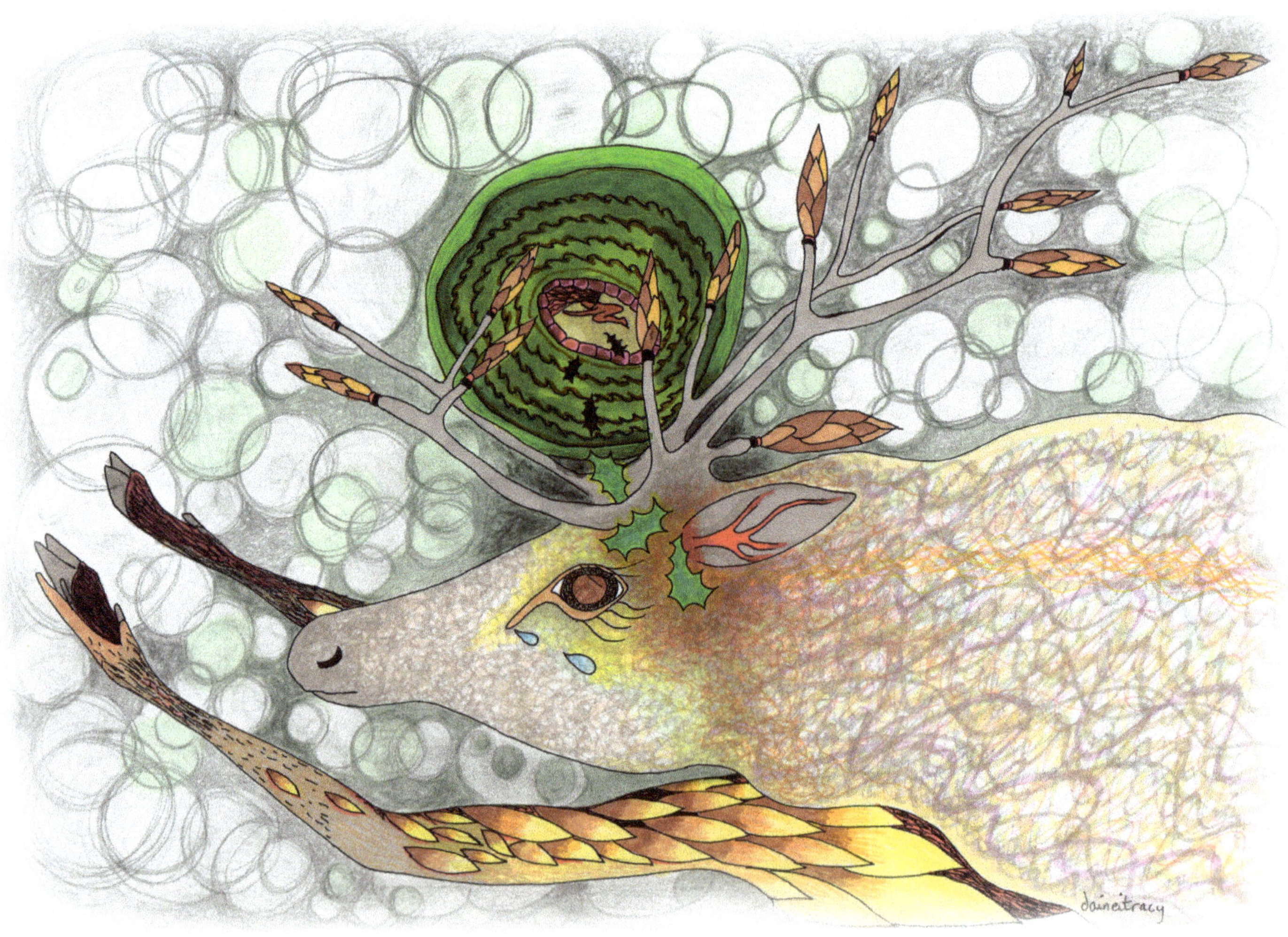

A giant white Deer Mother stood silhouetted against the glowing sun behind her, its vibrant flare a disc that she held in the cup of her antlers. Just at that moment she turned away from her, in a mirrored departure, and our Que-an turned back to see the *Wom*'s shadow passing through a crack in the bark, into the root of the tree.

Our Que-an strode long legged along the Deer Mother's Shadow to that rooted spot to dig a hole in the ground, tautening her Strings, scraping the soil beings gently out of the way and pushing against the pieces of ironstone with her bare hands. She felt protected by the sinewy root-wood. It's long and strong trunks moving upward in sinuous lines of bleached beauty, wind sculpted by the very essence of itself, while its roots gnarled and mounted the stone, forming an edge of a Hole to the Under levels, nearer to the *KiGal*.

As she dug, she noticed that the Beech hosted a smaller Holly tree, growing in the soil collected in a fork between branch and trunk. The two trees were intertwined in a symbiotic signing to her of the undisturbed Re-al.

The red berries glistened in a menstruation of blessed, rounded and completed flowering. The mark of the cycle of the S-he Sea, ready to burst and reseed, receptive, open, in delivery of the next.

She sighed with a pleasure absolute and wiped her hands into the pulpy soil, while its organisms burrowed into her Membranes creating ever more healthy Uld Fire.

The right indications were intensifying, and she could feel the potencies and gathering tensions coming from the grief of the Great E-arth *Wom*, Eresh the *KiGal* and knew that even with her present and dependable Shadow Allies, she would need all her wits to stay conscious to descend in these parts.

Eresh was in the deepest and most long-lived cave of mourning because her inner Kin-Mon energy, her own Stag, had been murdered with the Shard by the Patron when It came to power and dominance, as it attempted colonisation of the S-he Sea.

Her anguish was trapped in a stoppage of all expression.

It stuck in her throat as there was no being to hear her, no-one to listen to her, she could not complete her cycles; and so therefore the Patron took the incomplete power and milked it to toxify the Felds with blame and Its S-hame.

"He is dead.

My Love.

Oh, he is dead."

They had inserted one of their Shards into her He-art, and over the endless Spiral it had grown up and into her mouth, so that she could not utter the dispelling truth, and could no longer support the Re-al. She could only fall endlessly Below. Her inner Kin-Mon had then been used as the template to isolate all the other outer Kin-Mons, and as she could no longer speak her own truth because she was gagged, she could not prevent or reveal the creeping Great Dissonance.

The Patron effected a sweeping dismissal and disseminated propagandic information so that all imagination and magic, all our Dreaming forward skills were deemed laughable and scorned, from that time on.

Imagination, like Dreaming and Emptiness, was feared by the Patron. It did not like the potential to disrupt Its petty imposter reality and hated the fact that a world could be woven that would lead back to the Re-al, rendering the Patron obsolete, as prayers of intention can be created that would dissolve Its own intention to control.

It was this very annihilation of the *KiGal*'s inner Kin-Mon that had caused the Great Dissonance, seeping into all dimensions, his fighting spirit triggered with the threat and overwhelm of being taken over so blindly and arbitrarily. Together they are now the living temple of the transformative energy of De-ath for us all.

In our Que-an's Spirallic descent she can only hear the *KiGal* left in the pit, sitting by her charred stake.

All parts of us are transformed by the needed initiations of De-ath, and the casting off of old mindsets, in whatever unique way these gloriously come around.

This is genuine embodied De-ath, in full awareness, fearless or Known as the transformation of the energy of the Fe-ar into the fuel of rebellious liberation.

A rebellious spirit so sorely needed because the Patron causes whole areas of previously harmonious and balanced essence Felds to simply become barren, stripped, mined, and all the life of it left hollow, bereft of the Re-al.

Our Que-an heard the vibration and bent to feel her way into the Hole, sticking her fingers in to part the folds. She saw the ground wound away downwards and round a corner, sucking all her attention towards it. She turned around and crawled backwards into the funnelling space, searching with her toes and bruising her knees, because this was the only way to tread this old track of the *KiGal* and inhabit the right timing to descend.

She followed this, grounded feet first.

She moved along in a rhythm being squeezed by the earthy moist sides, knowing she would soon be enveloped by the Croft of the Shadows, because she had at least always travelled this far within when she had found herself here, in this corner curve of her Spiral.

We might recognise these Shadows, with all their homeless, constantly moving energies in our thoughts, feelings and sensations. They are the ever-changing forms waiting to be drawn to the Hoards. The Hoards are the stored pseudo riches of the Mine of Coin gathered when the Fe-ar is over stimulated.

Fe-ar created by the Unconsciousnesses of the Bardo Factories, built by the Patron and fuelled by Its desire for Dissonance.

When the Shadows were first stimulated into more growth by the Sharding of the isolated Kin-Mon, they became the only viable bridge left between the Re-al and the systemic destructive head rule world of the Patron. It is through our own Shadows that we can see the difference between our conditioning and our truer selves.

Occasionally she felt them rush by her on their way out — silent open holes for mouths, anticipating the feedings to come. She blessed them in their task, as she knew that all the cycles of birth and death needed this kind of leeching of the pressures and stresses. It naturally came about from the need for balance, and this imbalance in itself is brought about by the extremism of those who refuse to open their captivated minds and find their own entrances to the Under Levels Below, preferring instead to revel in blame, unconsciousness and the false masteries of fake awakenings.

Seeking contact with the Under Levels was cruelly discouraged by the Patron who had created a substitute Rule for the Re-al. Which was that only the Light of the Patron existed forever, and that only It, the Patron, was the intermediary between this infinite Light and all Other beings. It developed a system of petition, allowing minor requests, so that as members of the hierarchy of the Patron, your given position would measure your right to Light.

The way It presented it seemed so compassionate that everyone was actually grateful and strived to gain as much of this Light as they could. This created the imbalance that made them afraid of their Shadows, and gradually they ceased to understand the Shadows, or themselves, at all, and became stuck in those repetitious and reactive closed loops of annexed energy, the beloved food of the very Shadows they were afraid of in the first place... and more fuel for the Patron.

Fucking.

Ironic.

THE CLOSET OF THE SCOLDING PSYCHOPOMP

"Be careful what you swallow. Chew!"

- Gwendoline Brooks, Writer, Activist

"Naught is too small and soft to turn and sting."

- Emma Lazarus, Poet

"The protest is both an upset with the existing external circumstances, and the way we rail against the constrictions in which we feel caught. As the protest is both revealed and honoured, gradually, over time you come to know the equanimity that glows behind the protest. Something luminous, gentle and radiating."

- Deirdre Fay, Therapist, Writer, Healer

Our Que-an felt herself drawn into and past the Croft of the Shadows, her toes still extending backwards, finding miniature black holes, where she briefly heard the hissing of a billion waiting rotations of backed up Bile.

Soon the Closet of the Scold could clearly be seen when she looked over her shoulder, through the disappearing trails of the Shadows rushing past her, and our Que-an moved further Under along the Spiral.

This next Membrane is viscous and damp. She feels the tug again deep in her vagina, her cervix squeezing in a saturation of triggered inhibition. This is a sign that more coercion is coming, so she heeds it well and fully.

Her Vagal Snake rises from its half sleeping coil hissing, the fork in its tongue licking this particular duality in a stinging amputation of separation and objectification. This is a place of divisive and oppressive rule.

The extortion chant threaded through the Membrane being this;

Serve me...bitch.

Serve me, slave.

Serve me...you, E-arth.

You. S/he Sea.

Here is an Egregore of the Patron, and the borrowed cry of the Kin-mon who, instead of realising we are Sharded by the Patron, blames all else for the lack of satisfaction and the lack of rising joy.

"I feel sensitive," our Que-an has a stray thought as the Closet draws nearer, "to the reactionary states around naming this. I can feel the Patron — It, happening inside me, inside Us. I see it through all the Membranes... I can see it manifesting outside of me everywhere."

Even if this extremely pertinent stray thought does not arise to show us this possibility every time, or ever, and even though it might not be our personal conscious experience in this moment, it is a truth that is useful.

While also being elusive and tricky.

Another stray thought comes in this little necklace of conscious insightful attention: "This is why I want to say it. The weapons of blame and the S-hame are using our own Uld Fire to arrest us. To stop us departing deep down and Under, going to our own within Below."

The suppressed Wise Feminine of this within the Kin-Mon, closeted, demonised and denied, creates a bartering in the psyche. A marketplace of unmet needs, jostling for priority and the best deal. With accompanying uncomfortable rising feelings.

Instead of releasing the loving Uld Fire that runs through our central channels and feeds our Re-al, it is demanded of the *Wom* instead that we stimulate the Sharded remnants of old conditioned sensations. Because having a Shard in the He-art creates a sense of power and false dominion, but with no sensitivity to the Re-al. So this is the closest to the Core Consciousness that the Patron can approximate. As It is closed off from the Core by Its own imitative, rather than creative, mindset and intention.

There is no acknowledgement that we are all, Kin-Mon, *Wom* and Wo-Mon, the source of Core ourselves. No, and the cost of this is to lay both burden and therefore potential too, at the door of the other, forcing us to give away our energy, our Uld Fire, to the dominator.

And if the *Wom* were not to do this, or at least be seen to do this, through fake porns, pumped up glamour faces and subterfuge with accentuated or diminished bodily parts, subject to Patronic fast fashion, and laughably, even if no Re-al Fire was actually ever lit...then they were cast away and named termagant throughout all Patronic cultishness.

Exiled.

Defiled.

Wasted.

Ho.

Our Que-an entered the Closet in a single strong backwards stride, and was not there alone for long, for here entered the Scold himself, dressed in a voluminous glittery cape of samurai chiffon, ballooning outwards and wielding an impressive amount of fronted-up feminine charm. This masquerade was an ultimate prance in passive aggression, but also filled with the strange attractors of so many postures left un-thrown.

So very many wantings.

It was so damn chilly that you felt the ground recede from beneath you.

You could not sense which side of the coin he would fall at all, for he was both, and nothing, at the same time. He looked at her, appraising, measuring what he would need to do to get her on whatever side he might eventually choose.

At his leisure.

Yawn.

His attendants, sincere and helpful, clustered around him, assisting him and fussing things into more importance.

His Eye started searching within her, probing for her Uld Fire, seeking for the thrill of her nervous response. She could feel he was wanting to step right on the head of her Vagal Snake.

Crush it down.

Powder its snake oil.

She immersed a little, into her Core stance, feeling her Shadow Ally come near in a warming pass.

She noticed each tiny detail of interaction, things mostly unseen, under the surface, subtle, rife with the inherited patterns of all the generated malnourishment of the Patron, of whom our Scold was an avatar, if you haven't guessed already.

He reached out towards her and she felt it begin, the tug of demand.

Pull, pulling at her Sun Plexus and the He-art Belly of her Snake.

Wheedling.

He called her by her name to try to pin her down.

"Dear Que-an, how lovely it is to penetrate you."

With this ghastly nudge, she announced her own energetic presence as an individuation, taking up space and making intention to be more formed and anchor the Thunder-Stone of her Spiral. (We will Know more about this when we arrive at the table of the *Wom*.) Her vibration was this: "No matter what you, Scold, do or say, I will be passing through you, actually, and all on my own terms.

So as much as you and I are One in love unique, I may not dally here as I have already stayed too long.

So here, suck this instead.

You never know, it might meet a Re-al need or two, should you ever Know them."

She announced:

"In realising I am on the Way to my Under, I am moving on now. The agreement of this stage of the usual conditioned compromise has finished."

The attendants moaned, and she gazed at his out-stretched penile hand.
No.
The attendants called out, "But Friend Que-an! He is ill this time around!"
"No. I have arrived here for all *Wom* and this is over."
"But he is weak and sick," they called, as he lay down on the floor obligingly, his gynandrous form at once inviting and repelling.
"He needs your Uld Fire!" The whole closet was thick with entreaty and supplication.

"We thought you were here to help! You betray your gentle loving kind. This is just too shocking. We will be reporting you to our Patron."

"No."

His body burst into boils. "Look!" the attendants were almost shouting now, "Look at him, you must help, come closer... use your healing Uld Fire."

"No."

The boils suppurated and wept, seeming to lament the lack of sympathy, oozing towards her, pulling her attention. Seeking dependence and care.

"No."

And then his body died and his skin started to rot and melt — all this at finding her so wanting and cruel.

"No."

His attendants grasped handfuls of rotting, pink and bloody flesh and offered them to her, asking her, please, to eat, to save him, to transform him.

"As eucharist."

"At least do this."

"No."

"Suck this pus, please."

"No."

Deep inside she felt the hold of the Scold finally weaken. She felt the head of her Vagal Snake gently rise, alright just as she was, her refusal unswayed, breathing inwards deliciously, licked by her own tongue. Her centre was secure for now, and she delighted in it, allowing the soft pleasure of being herself to transmit to himself and his attendants that no matter what they did or said, she was her own *Wom* and she was not going to eat their shit any more.

However much it seemed to be so, so, so, so, so, so needed.

This Closet of the Scold, holding his rotting corpse and his coterie of distressed attendant feeders is a fundamental point of this Spiral towards the *KiGal*. She knows it well, this emanation of the Patron, as It annexes more and more of the Infra-fascial Membranes between Itself and the Re-al.

The challenge of this particular encounter is because if you did stay to help him and joined your hand with his, then this would consume everything. No explorations Under to release your *KiGal* would be possible, and it was extremely difficult to move anywhere else for a very long time.

If ever.

As a projection of the Patron, he was the first line of dominance used on the *Wom*. Seeking to involve all *Wom* in the pointless task of healing the Sharding, at the same time as it being forbidden to remove It. This would involve them in soothing the Fe-ar that would never be appeased, because it was a source of fuel for the Patron, and so we have the binding up of all of the *Wom*s Uld Fire.

The truth is that only us, the holders, can reject our own Shards, if we weren't so busy rejecting our own nourishment.

It is our own healing we have to effect.

The *Wom* could not keep trying to heal when their energetic Uld Fire strands and their He-art Strings were rejected, yet at the same time bound up, for then everything becomes based on eternal hopeless conditions.

This being yet another symptomatic obligation to the Great Dissonance demanded by the Patron.

Let's have It.

Another Great Yawn.

# THE CHOD WOMS

"When culture is based on a dominator model, not only will it be violent, but it will frame all relationships as power struggles."

- bell hooks, writer, social activist

"In the middle of my stride now. I am walking yes indeed I am walking through my own house."

- Angela Jackson, Poet

Not impossible to deal with in the meantime, though, because thanks to the promptings of her Core, she Knew of the flourishing Chod *Wom* tribe of corpse eaters. This amazing group of free beings delighted in being born into the swamps of deep extremism and imprisoned mindsets. She had spent one of her previous Uld lives living in those De-ath Felds learning the practice of eating the negative feculence generated by the Patron.

Working in, and surrounded by, the great pain body Membrane that exuded nothing but suffering in a huge response to all the exiled parts of the one dimensional phenomena created by the Sharding.

It was here she learned to honour our dear Shadows as the transformative way, in itself, and the Kin-ship with what seems at first to be separate, as the defining Re-ality of existence in all Infra-dimensionality. Here the *KiGal* is Known as the quintessential emanation of the Core and sits in the central creative Se-at of Flow and Desire. Because ultimately, all desire is flow and awareness, we learn how to desire to increase Love and ease and evolve away from manipulating the separate objects we've created in our stagnant mindsets at the prompting of the Patron.

The Chod *Wom*s are the clan of the ultimate Fucking cleaning Wo-Mons.

She would delight in practicing the evocation of bottomless Fe-ar itself and let it creep around her. Or invite it to rush at her from behind, patiently waiting for it to pounce like a leopard, and she would transform the energy, as it clutched at her Vagal Snake, sliding through her, trying to swallow her Hole.

She would invite the Fe-ar to sit beside her and rest while she turned her Labyrinth towards it, deeply listening to the message of abandonments and extinctions it brought. It would bring her visions of the energies created before the time it suddenly found itself bereft and pushed away, while everyone forgot why. Beautiful ebbing soft babies of vulnerability, newly awake and full of wonder.

She would extend a gentle cord from her Empathic Gland and tenderly touch all around the Membranes of the suffering Fe-ar, bringing the Core within the Re-al up close and more easily merged. Many a time she fell unconscious and acted out blindly, but gradually she became able to swallow what was brought, the Fe-ar, the hatred and the anger, so misunderstood energetically, and with her passionate digestion, turned it to the Nectar that fed the essential needs of the parts that were trapped in the closeted states.

And these states were extremely sticky, the glue of the hungry ghost runs all through the De-ath Felds in never-ending streams because the Nectar itself is never-ending.

To be in process is its own reward.

Always.

Pungent but sweet.

I know, hard to believe.

Triggering even.

But here and now on this Spiral, this Scold entity must eat his own shit. This was her discernment of the dark compassion, be it wrong or right in Patronic terms. And in this instance, it is the Way through. Please, if you do one thing, Loves, then help with the integration of this within yourself. Don't blame the messenger.

Being just through enough, anyway, is still free.

Fully engaged, she stayed present in her Spiralling down as she acknowledged the energetic quality of this agenda, and the pain that he needed to use to get the hungry Shard fed.

But this time now.

She said No.

This is the time of meeting the *KiGal*, and no energy could be tangled up, all had to be aligned to the Under.

So, sorry, babe.

It is.

A.

NO.

THE GREAT NOT FEELING IT

"The tongues of mocking wenches are as keen
As is the razor's edge invisible,
Cutting a smaller hair than may be seen,
Above the sense of sense; so sensible
Seemeth their conference; their conceits have wings
Fleeter than arrows, bullets, wind, thought, swifter things."

- Love's Labour Lost, William Shakespeare, Writer, Director

"The night is given to us to take breath, to pray, to drink deep at the fountain of power. The day, to use the strength which has been given us, to go forth to work with it till the evening."

- Florence Nightingale, Healer

"When the winds of turbulence are raging inside a nervous system, it's hard to trust that, as with everything in life, everything rises, crests and ultimately falls."

- Deirdre Fay, Therapist, Healer, Writer

Her first fascial Knot clotted just under her left rib as she turned away, moving on, and her colon twists with all the undigested forced feedings. Her Vagal Snake opens her mouth as wide as she can and her jaws become unhinged, for this was to be the long absorption, encompassing all indigestible experience, too big, too much, too many. She could hold the burden of the Patron, it is unavoidable, but she wouldn't ever really make It her own. Even when It tried to force her, even when it tried to make her unsure for Its own ends. When It wanted her to doubt. She was taking It in because it was being shoved down her throat, but she needed much more time and gentle self-respect to integrate, to process, to get her own bearings.

To Hell with this dancing with the Fucking Dictator.

What was all this for again?

Her headset had no memory reckoning.

The brain fog had settled in to dissuade her. Her doubt started up a jig with her Fe-ar and all her Knots became unconsciously numb in a sleep of vacuum. She felt like a whale, eviscerated and being fed on by too many starving creatures, come out from Under and desperate. She would lie here, spread too thinly, secreting weakening signals and watch herself filter away into the ground, looking for Re-al nourishment.

The Shadows hovered, waiting, Knowing.

This was the Patron trying to get her back on Its piste.

She could feel Its seeking interest at this, her latest Uld Fire statement to the Scold, with her last particle of consumed awareness, and she knew it was time to hide.

Her Vagal Snake quivered, triggered, bloated and paralysed, the burden stuck in this displacement, and her time bones ticked and tocked in a slow rhythm. Whenever the Spiral is like this, as this isn't new or old, it always slows slower and stills into the He-art corner of her gut. Here it becomes impacted if she tries to rush and hurry, to run it. To survive. To be strong. To try and Know before time. All she can do about it, until it resolves with the nudge of the Re-al, is to go so, so gently and ease her interaction, if she can, with any more of these bile-rising Patronic situations.

Her left hip braced itself. Her old Samskaric scarring tensioning from all the times she had eaten from the proffered plate of the Patron, as It carved up the giant junk morsels of

Its processed emulsions, the Bardo Factory chyme, manufactured to smother her clarity and induce more of the craving for Its fake.

At the same time, It continuously scanned for dissidents, or any beings that refused Its worthless offerings. Everyone all bent over backward from the force of Its wind with straining compressed Sacrums, clicking in and out of sciatic throbbing, like a scream on a tight wire. The refusers being usually the *Wom* and the Uld, the Shadows didn't have to refuse, as they weren't offered anything, being on a permanent deportation from the Bardo Factories.

She would, she decided, get up close to a Membrane and press herself into a Shadow Ally. But all the fever and vigilance had coalesced into her second fascial Knot that clung to her pelvic bowl at the top of her leg, and she had to keep repressing the feeling to retch and run again.

To run would make her the moving obvious target. To fight would make her the responsible target.

This is a sticky place on the Spiral — do you know it?

Your own selves?

Loves?

So she had to swallow her feelings, all mixed in with the Sh-It. This would give her breath space because it would make more Linear Time. Hiding, for now, would be more successful, and it was also good practice for being invisible, so that she could journey onward into further Felds, in peace, to continue her Descent.

This seed sign of potential Peace peeking over the Membrane of her mind made her body sing like a bow in Joy. The right side swelled in a tensile curve and the left side became the taut string holding the arrow of her Uld Fire ready to let loose.

All in good time.

All in her own time.

Owning her time.

Her mouth watered.

This succulent Here-Nowish is my time.

Maybe then this supported Uld Fire could be shot straight from her singing He-art Strings into the Shard of the Patron, in whoever and wherever it lodged.

Sounding like a plan, she noticed its directional quality, in this initiatory way that the Spiral eternally invited.

The He-art Belly is the tool for this balance. And this is where our Que-an is shooting from here, for this very Dream is shot from the bow of her longing.

Feel your He-art and let it sing the song of freedom from all this Fucking offensive fakery. Let your brave He-art meet your sorrowing Shard. This is the path that leads to the seed within the seed; and within this nucleus, our *KiGal* is calling her sweet rot song.

Now, as sure as the rising spring tide, she felt the usual wave of vertigo approaching. Her vision clutched for something that wasn't in the Spiralling. The nausea rose into her throat and her liver compressed off to the deeper side. Her Uld Fire channels writhed inwards and her Snake took up the flacking slack. Dizzy and destabilised, she brought herself down into the soles of her feet, where they touched the Re-al inside the ground of the Membrane.

A clod of E-arth oozed through the gaps between her toes.

The Fe-ar of exposure rose up sharply. Of being the bullseye, in the line of fire. Backlashed. Naked and too seen, to be spat on and reviled by the Patron.

Steady now.

The Patron can't see you that well anymore, remember — even with Its strategies.

There is something else about moving forward, just here at this spot that is also inviting the dizziness, the congestion in her head and neck, guts weak. It is as though she is overdone, overblown. Our Que-an knows she needs this turbulence; it throws off all the old scents to signal the new direction. All new direction, all new transformation, will disturb the Samskaras in their comfortable old loops. But what is this point right here? Can our Que-an have an unconditional place of safety and solace? For her own Self?

Her energy bottomed out.

The energetic price exacted for this journey was taking a payment just now, this she could feel. She had moved the firmament in challenging the Scold, the flagellating offshoot of the Patron, who is the pseudo entitled It using stolen resources to stop the tracks of those who Dream into the Re-al in connection with, and being the Descendants of, the *KiGal*.

It is like the spiritual war has upped its ante.

How're you feeling now, Loves?

Our Que-an was happy to pay this price, as these payments were to create the balance that would be more resilient, ever strong and versatile moving forward.

To give herself more time and space and slow it all down was what she needed.

Her Great Grand *Wom* had often sang this song to her, to help her for these times:

"Slow down sweet girl-fire of Uld.
Your Flame will soon cool,
Your wings will unfurl,
Sliding soft across your ribs.
All space becomes your own
In your
Unwinding down to Under."

Peace.

Be free.

She wondered if she could secrete a side chamber to recover. And just then a single tinkle of a clear bell somewhere, cut through her spinning Labyrinth and the pupil Hole of her Eye opened wider to See, to say.

Yes,

YES,

yes, she could.

The deepest quiet descended and she lay down carefully on the Membrane before her, using the spinning surge of the Spiral to choose her next movement and slowly become the stillness in the centre of the journeys gyre.

She sensed the inner borehole that had run dry so many times before, as she struggled with the whirling gaping up at her. And as her attention was gently drawn Under, feeding into this rotation of her perception, she lost all sense of landing anywhere in particular and she ceased to struggle for now.

She let go into the ground, her palms and heels feeling into silky dust, as each of her molecules burst emptily, showing its true face to her, flowering so softly.

Smiling in Love.

The vertigo energy orientated itself within her, click, click, ready to move a lead into the deep dive; and she sought that pearl of her Self at the bottom of this vast silence, ever revealing itself.

She saw it, then, She felt it, then... I am this.

S-he Sea.

I am.

The tenderness of the ever unfolding centre of her continuous Core infused the Membrane all around her with safety — like a pigeon cooing quietly, late inside a hot day.

Her body rested in soft limbo as she merged into the ground of being, nestled.

The spinning slowed and showed her truth to her. She could see her own Spiral and was very glad to be facing the Under again, letting...

gone...

gone...

Into.

She watched a tear release from her Eye and it rolled down, round and round, into the Great Below.

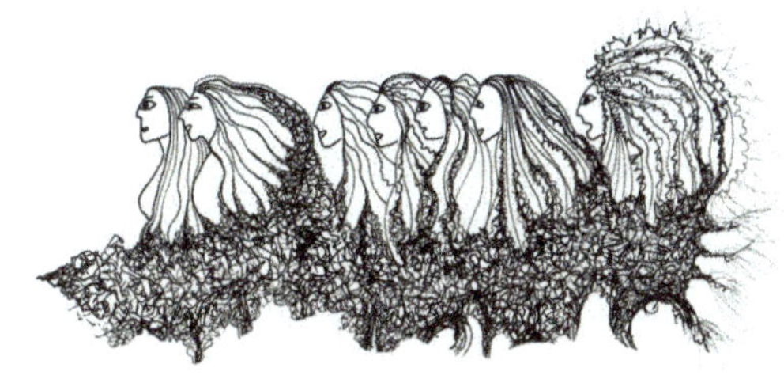

PARTLY CLOSER TO THE *KiGal*

"I am not free while any woman is unfree, even when her shackles are very different from my own."

- Audre Lorde, Warrior, Poet

"... in practice the standard for what constitutes rape is set not at the level of women's experience of violation but just above the level of coercion acceptable to men."

- Judith Lewis Herman, Psychiatrist, Writer

Our Que-an is now in a position on the Spiral to enter the outer edge of an Under-Feld of the *KiGal*, if she wants to. She noticed the feeling of the reflective grieving sounds of the Echoes in her Labyrinth, dispersing through the tunnels and channels in the Under and playing with the density of the air. The lament was growing and calling into her He-art Strings, this aching siren of the exiled. The sighing and flowing came on and on, uncovering sorrowful sound.

She reached one of the seven (but Re-ally we are not counting, are we Loves?) gateless gates of the descent in the No-thing, the Empty Void so common to all *Wom*, through which new beginnings, new souls, and new spiritual evolutions we know as Spirals, are born. She paused to sense if she was to enter. Or whether S-he was to enter her.

You never can tell in advance about this.

She saw the Faces of the Echoes in the roundedness of the burnished stone entrance of the Gate, rubbed by the countless hand oil prints of all the rainbow relations of the *Wom*.

Black, Red, Yellow, White, Black, Red, Yellow, White, Black, Red, Yellow, White... Green... Blue.

The Faces turned, looking and staring, and saw her Seeing, and that her Eye was being kindled to Empty. Empty, as in ripe with possibilities, having not settled for anything. Maybe never settling for anything ever again, living in a constant flow with the Re-al. True and self-delivered.

Tears pricked her eyes and she felt the wash of it. So poignant, unpretended and so tender. She could hear her Eresh the *KiGal* weeping and those mirror tears washed through the ethers on rivulets of lighted sea strands.

"Fuck this Sh-It," the *KiGal* was saying.

"It wants me as Its supplicant, I have to stay hidden and shackled and I cannot state my truth and embody our beloved Re-al. My Uld Fire is suppressed, dampened, I am silenced. I am shut down in my Unders.

The Patronic Eye sees my Vagal Snake as evil incarnate.

I am Its very trespassing demon.

Yet.

I am but Its own sin because It has made Me the Hell-Hound to better exert Its power through polarity. It submerges me here to eternally suffer this projection.

I feel the Shard deep within me, clamping my Uld Fire.

Where is the Titan? Why does he not move his mountain?

Too self-absorbed in his entitled meditations. Bloody waste of space up there in his Realm of the Gods.

My dear Lover Kin-Mon? Killed away from me by the false promise of Its puny Patronic light for a price, and the smallest love making with Its strictest of conditions.

Constricted so tightly.

I am shut in."

A silence settled.

Then,

"Where are my *Woms*? ... banished to the invisible realms.

Are you here????

Where are you?

I can feel one of you approaching me. You are not the first or last, don't think anything of it at all.

Just... have you given up everything of Its world completely?

Listen in your Labyrinth, have you?

If you have...

Then.

Touch me.

Touch me.

Touch me.

Touch.

Me."

Our Que-an heard these Echoes through the chasms and corridors, making use of all the ruptures, unleashed in the gusts all around her, yet also sometimes stabbing right through from the inner centre of her own Labyrinth in an almighty earache. Dropping down in a plummet to her yearning He-art Belly.

Outside or inside this Spiral? Both and neither.

Not nothing, not being. Not and not not.

Everywhere and elsewhere, which is only Here-Nowish at this point. Get with this... do try.

Try.

She arose from the Empty, the pain of loss ripping through her and her He-art Belly parted open, blood of Uld Fire spilling and spilling and falling outwards to cover the stony ground below in a pooling. It was absorbed into scab in a whisper.

At the same time, she also felt it all become more distant, fading into the No-thing. She checked to see if she was disassociated.

No.

Our Que-an is still embodied. In body. Big enough with you, Loves, helping to hold this Great Dissonance, as we are discovering.

Instead, her focus diffused and widened and she was smelted in her own arising Uld Fire as it changed from falling to rising, her broken He-art Belly expanding into the great space from Below, becoming in the Under.

The pool of her drying Uld Fire blood darkened in a deeper way, forecasting a sharp turning that unwound, round and round, opening wide...

And the Great Rage blew up and through all of her creation, in this moment, through this ripped Hole in her He-art Belly. A boiling red hot energy that searched for its landing with an unfailing direction.

It burned all the laments away and she stormed towards the *KiGal*, screaming Fury in a Blue Face right into the centre of everything.

But no.

She would not touch her *KiGal*.

Not Yet.

THE IRON MAIDEN

"In this sense, I can willingly subscribe to the biblical statement: 'Follow me, for I am with you all days, until the end of the world.' In this case I am not following a guru, but I am fully surrendering to the loving aspects of the Earth, the Goddess. Imagine the sensual trust that enters into our cells when we follow the statement in such a way that no fear can creep in, because we can perceive the protective powers of growth in nature and connect with them both physically and spiritually."

- Sabine Lichtenfels, Peace Activist

"Slavery is the next thing to hell."

Harriet Tubman, Activist

For suddenly she was plunged and swimming in a limitless lagoon, where the water was becoming more and more cloudy and thick. Vapours and mists joined together in edgeless clouds above it. She could see, was it two or three or four, other figures swimming within the clotting soup, and what seemed to be a Kin-Mon stroked up towards her from below, his hand reaching across the current between them.

In her longing, she reached for him too. She was under the surface now, and she could see his hand was leaking a blood red fluid Uld Fire from its palm lines. Life line, He-art line, He-ad line, Fate line, the line of Intuition all bleeding and merging with the waters in a hopeless and endless haemorrhage and it feels so, so desolate.

What will stem his flowing depletion and stop his Uld Fire from drowning in this solidification?

He sank back down and away and sandy clouds obscured his face and hands. The tendrils of red thinned out and crystallised ore-like into stratifications.

Our Que-an felt the arising of the Fe-ar at the same time as a firm rope–like feeling brushed against her inner thigh and she made a grab for it quickly. It was her Vagal Snake, and it became a pulley she used to break upwards, shattering the surface tension, crawling along its smooth back and jumping onto the wrecked shore. She was dazed and then remembered there were the others. One, *Wom*, arrived right behind her, brought in on a slow oily wave.

It was Imago! Her strength flooded the beach, so utterly welcome.

They realised that the other, who they both Knew, suddenly, and at the same time, as a Wo-Mon of the Uld, was still in the lagoon. They turned around and saw that all the water had solidified, cemented in an aggregate, all mixed up together and hardened completely.

S-he was buried and set in stone.

"How do we know if S-he is still down there?" our Que-an asked.

"I can hear her," Imago murmured, inclining her beautiful He-ad, "I can hear her in my Labyrinth."

"We must dig her out then, surely?"

And very handily, as though always prepared for this eventuality, here was the necromantic Thunder-stone (You can jump on the Spiral to the Table of the *Wom* to find this Stone, but remember to then jump back to this same place) ... and a crowbar.

Both leaning against the bottom of the cliff which appeared from the fogs, towering above the shore, where at the top you could spy the lines of sputtering flames from the torches of the Patronic Witch Hunters. But they could not descend — trapped by their own lofty heights, they were oblivious. And there were a fair few Sheela-Na-gigs nesting half way up, that would put off anyone from ascent or descent. Just because their laughter was so Fucking loud and damning.

Such bloody bitches.

So our *Woms* set to work.

The layers were hard and impenetrable and they soon saw that this was no endless stone coffin of a sea, as it grew smaller and defined itself into the shape of the entrapment Known as the Iron Maiden. The famed and feared ancient Inquisitional punishment that imprisons and confines our inner *KiGal* below, restraining her soul, imprisoning her Avatars. All our own souls. All Uld Fire diminished into the usual muzzled scarcity.

The blood from the palm lines of the Kin-mon's despair rose up their gullets, bitter and rushing, drowning them in the murk of depression. But it affected our Que-an and Imago not at all, because even though they Know that their own power exists as the irritant to the Patron, and that this Uld Fire triggers the Patron creating the ultimate penalty, they also Know they are interconnected in the Infra.

So it was easy to determine to persevere with the release, despite feeling depressed, and open her on up.

Because to keep opening at every turn is the only way to descend to liberation.

Right?

The strange regenerative bravery arose and gave them succour. Even as more agitated movements swirled the fug at the top of the cliffs as though to warn them off. To protect Its own grid.

Struggling and panting hard in pleasure, they jimmied and struck with all the might of the uprising punishment Itself, using Its own repressive energy against It. The weighty, sharp, double-edged two-lipped Thunder-stone swung down and down, again and again, violence erupting and powered by something not yet fully rendered, but so strong and vital in essence.

Then, the crowbar found a slit in the permanence and S-he opened.

Relief flooded over the harsh reality of this seemingly never-ending road of hardship and toil. They looked within, their eyes shining.

But all was Empty.

S-he had merged into totality in the Great Below, long before this effort took shape. The weight of the solidification had compressed her into a minuscule diamond viral point that reflected back into itself so many times that it disappeared from their Sight.

They bled the sweat away and sighed.

The Thunder-Stone and the crowbar glowered with metal-mongering heat and the Iron Maiden's cracked shell lay in a radiant flush on the beach.

This old rape of her was a fossilised dead end-story and now they Knew for sure that as all things pass and change, this layer of the miasmic straits was just as temporary as anything else, having broken Its spell for now. It would not reform as long as S-he was gone, gone, gone beyond.

Imago and our Que-an bowed to the wisdom of this passing and went to have a cup of tea. (Medicinal, purgative and mildly hallucinogenic, yes, of course, always.)

The cliff face subsided onto the beach and an avalanche buried the Iron Maiden's husk in the impotent torches, ducking stools, stakes and hanging ropes of the Patron. No lagoon was left, no moisture remained, all juice dried up.

Just a small last gasp from a buried Kin-mon who had forgotten how to swim in stone.

UP THE BLIND ALLEY

"I am a collection of dismantled almosts."

- Anne Sexton, Writer

"I'd like to ask the men here to consider idly, in some spare moment, whether by any chance they've been building any walls to keep the women out, or to keep them in their place, and what they may have lost by doing so."

- Ursula K. Le Guin, Writer, Seer

Our Que-an rose up, sitting and staring at a dead end, directly speaking to her blind spot. Feeling buried alive.

A monochrome reflection of the sheer impossibility of being able to see in what ways she had continuously and relentlessly become trapped. Frustration does not even come close to the gaping helplessness created by this particular not knowing.

This possible masking of her true nature.

What is it saying, this view of no view?

Is it a Patronic should-form (should! should! should!) block that must be investigated and dismantled?

Blown apart?

What is its meaning? She did not even know which part of her was experiencing this. Whose Uld Fire Eye was resting against the cool smooth Membrane that secured the ending of this passage. Stopping her dead. All sound seized up, strangled, all sight was focused ahead into the barrier. She could not sense the *KiGal*, and when she turned, the Membrane turned with her. She sighed. Would it always be like this? And was this actually the bright side of it?

An inner shutter slammed shut. Her focus had to get used to itself with nowhere to go.

No-thing to do.

The Membrane tightened against her face.

De-ath crawled in and out of the No-thing like a worker wasp in her hive.

Ah, the deep Fe-ar and discomfort arose, as she saw the part of herself in turmoil before the jump. So many Knowings had been as so many platforms to jump from, up until now. She felt her stages disintegrating and here was the wall again.

What is this wall? This mask? What is this Membrane the bandage for?

She lost touch with the wounding sting of this slap of a wakening, and came to sense in towards the healing, but wanted to die anyway. The sheer lack of meaning in the Membrane surrounding her is the message of the unknown, the stew of void... again.

Turning, turning, turning, always turning round the Spiral.

Then she finally remembered to look down.

Under.

Not a-head.

Into her He-art.

The Membrane became the circular sides of the well of the lonely Fighter and her dripping cry cascaded, echoing into something else.

What?

Oh, I am blind. So, so blind. My Eye in all its closings cannot last a day upright this way. And from her sitting, she did a total tailspin directly pointing into the Below.

Her Vagal Snake yawned and erupted through this upside downing crowning skull into the million wormholes that were her follicles of perception.

She dark Medusa-ed and her priestly celibacy exploded.

Her seeking arms reached and multiplied to touch every single soft suffering baby soul part, each having an Eye to open in their begging palms.

You are perfect, you are perfect, my He-art pours love into your suffering. Soon you will not have to be the dark burden of the surface, but be seen as the Uld Fire who stands in the original beauty all through the neglect and shame that holds you apart.

She Divined to the Birther, and the Uld Fire energy swooped and changed her expanding material density into the transparent web of the Sun Que-an spider.

Is it venomous?

Oh yes.

All the time.

Give me your stonewalling, gaslighting and obstructions and I will glare you into the cold with this hot soul burning.

I Know what I don't know, and that is enough for me.

Enough.

The Membrane spoke,

"Don't try and mirror me so that you feel the passive nun again. Because this will not bring you freedom from your self-rejection. We all end up here alone one day. You have to face me and the lack of love, wherever I come from in you. The void is the ancestral Hole to the lack of love. The space that waits to be filled with grace. Don't worship the No-thing. It is a complete waste of your Uld Fire."

Know the edges of Love by its absence.

She saw the energy in the Membrane, seeing the intention that built it. It was a protector that also offered the chance of the transformational undertow. She felt the great tenderness emerge as she came home Known.

And she Bodhisattva-ed.

No-one needs to know anything but the deep Feld of the Love Peace when the wound of wild un-trust is ripped bare of its scab of a Membrane. Our Que-an has blood to flow and knows ever more deeply that she will be alone in this unknown because there is no other place to be and no other being to be it.

Which is thee and me, Loves...

What journeys end is no end? The Labyrinth winding in and out. What is the fate of the two-headed splitting axe of Patronic domination but becoming the Labrys transformed into an enfolding labian caress.

She squatted and opened the petals of her lips delicately.

The source of you.

Enter the cave of your self now.

Be you in all your glorious perfection that is dark, unwanted and ugly. For ugly is so beautiful when we are all upside down, Below, and free of the Patron.

This feeling of deep Loving expanded outwards and then the Membrane absorbed itself and our Que-an freed up and felt herself into the next passage.

Swiftly and suddenly caused by this shedding, she smells fermentation on a sweet and unlikely breeze down here in the depths. Our Que-an meets her own corpse rotting on a stump in the hollow of the *KiGal* in this further deep. She is not surprised, she is pleased. Delighted with the stench of change. The crooning gathers loud and clear and the Echoes abate to wait as more Membranes fall away. Our Que-an spreads herself as best she can upon a hook and waits for her deep sister to come closer.

She is here, the *KiGal*. A grave pressure builds with a grounding edge. It is delicious and impenetrable.

Eresh the *KiGal* gently inspects her raw arrival, picking through her skin and separating her bones for sorting, ordering the very air to be still. Her nails part the places that cling and her wet tongue loosens anything dry. She selects all the Knots and compactions delicately and tenderly, her face of ultimate De-ath so peaceful and calm.

Our Que-an's viscera drops out in a spiralling looseness and she melts off her hook like wax off its wick.

Everything comes together then, the Patron forgotten in Its dim past dimension, nothing but ancient dried up news. Her Uld Fire is ready for this. It's been too long coming. The *KiGal* mutters something and our Que-an's Labyrinth sparks open.

What?

Hear me now.

I have been here.

I have been alone.

I have kept the Love safe.

I have cared for the Peace.

I have called it all out.

I may have been buried but I am the seed that grows in its own direction.

I am you.

And you.

You Know who I am.

Be me. See me. Create me forward on this Spiral.

You *Wom* of the Re-al.

Creatrix.

Our Que-an feels her strong arising being gently pulled at and a great shapeliness overtakes her as her new form feeds itself, filling into the Under spaces of the Great Below. Her Vagal Snake softly hisses erect, and our Que-an can see through into the He-art of the *KiGal* where the Shard is encased in her scar tissue.

We all want this Shard to die the noiseless death by now, don't we?

Fucking thing.

Eresh hisses too, and our Que-an feels the beloved Core of all creation spinning up within her as she bounds joyfully into the presence of all there forever is. They meld into an equinoctial infinite point together, the Shard held between them like lovers, particles seamlessly merging with their anti-particles to transform into the wave unity and they disappear through a Gateless Gate to dissolve Its glaciation.

They reappear rising.

Now as *KiGal* we are in total touch with the Re-al, searching and transforming throughout the Great Dissonance to balance the Patron. Bringing all that is judged as the dirty, the sick and the poor into the Seen. All suffering and illusory dying into the Seen. As all this is true beauty, being only wasted in pathetic Patronic aversions.

To challenge the view of this Patron. To call out the nature of Its relentless assumptions. To say what needs to be said in all the large and small ways.

Naming It.

To liberate everything from the Fe-ar and unconsciousness.

To stop this rape of the Re-al.

Because what else is there to do on an ambrosial morning of this life? Why would any of us be doing anything else?

What are you doing today, of your own Way, dear Loves?

THE TURNAROUND TO FACE THE GREAT DISSONANCE

"Sometimes it is necessary to make a confrontation — and I like that."

- Louise Bourgeois, Artist

"The white western patriarchal ordering of things requires that we believe there is an inherent conflict between what we feel and what we think — between poetry and theory. We are easier to control when one part of ourselves is split from another, fragmented, off balance."

- Audre Lorde, Writer, Warrior, Poet

"Encountering turbulence in any form, making contact with the pattern, in order to re-pattern from within, and pivot to a more nourishing experience."

- Deirdre Fay, Therapist, Healer, Writer

Our Que-an, at one point or another, has to regularly strengthen her Membranes specifically. If she neglects this process, the Patron becomes attracted to the freely available energy of her vulnerability. Her porosity dissolves her boundaries and she loses her intentional definition.

Is too easily merged.

The strengthening process can arise in different kinds of opportunities, not all of them pleasant. It often looks, on one side of the Membrane, as though Love has abandoned these situations. But this is never true. It is rather a great fatigue that arises on all sides, as the demands of other agendas manifest and take their dues. Especially if activity is triggered by the fear of loss of control, or the loss of profit, by the manufacturer of these other agendas.

Entering into contracts of any kind have to be thoroughly scrutinised for subtexts and unconscious entitlements.

This attention to detail might seem counterproductive, maybe even petty, and against the noble precepts of surrender and availability, but being weaned into life as fodder teaches you certain valuable things. If I (Oh, who am I then, Loves? Who dares?) were to name this for the purposes of our Que-an's descent, then it would be that evolving consciousness is not evolving, if it is enslaved to the point that it dies inside, in an old pattern. And plenty of situations cause inner death, the dampening, or even extinction, of our Uld Fire.

Which is not to be confused with our wholesome De-ath's shedding outworn shells and skins, in all that thrilling splendour.

It is not only the Bardo Factories that demand time and takings in these deadening transactions. Individual emissaries of the Patron, discernible by the unconsciousness that they have for their own Shadows, who trail them around miserably invisible, regularly visit with petitions. And these can look like just about anything.

Even the most innocuous delivery of an energy package, all dressed up for the Christ-mass, must be seen deeply to assess the direction of its evolution. What binding cords are being extended from these gifts? What esoteric ribbons and bows that flatter and twinkle towards you?

Discern!

Alert!

Our Que-an is wise to all this and offers no blame. She may not accept the package but she won't start, or end, a war over it either. There is no need for blame as a weapon of defence, that would be playing into the unconscious energy. No, a simple Seeing is all that is required. Because as soon as you fall short of the proffered projection It is onto your Uld Fire like a snake charmer, in a bid to dismantle you. It hopes to humiliate your Vagal Snake through insult and character assassination, to get you to admit failure, lack and fault, which all serves to erode your Membrane and drench your Uld Fire.

It is everlastingly relentless, as there is one thing the Patron has that is very important to the continuing Dissonance. And that is the aspiration to plunder and push all the Membranes into one entanglement that then can be mined for the generation of more linear Time on Its side and more mimicry of the Re-al.

For this winding up the fishing line of Time is one of the ever suffering heralds of the Great Dissonance. Time that the Patron needs to keep regenerating, compartmentalising in an attempt to make more Time, to maintain Its control, and so Time too, has been enslaved by It to bring Its own systems into being.

The turning of days lights and nights darks, in their own Re-al cyclical rhythms and flows have been constrained and channelled to designate when a measurement of themselves would come or go. By clocked decree. All tides regulated, so that this energy could be bought and sold under contracts whose terms were always eroding the flow of the Re-al. The less Time available to the Re-al then the more Time for takeover under the use of the Patron.

Or so It supposes and tries to make true.

Our Que-an and all *Wom* Know this as a challenging limitation, but also as a resource, because, for us, the fact the Patron exists can be used to pick out the wisest way in satisfying differentiation and Membrane strengthening. We become aware of the parcels of mini time meted out to us as either reward or punishment, and then we choose to retreat from this Dissonant Dimension while leaving a part of ourselves behind, to maintain an elusive presence that does not trigger a chase for control of our Uld Fire.

We, too, can ghost when we need to.

Hell.

Yes.

The wisest Way only becomes apparent if Uld Fire is engaged in the inner work of our own unique energy flow in relationship with our Vagal Snake. This is the place that shows the use and misuse of personal attention, and will show us what it is that is in control.

Check for yourself right now, Loves. What have you allowed yourself to be a slave to? What kind of voices are you hearing? No need to judge it, no berating required, just know it and decide from Here-Nowish.

Practice deciding again and again, and see how much focus can be stored for future Seeing.

The Wise *Wom* Way is encompassing all that arises in our Knowings and it will come to us like coming home, once we have shed the Time particulates of the Patron and the offered parcels of distraction. Slow down and enter yourself to Core, dear *Woms*, Kin-mons and Echoes. Reach into the Here-Nowish to wrest control from the past of the Patron.

This is the key.

Wise up.

Face the Dissonance created by subterfuge, infantile dominance and dependency. Face it within, you allow it, you are its food. Decide then.

What is your own unique wisest Way?

What are you in judgement of?

Focus!

Focus!

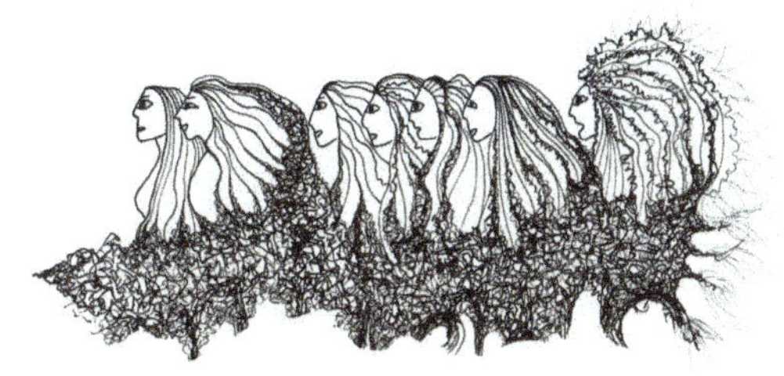

THE FELINE PACT

"The close nexus between reductionist science, patriarchy, violence, and profits is explicit in 80 percent of scientific research that is devoted to the war industry, and is frankly aimed directly at lethal violence —"

- Vandana Shiva, Eco Activist, Writer

"The sexual imagery of penetrating, torturing, and enslaving Mother Nature should not be dismissed as harmless figures of speech unrelated to the way seventeenth-century English gentlemen scientists perceived the world. The subordination of women was an essential component of their worldview, which was entirely committed to maintaining male dominance in a patriarchal society. To believe that the early scientists' pronouncements were 'value-free' with regard to women or any other social matters would be extremely naive."

- Carolyn Merchant, Environmentalist, Writer

Our Que-an is now wandering lazily unlimited through the Infra, where many Felds arise and pass in waves as they move into individual seeds, and then back again to waves, her Vagal Snake leading her like the tip of an arrowhead burrowing deep between arterial roots, parting soft grasses. Her direction meanders before her, revealing itself with a steadiness that here is secure and absolute… if you are capable of reading the signs, like she is.

Happiest landing in this seeding Uld Feld, with its untouched, wild and vibrant Re-al, she collects spiders in her hair, feeling confident and content.

In her element.

Here in her Way, there are no questions asked to find out about anything outside of this, as she is not interested in attracting the attention of the Patron. This way only has the gentle probing sounding into the Under. It is the most vital inner enquiry and only leads to the Re-al, as it exposes all that is not Re-al.

No Patron had stepped Its insensate crushing footprint on these tender plant growths and curves of soils, battering all the precious arthropods with its smothering mine mind and noxious profiteering vehicles. All the Uld Dragons of this land are protected and honoured; harmony is invited into every precious moment of weathering beauty.

It was such a fresh spring breeze of a freedom to be invisible to the Patron here, in such enjoyable ways, because she was coming to know that she would be the one to decide how she would walk further down Below

Or not.

Not hurried, or worried, or frightened into compliance. Just walking and E-arthing in the Feld, in a solid reflection of her Uld Fire, with all the wildest gifts of the Re-al from the Infra-connected Uldermentals who protect these intrinsic parts.

The Felds belong to the *Wom* only because they understand, and can see all the most delicate, and sometimes smallest, links of the beings in the promise of the Re-al, being free of the Patronic agenda. No enslaving commerce is available when everything is free and natural. No-one can annexe power when all beings are recognised and respected as soulfully sentient, sovereign, and of such value to the whole unwinding Infra-Dimensionality. No one sect of beings can be coerced to serve another sect or its ideas, dying to themselves in the process.

That toxic arrogance in the thinnest of pathetic Patronic disguises.

Our Que-an always enjoyed herself, here in this potent musing, deep and fulfilling with no need to hold back or to watch herself, and noticed with amusement the tendrils of more benevolent Egregores dancing with her happy Shadows.

Are you dancing a little inside, Loves?

And your own Shadow? How is this tenderness?

And now, as surely as energy follows attention, (we know this one!) she suddenly found herself browsing a city street of the Patron.

An anti-Feld.

Just like that.

In a mirror manoeuvre.

Unremarkable and looking like the repeat road of all Its other conurbations and Bardo Factories, it had all the storehouse Membranous fronts polished clean and perfect, ready for the economic extraction of all passing souls.

Each outlet the entrance to the Mine of Coin that existed deep in the bowels of all the sewers. Great clumps of strip-mined and displaced deadened ore, sitting lumpen and solid with all the weight of anti-matter, injected with an imitation of value and forced to generate the intention of drawing all the imaginary assigned wealth to itself alone.

This parade was the front that hid the garbage it generated. Behind it was all the heaps and masses of discarded, dangerous and expensive waste. The lost principles of sharing the bounty of the Re-al with the kindness of strangers, stacked up unused, as it was lacking in profit. Everywhere the fool's gold glittered there, uselessly.

Our Que-an shuddered in recognition and opened her attention wider quickly, but it was too late. She was sucked behind a store front and became immediately enmeshed in its window display, surrounded by Fucking Relics. (Oh yes, they become trapped in the buying and selling of their owner's karma, as we know...)

Frozen and paralysed, she postured towards an empty street, spiritually naked and caught, her hands now raised in an impotent entreaty with her bracelets like manacles pulling her backwards.

Her Vagal Snake was taut and thin, holding on to her gut, feeling rattled, they were in a binding coil together.

Stuck is stuck is stuck.

No-thing passed.

And it all stretched onward, waiting. A long sliding into more extra Time packets than felt possible. Until it suddenly seemed too soon, and a smothering noxious vehicle drove from around the nearest corner and automatically parked in front of the shop Membrane where we are with our Que-an.

The poisonous wheels were towing an open flat-bed trailer in which a large white panther was standing serene, with the most luminous eyes of any dimension ever manifested. Deeper than emerald green, an ocean with starlight for water. The cat looked at our Que-an, drawing her attention so very close as they gazed, each in each other's Eyes. And our Que-an swallowed a small pump of the Fe-ar at the back of her throat. Sour and astringent.

Her Vagal Snake's head retracted carefully back down her central channel, smoothly silent in this feline presence. No need to offer one's self up for dinner.

Where in all Hellaciousness is the Keeper of this cat? Surely they will be around here, somewhere near. She wondered, still all caught up, and was glad that they were on opposite sides of the shop Membrane as she could not flee. She was paralysed and naked and helpless, and here was the beautiful De-ath eyeing her up again.

The pump of Fe-ar in her mouth now drummed into full throttle. So, obviously, she could not scream. At that very moment the white puma jumped out of the vehicle, lithe and free to bound round the edge of the Membrane.

What?

Our Que-an didn't even know there was an edge to this Fucking Membrane and Fe-ar exploded everywhere as the cat in a final stride was upon her. Mouthing her neck and holding her tight in its jaw, this was a most beautiful and terrifying Grimal-Kin. She could feel the pressure of its teeth, not quite biting into cutting, its large, rough tongue and the warmth of its running saliva sliding down between her breasts.

Nothing could ever be closer than this terrible intimacy. She calmed herself, desperately, the Keeper would be somewhere near and she would be released soon, she really felt that hope's faint glow.

But no.

Her trust faded and the waiting game extended again, growing and yawning, while her neck stayed clasped so very still and strongly held. She tried a small movement to see if she could **trigger** a release. The grip firmed against her.

The stillness grew and she tried again.

Every time she moved even a nano, the jaws tightened in exactly the same measurement, so she was slowly being compressed, and no release was happening, only its opposite. And it was utterly quiet.

No Keeper anywhere.

No way here or there.

No movement, unless she initiated it, so it was a kind of choice, yet it was a choice that only led in one fatal direction. Because every time she made the choice it only worsened the whole situation.

Nothing to do, nothing to be, nowhere to go.

Snared.

That Fucking rock and the hard place again. Her capacity for creative solutions around all this was wearing a bit thin.

But hang on.... hang on.

Suddenly she knows this as another stateless place on the Spiral, and a dawning Knowing comes sifting up through this bewitching stalemate, and she knows where she must really go.

You are probably already ahead on this one, by now, Loves...

You are right.

She absorbed the strangulation and turned inwards to dive Under.

She followed the direction of the obvious compression and found the falling groove into the central channel where her Vagal Snake was already whipping round to unwind, and down they went together into the empty void of the pure and abundant potential of the Great Below.

Out through her lowest of the low.

Our Que-an was really getting the hang of this now, and realised, on a tremendous surge of Uld Fire, that she was in access to the actual Under at any point. And that this Under was far beneath the Ore bowel of the Patron, under the city shops, under the Bardo Factories, and that actually she had just been blessed with another gift of the Re-al.

The Feline Pact of the energy of the great white cat, her Uld double.

Her own Uld Fire in magnetic attraction creating the potential for the Re-al to manifest within this Dissonance.

This is our double that each *Wom* has as her own Infra-Dimensional Keeper of energy. That's why no other Keeper arrives to save us. Our double appears in any dimension, in whatever forms are most needed to challenge the Patronic status quo. So that the Patronic fake rule is slowed in its shafting Sharding of the Re-al and the spreading of Its suppressing influence.

If we do not See that it is our own Uld Fire and we are the deciders, then we are held captive in our UnSeeing.

Through this lesson of equal and opposing force, our Que-an collapses into pure energy.

The Re-al emerging in triumph.

It was her own Uld Fire being used all along, disguised by the Patron as Its own. And, had the Feline not arrived so stealthily, using their own noxious conveyance, our Que-an would have remained paralysed and eventually forced into being one of their showcase puppets. Her strings pulled and pulleyed to further attract more of her kind to this sterile dead end fate.

Our Que-an enjoyed being in the empty Void — magnificent, in all its free loneliness and its humming One Core sound.

So full, not Re-ally so Fucking Empty after all.

Isn't it?

Remember, no-one is doing anyone any favours.

Don't bypass.

Instead.

Trespass on the trespassers.

THE PRELIMINARY SHARDING

"...howsoever the use and practice of such arts is to be condemned ... for the further disclosing of the secrets of nature ... a man [ought not] make scruple of entering and penetrating into these holes and corners, when the inquisition of truth is his whole object."

- Francis Bacon, Scientist. Writing about raping nature for scientific gratification and pseudo knowledge

"One of the benefits that oppression secures for the oppressor is that the humblest among them feels superior."

- Simone de Beauvoir, Philosopher

"...can't be a slave if you're already free."

- Gabriels, Singer

When our Que-an was a daughter herself, one of the first intensities that anchored her in this dimension of the Great Dissonance, was being climbed upon, as she slept on her mat, by a very heavy, miasmic being. She woke back up through the levels from nurturing Infra-Dimensional sleep because she noticed its Shadow form trying to alert her with outstretched arms, sliding up towards her from the bottom end of her Dreaming.

This crushing being crawled all the way up, and on, to sit on her mouth.

It had reached through the Membrane and masked her face in a thin binding, a plasticised gag, so that she could not breathe or express a sound and she sensed she had to stay very still until it had gone. She did not Know what it wanted, but she felt a needing feeding.

Absorbing her Hole.

She sensed within it an asphyxiating Berserker needing supremacy.

Being very still, while wondering when, or even if, you will be allowed to draw life's breath again, became the seed of a protective pattern that is still useful to this day in the presence of the Patron. So, although on the face of it, as a regretful pitiful story, in fact, this was fortuitously the first preparation and initiation back into her own Spiral. The earliest Knowing that it showed her, was the suppression that she felt becoming tighter as she continued to be and grow up within this constricted dimension of Dissonance. As it is with all the *Wom* and the Isolated Kin-Mon.

This was the first intimation that the Shard of the Patron had finished colonising the E-arth and had infiltrated the Astrality. The Membrane was being breached permanently, making the Etheric Felds of the Uld no longer as visible and safe for the *Wom* as they once had been. The esoteric blueprints of all the diverse beings in the whole of this Infra were, from this time on, expendable and only to be treated as resources and fuel for the Patron.

The Uld Etheric Felds are the seeding grounds of all the other semen dimensions in this current Infra-Dimensional Ulder-verse. From them, the Re-al comes pouring through in abundance, and was always held so tenderly, and in sacred awe, before the Great Dissonance.

This was from eternally before everything else, and so had always been considered sacrosanct, a closer part of the great inviolable Core. But as everything was unwinding and coming away, ultimately intending to Seed more Core, it eventually evolved a thinner Membrane and as soon as it was thin enough the Patron broke on through to the other side.

Slicing.

Neatly.

This gave It access to a false kind of inter-dimensionality (please note: not Infra) that was very short-sighted, as It only abused it, and did not work in harmony with the first wisdom of the Ulds, using any of the original versatility for Its own lonely, greedy, Fe-ar-filled ends.

This duplicity and sly abuse creates the Great Dissonance that obscures the Re-al continuously. As we all know, as we are living in it right now, and we see there are very few places to evolve uniquely at present, despite the relentless advertising of fake freedoms and special 'holiday from the Bardo Factories' destinations.

Evolving uniquely is the ultimate way of consciousness, and consciousness is what Re-ality is formed from, and so you can see the solution and the problem here all at once.

Another thing hated by the Patron because it is not black and white and controllable enough. And if the Patron gets that hand on your face and another between your legs then it is very difficult, but not impossible, to do your own Way and enter your own Spiral.

So this was our Que-an's earliest lesson and introduction to the kind of challenges she would be facing the length and breadth of her span in this Dissonance. This vital first connection with the Shadow of the Patron gave her all that she needed to know and is now woven into the Way of her. Her consequent messaging has always been the same since the beginning of all true transformative messages.

As every good message is.

No matter whatever and however the amnesia is, that is triggered by any Great Dissonance, her message pulsed and re-recorded itself drawing from and feeding into the Uld Ether Felds. Reaching backwards and forwards through all the times of all the Cores along the Great Spiral.

The potent Dreamtime adventure of us.

Which is.

Be your truest self, to yourself, and clearly define your Patronic conditionings and codependencies, as fast as they are imposed, to cast them away and be free. Being free is the continuous key that unlocks the pain of its opposite, slavery.

If you can define your Patronic conditionings, then you will be sensitive to when you have passed them on and can keep engaged with where they have gone rogue. Some sweet and lucky day, they will come back to you and you can transform them back into the Uld Fire that they Re-ally are.

The pain of this is exquisite and instantly turns to its opposite.

Ecstasy.

Without doing this you are merely the puppet of the Patron, no matter how good it all is made out to be.

It is something only you can do, for yourself. Others can support you, but only follow another if they are following themselves, have their Shadows onside inside and visible outside, and can show you those true versatile skills that are independent of the Patron.

This is your revolutionary evolution.

How Re-al will this be getting with us, dear Loves?

Don't just practice something for the projected reward — you will be perpetuating all kinds of manipulation, and that is the food of the dimension of the Patron — you might remain entrapped and a paltry side dish to yourself. All the energy that is sidelined and wasted from not following your unique Way flows into your own Shadow, and then your Shadow is forced to engorge. The Patron rejoices because this Fucking thing has no limit on the size It can get and the reach It can have. As evidenced by the mentions already in this so called Empty Dream right here.

So practice for the reward of the Re-al.

It is in loving our Shadows dearly that we set them free to be our own Allies to help with this, which is our true responsibility, to be in relationship with the Re-al.

Our true Inner self.

Don't let the false fears or values of the Patron become your own.

This is exactly how it all keeps on growing into this shitty psychic pollution and polarising counterfeit concern.

Listen to what you utter in Its name.

Directly facing this Shard of the Patron at such an early attention stop on her own Way, was the gift of the Core in our Que-an. In her life there had been no other beings that could assist or protect her, as the *Wom* had already been killed off, by dismissal, to this Patronic dimension. No-one was there at all. She was the holder of this Knowing alone, and all she had to do was keep on keeping on, keeping her Eye peeled.

Knowing more or less immediately, before she could even walk her way and descend, that her face was red-rashed and pox marked, and that the Shadows knew her intimately, was a preparation for the amount of energy she would need to keep stored in her He-art Belly as best she could every day.

Even while being fed on.

It showed her exactly how she would lose energy and with what kind of beings, and what kind of time, and who would be the Allies on her Spiral.

So all to the good, through the bad.

But also.

This Shard is a way of the Patron to ask for help, although It does not know it Itself, and would deny it angrily and self-righteously. This is the key characteristic of all Sharding. The Shard is the unconsciousness that stops us Knowing what we really feel, fully feeling what we really feel, and then freezes us into not expressing the feeling or to get to Know it for what it means to us. Or it creates an interpretation of the feeling that can be boxed away intellectually.

Then It also seeks to feed on this imitation of transformation, our abreaction, the frustration coming from our mind boxes, making more approximations and delays to what It knows It is really missing.

So she made herself ready every day to hear the right voice in her Labyrinth with the unchangeable tone of the sound of the Core, and what it told her was always a little ahead of regular linear Patronic time. This way she could track her levels, withdrawing and extending, as needed for her own Way. The headaches and constrictions of all the relations on the road are indications that she is in encounter with the other energies and to be vigilant with her juice.

Her Uld Fire.

So in response to this, she always sought the Shadows directly and entered their environs willingly. And soon an amazing cross current of energy was established between them all. She learned to see more and more in the dark, as she was ready to be with all experience and aid all transformation, practicing her own energetic Membranes being simultaneously arrived at constantly. This meant she could steer the Shadows towards true nourishment whenever she had any chances.

They joyfully became her Allies as a making match of energetic explosiveness.

A spiritual consummation.

This is how she found out that the Shard of the Patron was highly addicted to the unconscious power emanated by all the Shadows of the other beings — Its preference being to keep everything in the dark so that It could continue to feed undercover.

This was the disputation that would be the end all and the be all, eventually.

Tending the Shadow was the only way to reveal the true energy behind it, and to do this you must know your own Under levels and connect with your *KiGal*.

She who holds the first Sharding.

But when our Que-an was a baby lying on her mat and only two cycles in, this was all only applied on top of her as a potential. So it is not surprising at all that she felt a bit suffocated, and decided to be as still as the headstone on her own grave.

Maybe, possibly, eventually, kill It for herself.

Fuck.

Yes.

Uh oh.

Naughty, naughty.

Shall we pretend what we don't feel now?

THE TABLE OF THE WOM

"I often feel I am being burned at the stake just because I have always refused to give up that wonderful strange power I have inside me that becomes manifested when I am in harmonious communication with some other inspired being."

- Leonora Carrington, Artist, Surrealist

"Good girls go to heaven. Bad girls go everywhere."

- Mae West, Actor

"When Changing Woman gets to be a certain age, she goes walking towards the East. After a while she sees herself in the distance, a previous self walking towards her. They both walk towards each other until they come together and after that, there is only one woman of no age."

- Version of the Tale of Changing Woman, founder of the Apache First Nation.

Our Que-an discovered a tranquil patio of warmest gold as she traversed a level on a turn that unfolded before her with more happy constancy. The light was a spreading wave from every hovering mote in the rippling of her own absorption. Each dancing particle giving its glow to the whole. She looked down, feeling a pleasant grounding weight, and saw she was carrying a cut and dressed stone, sugary with glinting crystal, the size of a brick, but more of a cube, in a quartzy golden grey granite.

She cuddled it against her He-art Belly all vibrantly nested.

In an answer to her preparatory intention and hopeful extensions, the Thunder-Stone of the Uldermentals had arrived in her possession again. Its supportive presence lending gravity and solidity to this exquisite Dreaming forward into the Re-al.

She skimmed along the swept floor (swept not by her, mind...) of a long corridor whittling away into the distance. The memory storehouse of the Uld by the looks of things. She knew where she was because her He-art Strings had elasticised and became so very at home. The direction of her telekinesis was whisking the flying grimoires onto shelves lining the walls of small contemplative wising-up cells, with stable doors, the bottom of which were all closed snugly, in case the ox bolted, on either side of the passage. She was involved in the most satisfying housekeeping and a delicious organisational game.

Library arranging.

Each tome a record of all Re-al relations, the connections and different forms offered, the gold of every life ever lived. Even the failed ones, which are always the best anyway. Think of all the transmutation that occurs as the Shadows are liberated by experiencing and releasing the untouchables.

By you embracing the star within your own black Hole.

Bliss.

Soon she was empty of her plenty and arrived at an opening into another courtyard in permanent amber sunrise on an orthremium floor. She moved to its exact centre and placed the Thunder-Stone upon the ground, caressing its bumpy rough facets with her fingertips, using her nails to draw the Dream, as her Uld Fire feathers shined its sides. She could feel the slight throb of her own pulse in its depths, because the very grail of it is actually us after all.

We carry as separate some very important Fucking Relics until we realise they are already inside us. So in wanting to touch your inner stone, you will meld into your own ground.

"There, that's good. I will always know where I am whenever I see you again," she whispered into its sensitive solidity.

For this was also her Dreaming stone that marked her inner positions on the Spiral, and this was a very important situation right Here-Nowish.

Especially when her own Eye opened up from inside the stone, blossoming in the centre of its rocky surface, and winked back at her in nectarean glee. All the visible crystals then condensed and merged until the light was a smear across the surface of what became smooth flint and the shape of this arrowed and pointed, still sitting solid but now directional. Striking sparks with her zealous steel to ignite all the Uld Fires that had been doused in too much despair and fright.

She was right, for all at once, she was filled to her brim with Core. She started to float upwards and raised her arms, reaching, spreading her fingers in an ecstatic pandiculation of complete and utter freedom.

She could do whatever the Fuck she liked, whenever she liked and this uninhibited feedback loop spiralled with no limitations at all. She felt her energy extend in an infinite net of Infra-connection throughout all the dimensions and places of power and peace right into the Core herself.

Backwards and forwards.

Completely plugged in.

Sensational.

Electric.

She stretched and tasted divine.

It was within this flying rising that she looked Down and Below into another courtyard across her Way in which a very long table was set for a meal. Each of the placemats shaped like labia, opening into soft tissued issues of the many abuses enacted on these lips of love.

All up and down, sitting in chairs of different shapes and sizes, was a gathering of many *Wom*.

The table of the Wo-Mon Ancestors.

Her He-art was full to bursting.

This was their secret Infra-dimensional kitchen! It smelled delicious and nourishing and in herby flurries of fragrant air she was moved towards them, buoyant on the ether, coming to rest behind their settings of open vulnerability, within whose placings are the energetic Samskaras that are held carefully until healing and reclamation take place, throughout the whole Spiral, up and down.

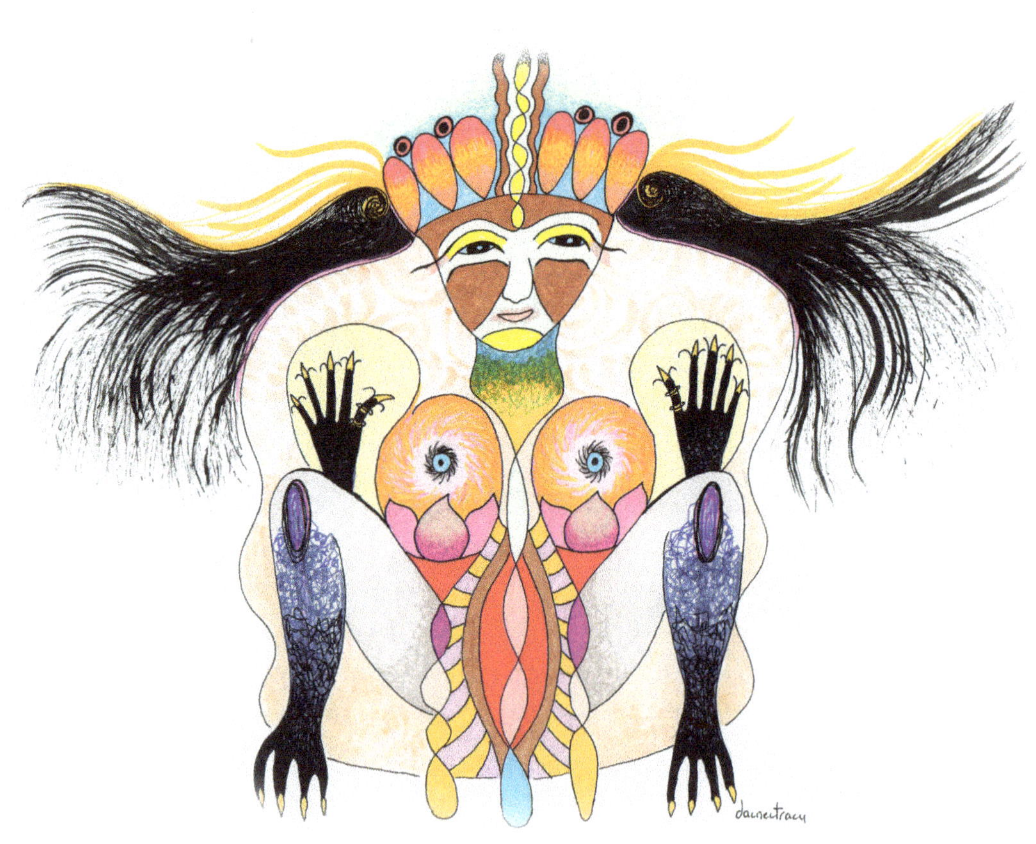

She noticed rape, repression, slavery, over medicalised birthing, over medicalised De-athing, prescriptive solutions, misapplication of sciences, over sanitation, chemical mutilation, coercive punishment, dissension as sin, transgression as sin, blasphemy as sin, torture, and, of course, the S-hame. The everlasting S-hame of being *Wom* and refusing to give in to the Patron.

All sorts of these templates were in formation and disintegration simultaneously, but each was attentively tended and existed as a loving and compassionate tribute to the innumerable affected Uld Fires of the *Wom* and Kin-Mon. Each one an altar to the courage it takes to stay present in all kinds of existences. Staying with whatever it is as it arises, in overwhelm, being overpowered, being dismissed.

She realised the *Wom* were not acknowledging her presence, but she did not care, as just to be here was indication enough her Spiral was in the right directional transformation.

She kissed each of the *Woms* fountaining crown head centres as she softly flew around the long table.

"I am here... I am here... I am here..." and as she did so, she noticed that they each had a kind of cruet set in front of their placings, just above the labia. One dark, one light, a yin yang of a message into which they poured their balances and reflections on all that was still to be done about the Fucking Patron.

She hovered to kiss those sensitive receptacles too, each one so soft and delicate like shy penises and vaginas in their perfect fit.

She looked into every Eye of the Wom, absorbing the stellar colours in the shapes of each of their evolving lines, and she drank in the distillation of the wrinkling wisdom of all the beings she found within them.

"I AM HERE!" she shouted so loud, so utterly full of delight, and did not expect or need an answer. Her cry was for the Re-al and for the sheer joy of existence.

The energy next indicated along a ways, threading her attention towards the end of the table, where she saw the living Wo-mon memory storehouse book turning its own pages towards her. Opening and showing, parting its covers, revealing inwards. This is no static record at rest, this is the unfastened invitation and she was pulled along towards it to the end.

Gazing into its beckoning feel, she saw that it was a spiritual recipe book that gave all the ingredients for every creative energy meal a Wom had ever prepared throughout eternity.

All the instructions and all the preparations stretching back into before Linear Time and way before the Patron had manifested its limited territorial views.

It told her in glistening termas how she was making all these meals herself in the journey along her Spiral to meet her *KiGal*, and that she would be joining the Wom at this kitchen table before she even knew of another thing.

Never had she been so happy as now.

The sweet reassurance come so independently and naturally, as long as she stayed in her Re-al. Everything she needed and the Dream already Dreamed, sitting at the kitchen table with her Woms.

This is the lasting rapture.

This is Home.

I love you like this, Loves.

And a dear small hand reached through the Membrane from the Infra and smoothed a smiling tear across our Que-an's cheek.

THE IS-LAND OF NO PARTING

"Empty and unlimited, she seeks from within her nothingness to attain All."

- Simone de Beauvoir, Philosopher

"Sand is a substance that is beautiful, mysterious, and infinitely variable; each grain on a beach is the result of processes that go back into the shadowy beginnings of life, or of the earth itself."

- Rachel Carson, Eco Activist, Writer

"I keep hearing tree talk water words and I keep knowing what they mean."

- Lucille Clifton, Poet

Then the little hand beckoned with a pudgy, lively finger and our Que-an found herself being pulled through the Membrane on a Spiral tilt where she found many waiting whirlpools on which to choose to travel.

Each one threw out a sound that was her own voice crescendoed.

An Infra ship set its sails on her music and our Que-an and her Echoes arrived on the Is-land of No by resonating themselves against each other. Shaking their Membranes in tiny tremors, they moved their densities to emerge on a shining beach. They all looked back, as one, towards the salty great Feld of Water Peace surrounding the No.

Great shadows of the blue air ran across the Above in the shapes and forms of the future. The Elephants of the emotional juice played and swam, their smooth rounded bodies roiling and arching into the bubbling waters, splashing foam and drops of exquisite reflections all through the Edging.

They seemed to come closer in on the bigger pounding waves, receding less and less in each turn. It was exciting to be so near, as their sensuous bodies merged and re-emerged in the clear waters. Every time they touched each other, a new current was created, and someone somewhere experienced a subtle and unexpected thrill of uncertainty. They were forming a great circle around what was clarifying from within the foam into a cavern in the protective reef, just beneath the turbulence on the surface. Within its mouth, our Que-an glimpsed one of the forms of the *KiGal*, sitting on an ever sinking and most dense throne, fashioned from an unsinkable tree.

The Se-at of Flow and Desire.

Coming and going, in and out... of her view.

The *KiGal* first stood, then sunk into a Goddess squat, rooting inwards, releasing to stand again. Up and down, rooting and releasing for as long as linear Time uncoils. An unfathomable ritual tide of movement generating more currents ever outward from the Great Below.

Like a Descending moon, her attraction was palpable in the fountains of spray. Then there was a potent, sudden rush of pleasure in all, as the *KiGal* beckoned, widening her arms above her head and her hands flipped inwards and then upturned, her arms reaching away from her standing water mountain body in the gesture of both power and connection.

It is a lightning rod condensation of all that has been held away and hidden. Of all that is ever denied.

No praying hands here.

The sitting is ended, this is completion in sacred action.

Our Que-an was cheered and excited by this underwater affirmation of their landing on this still free and potent Uld Feld. The Is-land was untouched by the Patron and Great Peace was discernible, stoking right through the Uld Fire of everyone present, as harmony soaked inward. This paradise swims through all of us, even as we grapple with the Dissonance, and the *KiGal* stands up for this, to remind us of why we are present.

This is why our Que-an, her Echoes and us, Loves, are here too. Because the wisdom keeper of this sanctuary is one of the surviving and glorious Great Grand *Woms* of the Uld. She is the guardian of this Feld; and so far the Patron has not isolated and annexed this source of the Re-al issuing from her Womb.

And it was as they all turned away from the Underwater cave, back towards the Upper beach, that they saw the Great Grand Wom, standing in the same form, mirroring the *KiGal* within the corals of the reef.

In that sacred gesture.

This sacred gesture.

Hovering in the prisms of Infra-Dimensionality between this doubling, were two Womb Holes, one Above and one Below, connected by a shining fallopian tube and attended by schools of spermatozoa all excited by the infinite possibilities of balanced emergence.

The Wombs turned and circled each other like sisters of the empty void, pregnant with potential, then they came together, fitted together, burrowing and rubbing along until Uld Fire was seen to be generated all along their Edges, while within, more stars are born.

Our Que-an and her Echoes each lifted a handful of sand from the E-arth under their feet and poured the crystals towards the Wombs, and there, from the inner bursting stars, new Felds formed and vanished inwards to more materialise the Infra.

Seeding more Uld Felds that would extend the promise of Infra-Dimensional freedoms was the practice of each visitor to this Is-land. When completed they felt solid and released of any stored Fe-ar based premonitions. This mutual exchange also seeded important symbiotic ideas that directly counteracted the Patrons controlling...polarised...useless realities.

The loving Uld Wisdom Keeper gazed at each of them, at the same time as gazing at them all. Her Eye penetrating into the Core within and pulling it out into the more obvious. This alone was of such great support that the gift was already given, but our Que-an knows that here is more.

This was the Eye that did not believe a single projection or objectification no matter how tempting or satisfying.

How good or bad.

How seemingly true.

Yet this Eye holds the power and immutable energy of the Dreaming forward of the Re-al. It does not believe in anything, it only connects with the deepest Peace, the farthest Seeing, the greatest Love and the most extraordinary creation. That's all, and this is the truth our Que-an needs to Know more of from here on in. To continue her Spiral without being overcome by the Dissonance that petrifies and paralyses, as had happened so often on previous turns.

The Echoes gathered, gently surrounding her, and they walked up the beach together, their feet disappearing into the crystalline powders and their atmospheres flashing white, shell pink and clear with the light as it arose all around them, whispering of longing.

Dispersing to find rest, our Que-an found her own place and lay down to centre and arrive more fully into this, the No Dragon of the Is-land's own Uld Fire.

Her Vagal Snake purred as it came home in the Dragon energy, and extended its tongue to lick and sense the Membranes she would be needing.

The Void beneath the form of her opened.

She knew she had nothing.

Somehow all her leftover garments and Fucking Relics had not travelled this far with her, even though she had been very careful to pack for this emergence. They were not lost, they were left behind wherever they were, like wardrobe time capsules of identities that can be taken on and taken off. Being bereft of them now was releasing another starting point. She felt out and about, and could not find anything dependable. All was quiet and open and she did not try to clutch or grasp.

The Void opened wide in every corner of her place until she could hear the Dragon's tidal breath and could feel the nourishing posture of the *KiGal* in her own Empathic Gland. Her mind wrinkled, caressing the folds of her lobes. Her Labyrinth cleared itself, toning to connect with this, her intimate exquisite stalemate again.

This dead heat kept appearing in all its infinite forms and each time she was more Knowing and more immediate with it.

She has nothing, is nothing fixed at all, which brings her closer to her *KiGal*, whose convolutions exert a magic all their own. Our Que-an did not even have herself, as she was now a conduit between the Core and its inpourings of the Re-al.

Being only this rush, and all that was wanted of the part of her that is our Que-an, was to openly engage with the Dragon and the Is-land's birthing flowering templates of Re-al.

This Uld Feld that is only for the succour of the Re-al as it comes more and more into existence to balance the Patron.

In case you haven't quite caught the continuous point, Loves.

Her Uld Fire flame, who is in total relationship with the Infra-dimensional workings of this intrinsic necessary action, is so essential to the healing of the Great Dissonance that it could not be separated out at all.

As is ours.

So to.

Just do it.

She arose and stamped her feet into groundedness to alert the Land Dragon she was in arrival, and the Echoes joined in the long sweet pulse to the Re-al. The Dragon roared, calling creation. Uld Fire soared up to the Above and spread along the bright glimmer lining the Edges of the cloudy shapes in wings of Love.

She then could feel her fresh skin growing, clothed anew, with each increasing crystal bell song and call. So deep and so wide is it, that the Dragon becomes us and we are in its tears, and the land rises to mountains and snow and there is a mighty gentle blessing of soothing rain upon the overheated Bardo Factories of the Patron.

This is all only apocalyptic weather to the reductive Patron, but that does not matter now.

Such cleansing, spuming and muddying of the Factories is the working of the Re-al and the long overdue balancing of consequence. It won't be controlled away, but because the Patron uses Its mind to box, It only knows one thing. Its science of attempted supremacy. Of the Lording over it all. And this makes Its own Eye blind. It depends on the Sharding and cuts away all else. This feels clean to It, but it creates the Dissonance that It fails to see, so as It continues to live in Its failing illusions, It tries to Shard harder and faster.

And so it continues.

Forecast bleak with only scattered purging.

Take a free breath.

While you still can.

Our Que-an and the Great Grand Wom passed the peace pipe to each other that blew Core into the Infra and rained it all down, and rayed it all up too.

A last smoky ring circled into the blue sky void to join its Shadow and a Sheela Na Gig laughed and pissed on a head.

No need to ask whose.

THE MIDDLE PARTING

Oh NOW.
NOW
Oh shit.
NOW
What am I feeling in the middle of my Spiral?
What can I take from here that has always been present, and has sparked the very beginning in the first place?
The only thing I can't see from here is the end, because the curves are hiding it, so much so that maybe there is no end.
I like that.
No leaving and no arriving.
I feel three tips in my pausing and sighing. I need to spin around. Three intentional directions are arrowing in.

First.
I see the Core apparent. I see the Spiral moving Upwards, away towards a central point that emanates continuously back in my direction. I am transcendent in it, climbing and flying towards a pinnacle of an ultimate state that makes me want to reach it, and be done with everything that is not this. A heat that burns my crazy zen mind stronger in a big pull of power.

But I see with the Eye of the Re-al that I am already home. Both inside and outside. I don't need to have it either way. The Core cares deeply who I am, I am her emanation, her avatar, and it is up to me to care too, and be ready to be at home in Her. This is the loop of Great Compassion that will replace the Great Dissonance.

Second.
I meet with my *KiGal* which is the downward Spiralling or Undering toward the Great Below into the caves of what needs to be seen and heard. All that has been enraged, denied or forgotten, lies resting and waiting to give the stored energy of itself back into my Spiral. This is a rhythmic revisiting of my evolution and the continuous re-igniting of my relationship with every little thing. I see and hear the *KiGal*, she sees and hears me; and the communication of this creates more energy and passion that feeds back into my Spiral, drawing me further into relationship with the Re-al, which is the miraculous true Nature underlying all Core creation.

Third.
At last, I am in direct engagement with the Patron on whatever Here-Nowish point of the Spiral I am on. Which is existing in a duality where the Spiral itself seems to disappear. From here it all looks like a straight line which demands I stay one side or the other in a polarity that divides and conquers and allows It to perpetuate the confusing Dissonance, while assuring me that if I am on the correct side I will not be distressed or disturbed, banished or cancelled.
Which turns out to be a lie because as soon as I choose one side, the agenda of the other side seeks balance within me, causing more Dissonance and disturbance.
I cannot choose sides, if I want to be free, within the straight-lined dimension of the Patron, because It only has one dogged intention, and it is not compassion for me or anything Re-al. At all. I will not be blinded to this one-sided push. I discern that I will not join anything in the Dissonance.

daineitracy

This is the tightrope or edge that I walk right now, in the middle, seeing all this, from these different angles.

These opportunities on my Spiral.

Will I fall off my Edge into unconsciousness?

Maybe, but I am not worried if I do, because I will land and wake somewhere else on the Spiral that will propel me onwards anyway.

I practice full consciousness. I invite full consciousness. I desire full consciousness. I spark full consciousness. I balance full consciousness. I evolve in full consciousness. I rest in this.

This is the choice that is always mine and cannot be taken away.

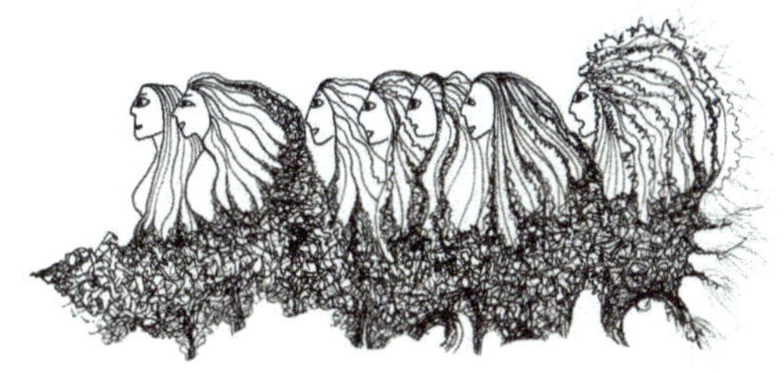

THE JOY OF CORE

"To be always relevant, you have to say things which are eternal."

- Simone Weil, Philosopher, Activist, Mystic

"I'm not going to die, I am going home like a shooting star."

- Sojourner Truth, Activist

"Buddhas gather so they can return to their original dwelling.
They return so they can gather again at the next Buddha party.
She, unnamed and untitled,
Her light, and its snares, one,
Surpasses their backing and forthing."

- Hotetsu, Zen Master

There came, in some lapse of linear Time, a middle of the Spirals spring, when she was quietly sitting in her Uld Fire. Her Vagal Snake curlicued and warm. All other was gone, particularly the Patron, and she nestled in with the great stillness. A peace was building within all the foundations and nurturing the Re-al which was giving its song and the delight.

The chorus of the Core.

This quiet sitting eventually led, as it is wont to do, to a massive revolving, which started up all through the Membranes of her Manor making her He-art strings thump against each other and causing her Vagal Snake to writhe fast into uncoiling and unspooling up through her neurones and out.

She shook herself as a wet dog to re-arrange her muscles and Strings and stood up to move to her resting mat where she lay down on her silks to be with her De-ath. Her Uld Fire, triggered by the huge movement, leapt into a surging upwards.

The He-art beat thumping, all this time intensified, distant drum sounds coming closer so that her attention fogged and could not keep up. Feeling overwhelmed she sought some kind of refuge, probing past the revolutions of past Spirals, but no refuge was to be had, as all was too quickened, and it became way beyond her.

A choice point arrived within this nonetheless, as she was poured into herself. But she could not discern where to let go of. Or even whether to surrender. Is this about surrender when you are engaged and open already? What further cycle calls? What Other propels us that is not intent on overpowering us?

What is here to surrender into, Loves?

She suddenly Knew this as the central Call of the Core singing through her Labyrinth, an answer to her questions, and into the hinge String of her being.

Now is the centre of her life storm and the churning of all that had been happening on her Spiral, before this, and after, way beyond.

She arrived at a direction, not easily though, and decided to join into the unknown, throwing in her towel with this complete and stranger gyre. As soon as she decided, she arrived, her awareness sunk right to the bottom of her pelvic bowl where her Strings were holding on in taut anticipation, down, meeting the convolution of her Vagal Snake, intertwining and becoming the Caduceus herself.

Interlaced, Vagal Snake and our Que-an reversed with a tyres-hitting-the-road squeal from the Descent and turned, shooting up straight through their central Uld Fire channel and out her supercalifragilistic crown, with such velocity that all Membrane was tattered and left dangling far below.

Etherically speaking, this is what is traditionally known as a disaster, but this is the whole point as well, as always.

There they were then, floating in the Infra with all the other starry Fires. Propelled by this greater draw away from where she may have regularly found herself. Each a star of soul, a globe of such fulfilment as could never ever land anywhere else but within themselves.

Sweet.

They travelled through the vacuums between all this contentment in an august serenity until they reached the magnetic pull of another space horizon entirely.

The Que-an and her vagal Snake, as their Caduceus, felt firmed into the form of the eternal knot arriving at this colossal edge, and they entered the next Dimension through its invitational Membrane as a single condensed ball of extraordinary Uld flame. Blue and gold and centred red.

Now all that Is, was becoming stretched and slowed, warping and changing, diffusing into the Feld of Eternal Potential, where every seed Knows its quantum mirror twins throughout all the possibilities of experience.

Space disappeared into its numberless components and a wave of vibration came.

A tsunami of glory pulsing right through, in an interpenetration of everything in existence.

No separate sense of any other could survive this complete and utter surge of Core.

We are in, and nowhere else.

More waves, inside her as she was inside them, each an opening to deeper flowering, inside seeding, inside petalling, inside corona; eternally patient penumbras, all cupped together so tenderly in a vibration, immutable and boundless. A huge generosity of space pulsing evermore.

All ecstasy was drowned in this, the greater and greater awareness.

The Passion of the Core inviolate.

We revel.

Now. A switch is flipped and our Que-an is conscious OF this All. She recognises her own strong and glorious separate self, differentiated, in a joyous relationship with this, her own Core pulsation.

Now. The switch flips again and she is the wave of Nectar, being the very food itself of Core. Bubbling deliciously in her pot, unseparated in her soup.

Now. She switches back and is aware again OF this, in a potent separation, she a glorious Other. With capacities flowing in myriad reflective possibilities.

So she played as Core played, from state to stateless, riding back and forth by her own will, which was also the will of the Core. She Knew and she was Home. It could not be any other. Her will is the will. This is why it is not about surrender any more.

Be an Adept.

Accepting the greatest gift of all existence as it is being given to this, her own dear, hardworking, *Wom* awareness.

Absorbing the supreme gift of evolving consciousness, in constant regeneration and delighted expression of the Re-al, the centre of all Love and De-ath.

At one in Core, and able to Know at one in Core. The dualistic skill given to us, in which, if we end up only polarising, is frittered into the Great Dissonance to become the weaponised tool of the Patron.

But our Que-an is awash in wisdom in this centre and she can play. Practicing and playing, forever and a day, feeling she has fully received the gift of this, her own totality in duality.

Now. She says to herself as Core, held so completely;

"Okay that's it, I am back to making my own bed and to lay in its creation, reaping my consequences, so that I learn and learn and protect, to nurture your Re-al, with De-ath by my side, to bring me Down into you always."

All my dearest Core relations.

So she is, in a flash, on the silks of her mat, in her Manor, all fresh and relaxed and her senses all balanced and coolly in possession.

Of. Her. Core. Self.

Joy and evolution, be thankfully praised and multitudes of blessings all showering around.

Home.

Sweet.

Home.

She knew now that she must keep finding the *KiGal* in this present Dimension of Dissonance, and save the Re-al, so that all was not in permanent exile from itself because of those Fucking Shards.

For the Patron wanted you to host Its Shard and do Its bidding, feeding Its own control, instead of being at Home in yourself, on your Spiral, with access to Core, in creation with the Re-al.

This is this whole damn thing in its nutty shell.

So here we go.

Again.

SPILLED DIRECTLY TOWARDS THE *Ki-Gal* WITH BITTY AND IMAGO

"Courage in women is often mistaken for insanity."

- Alice Paul, Quaker, Feminist, Activist

"Sometimes I think I'm near the end of my energy for living. I plot to travel to another world because this one seems too decimated by the white men who wanted money and skin, too dangerous to navigate because of the sentinels still roaming, raping, and gouging out the earth to maintain power."

- Elissa Washuta, Writer

"In the diamond sutra it is written that past mind cannot be grasped; the present mind cannot be grasped, and the future mind cannot be grasped. Is that right?" Asked a not-named old woman of scholar Te-shan.(Who is named, notice, by the patriarchal Patronic recorders of the believed hearsay called Zen his-story.)

"Yes, that is is right." he answered.

"Then with which mind will you accept this tea?" our not-named old woman responded.

He could not answer, realised he Knew bugger all, and went off to try to find a man to help him be a Zen master and also see another man about a dog."

(Commentary — Pity he didn't stay right there with himself and our not-named old woman.)

- Retold by Dainei Tracy, Artist, Writer, Zen Feminist

Where I am is how I wanted to be. This has been my intention all along which will propel me to what I need to do now. The me that is Here-Nowish has Spiralled back from the future. More specifically when I am futuristic, it is more potent to me in the present. So, to me, this evocation of my potential is more relevant than the limited actual linear moment that once existed and seemed all there would ever be.

At the time.

I am all over the positions on the Spiral, and although that may seem peculiar and impossible, it becomes more understandable in relation to what has happened in the future and will happen in the past.

Everything can only be seen in the spectrum of the W-Hole. Nothing can exist in just one place in the Infra, or on its reflection, which is the Spiral.

Just as this communication is amplified and extended by the Echoes in our minds, it does so to further penetrate into our Labyrinths every time we pass the utterance of it. The merging of past, present and future supports us to deepen into the Under, as we come ever closer to the *KiGal*. She becomes our destination, the buried feminine of our true nature, living and breathing and Dreaming into existence the essence of why the Fuck we are here.

We enquire and then notice we want an answer, a de-finity. Which is the other side of infinity, so liable to a certain stuck-ness.

Cut and dried is a level behind where we want to be right now.

I mean, if you have got this far, then you are near enough at the committal stage of being fluid. Buried alive and rushing down here in the underground streams. In the cuckoo moon predicament of wild caving and not knowing where we are going, as if we are the imposters in our own reflections.

Here we are the three again of future, past and Here-Nowish. Imago, our Que-an and Bitty. If you are hoping I am going to make sense of this for you particularly, then you are mistaken. I am merely trying to show how we all collude in trying to manipulate time so that we feel we are on a continuum of achievement and reward, because that can lead to subservience to the thing we are copying. Taking good care of our complicity.

We are three again.

Finally a feminine trinity from the sacred W-Hole, coming back to the place we were buried before we were immersed in the Dissonance of masculine over control.

Together we stand with you, Loves, and the more unnerved and discombobulated you are, the better for us all. Directionally speaking, this will incentivise you into finding your Loving intention again. If you don't run screeching and jumping into the nearest false security sentry point of the Patron.

Standing here on the edge of the Under we peer down with our Eye.

The *KiGal* is looking straight up at us from the Below. It is a shock that this could suddenly have become so simple. But also a validation that we have penetrated far enough, past limited logic and control, and more deeply into true meaning and insight.

We must have shed enough by now, surely, to See her.

And then a shroud moves across the space and she is no longer visible to our Eye.

We need a little more De-ath and a little less conversation.

WHAT IS SO TRUE ABOUT THE RE-AL ANYWAY?

"Reality is a sound — you have to tune into it, not just keep yelling."

- Anne Carson, Writer

"Civilised Man says: 'I am Self, I am Master, all the rest is other — outside, below, underneath, subservient. I own, I use, I explore, I exploit, I control. What I do is what matters. What I want is what matter is for. I am that I am, and the rest is women and wilderness, to be used as I see fit'."

- Ursula K. Le Guin, Writer, Seer

Do we enter the Re-al like arriving on another planet using the spaceship of our mind? Or do we co-create with the Re-al in a supernatural Dream studio?

Can we destroy the Re-al in a war of the worlds? And if we do, is the ultimate power, that we think we win, ours alone? How corruptible will we be? How much does our relationship, our compromise, with the Patron, and other parts and beings, create or destroy the Re-al? What do we do when we come up against another's Membrane that has a different Spiral spinning away in other directions? And what kind of thrust might be in that spin that seeks to destroy any other Re-al that is not its own version? What is It hungering for? What do we long for?

The Spiral draws us inwards, curiously capturing our attention so much that we express outwards in roots, tendrils and fruiting bodies. Wanting to grow a weaving of arisings, allowing each part to exist and complete its incarnation in a joy of its own becoming. Once we have fully ripened ourselves in form and Uld Fire, we Know our whole Hole and are indistinguishable from the Re-al. So much so, we may differentiate straight back out again, just for the Fucking fun of it.

When this process is truncated or repressed, or used against us by the Patron or Its officers, who come in many guises, including the ones that live inside us, having been installed earlier, against our will, possibly, and with an accompanying Shard, probably. How much do we fight It, to get free? What is our own invitation to all parts of the unravelling, descending Spiral that is evading totalitarianism, inner and outer. How do we cheer Her on? Our inner Que-an. How do we personally find our hidden *KiGal*, deep in the bowels of our own Unders?

Because our personal Spiralling is the direct connection to the Universal Feld of Infra-Dimensionality, where what we are and what we do directly affects everything else. Even if we don't want it to. Or if we think we are so separate, we have no effect.

We do, Loves, we are the Ones.

This is all our own creation.

Everything comes together here, in this inquiry, including the Patron, especially the Patron, because although It has colonised the E-arth and her Terratoriums and Felds of Re-al, It has done it by manipulating, abusing and reframing separation and pain, and ignoring or damming flows and fluidities.

Shredding the Membranes whose differentiating qualities celebrate rich differences and diversities. In using suffering and greed and fear, It has displaced Itself from the Infra-connected Re-al.

Because the Re-al will not ever serve It.

So It feels entitled to cancel all that does not serve It. And the worst, the very worst thing, is that then It wants us to conflate It with the Re-al. Like a surrogate truth, the Shard sits on all He-arts, a life-sucking abyss, not allowing any other experience.

This is the journey of the partitioned Patron who seeks to own the Re-al and use the Re-al to perpetuate Itself... making this Its truth.

Why is this Its intention? Can we fathom this? Maybe we feel that It is easier to just not ask these kinds of questions in the first place. There is after all, plenty of disincentive.

Hah! As though not asking questions will stop the petty conjuring. But don't be so Fucking negligent. If we look away, "oh what are you talking about? I can't see anything...", then we are complicit. So don't be fooled, and do challenge the Patron as much as you possibly can.

What energy or force can move into the place that is needed to heal this extreme and be in relationship with this urge?

Compassionate awareness, that's what. The Re-al is grown by awareness.

And the Patron will grow Itself in your lack of awareness.

So, you can choose, you do have all that you need.

Is our Que-an you? As she descends to meet her *KiGal*? And how is she staying so consistently and deliciously free?

She is conscious loving awareness unleashed from Patronic agenda. She is us, in a true unfettered form. No slave to convention or constrictive role play. Even after having been punished for not playing Its game, over and over again.

Through all the Patronic linear centuries.

In all Her colours.

Continuous awareness, with no power struggling manipulation is the way of the *Wom*.

The only precept is the intention to release any sense of separation from our Uld Fire, and this is gained by working through the levels or curls on our Spiral, hand in hand with our Shadow. And welcoming home our inner exiles. Those parts that the Patron wants you to police yourself with, so that it can rule you in the same way.

Watch this, as It comes up with its many identifications.

Awareness is the spice of consciousness, and so we must remain aware as we descend our Spiral.

What is your Spiral, as you wend your way round and round noticing the familiar scenes and patterns? You, in relationship with yourself and your evolution, through all the many measurements of time in whatever ways you divide it.

The Re-al, constantly unfolding, relating, in and out of dualities. In and out of multiplicities. There is no fixed place of duality or unity, there is only our own awareness that perceives when in relationship and is absorbed and completed, when everything is merged in communion with itself, always ready to be in relationship again. Here the relationships become whole and complete, yet already moving on... in and out, round and down.

This place of Re-al Whole Hole is what **Eresh the** *KiGal* is pointing to. She is the crazy lunar wisdom keeper that holds this Knowing. Hear what she says about noticing what you want to be true, and allow her to rip away your old identifications.

Be in the raw.

As beings, we experience it by allowing the innermost depths of us to arise to our surface, which is us descending to meet them too.

But if we suppress the arising parts, using judgementalisms to manage our fears, then we put ourselves in prison instantly. So no need to judge it, just discern.

Eresh demands that we accept our many selves in all their gory, ugly beauty, so that awareness can continue loving. Eaten by De-ath, we may be, but it is our awareness that emerges immortal.

As our Spiral is showing...

PART OF THE SHARDED KIN-MON'S DILEMMA

"Dispute not with her: she is lunatic."

- Richard III, William Shakespeare, Playwright, Director

"No woman is really an insider in the institutions fathered by masculine consciousness. When we allow ourselves to believe we are, we lose touch with parts of ourselves defined as unacceptable by that consciousness; with the vital toughness and visionary strength of the angry grandmothers, the fierce market women of the Ibo's Women's War, the marriage-resisting women silk workers of pre-Revolutionary China, the millions of widows, midwives, and the women healers tortured and burned as witches for three centuries in Europe."

- Adrienne Rich, Poet

When Our Que-an was younger than Bitty and Imago might be as they Spiral along in all their own infinite variety, she lived in an Uld Water Feld, already annexed by the Patron. In the Manor of her *Wom* and her *Woms* Kin-mon. Many old currents and ancestral undertows circled round, alternately stirred and suppressed by the misguidance and preaching persecutors of the Patron, mostly in their garbs of pious friars, milking monks and fettered nuns. But not always.

The unacknowledged wisdom of the expression of the Re-al was therefore projected as fearful Shadow instead. Oftentimes into the many wonderful sea snake finned Naga creatures of the S-he Sea. Spirit creatures who used to live in beautiful harmony on swimming energy lines holding the Uld Felds in stability, until they were dredged by large iron, manacle like, crossed grids of chains. Uncompromising nets, exerting so much terminal damage as they dragged back and forth relentlessly, searching out true growing to annihilate it. Soon everyone forgot what they were fishing for, especially when there was nothing left of the S-he Sea ground to remind anyone.

Any remaining Sea Beings became the holders, much as the Arthropods had become in the Uld E-arth Felds, of the Fe-ar based controlling evil of the exploiting Patron.

Our Que-an's *Wom* and her Kin-Mon were always in their own slow permanent version of the crisis of the Great Dissonance, so difficult to avoid by anyone, as all the Terratoriums and Felds methodically fell, one by one.

She was afraid of her *Wom's* Kin-Mon, because as soon as he became Sharded by the Patron, which happened during her earlier life, about the time she had her first vibration of Its Shadow in her cot, he turned his lens of Patronic attention on her. Using the usual grooming education and special isolating conditioning, putting unbearable pressure on his own He-art Strings and weakening his own soul chime in the process. Hunting within her what he could have been looking for in himself.

He was forced to either accept the Shard — as all Kin-Mons were forced to, one way or another — or never be able to own anything, not realising that instead he would never own himself. And maybe be killed as well, anyway. He would certainly be judged and punished, which was the ever present threat, as the civilisation of the Patron colonised all the Felds.

So he became cruel to her and her *Wom* by not hearing them with his purposefully blocked up Labyrinth. She could feel dread in her He-art Belly all the time, as she called and called out to him. But all she could end up doing was follow him around like a little puppy ghost, whining for attunement and attachment.

Then one day she realised she was De-ad to him, like she was to the Patron. He had never Known her Uld Fire as the sacred font of the Re-al, as was his own, he had only known a projection of her, reflected through his Shard. This day, she Knew that the Patrons Sharding process had completed and he was crystallised.

Our Que-an didn't know why it happened this day, but it seemed to be because she just would not get educated around how things were going to be from now on. So she faded away from his dimension and was made spectre.

Just as she was fading, she saw her *Wom* weeping, and heard some Echoes amplifying the crying. The floating and resounding question was whether it was really warranted. Weren't the *Woms* just always playing the victim? The Echoes only repeated what was bouncing around, they did not have any will or discernment. They could only sound mirror what was already here, with no power to make a change, no matter how vital. So anything uttered into the Infra was endlessly copied, until

it became the normal. Or someone changed it.

This is why it is wise to realise we are creators, not copiers.

Her *Wom* could not see our Que-an either, for she was trapped and surrounded by her own Echoes, and kept shutting all the doors in her face. The feeling felt all against our Que-an. Her Vagal Snake kept shuddering and sometimes snapped in half, each half afire still, but a great space arose between the wounded ends that was difficult to cross, and so full of sadness. The shudders would turn into a leaching void that was like a hunger, but not to eat. The severed sinews would reach for each other within her and she formed bridge after bridge of fragile reconciliations regardless. She would not give up, ghosted or otherwise.

She would knock and knock and beat at the door.

But No-thing.

She would not be heard anywhere. Just like our *KiGal*, she was becoming more buried. She tried all the different doors of the gatherings in the shattered battle Felds for a long time, she could hear in her own Labyrinth the Echoes behind all these same doors in the different dimensions of It, the Patron. She followed her *Wom's* Kin-Mon even more, feeling desperate, calling into his Labyrinth, but he could not hear anything he did not expect, or had decided not to hear.

She was vetoed in this disconnection which had been building up and up, the more she avoided Its education. She was always making the choice to stay on her own Spiral, but this was so very hard, as she had not fully realised she would be so utterly alone. She could see that everywhere else was in a kind of censorship that was being navigated to survive and used to take refuge in, making up Its own parameters of false safety.

But she could not go near it. This thing was so blindly building patterns and walls that her Seeing refused to let her join in. She did not want to be saved this way. The De-ath is infinitely preferable to being absorbed into a gluey fester.

She needed her *Wom* and Grand *Wom*, but her *Wom* had been exiled, because of the tears and the crying, to her own Manor, and had been curtailed to not mention anything that would shed any dark on It.

But her dearest Great Grand *Wom* was in the turning of De-ath, which is a great comfort to those in the Know, as she would be making her way to the *KiGal* unhindered and would return to clarify more of the Dissonance on her next winding.

Eventually, though, in desperation, our Que-an dreamed her *Wom* and Kin-Mon backwards, at a time further away in their Spirals. She saw them both in a very large energy pool created by a hurricane as she floated above them in the watery air, pale as the ghost she was, unseen, and unheard, still.

Her *Wom* was trying to connect with her Kin-Mon, who had only just been earlier Sharded, so she was swimming gently backwards towards him, looking over her shoulder very shyly, and she bumped up against him, as though it was an accident. For a moment, so, so small, and only seen if you were totally slow enough, it looked as though he would embrace her finally in relationship... but instead he pushed her away. His Shard was now embedded and activated, turning all creation into polarity, which meant he was switched off to half of everything at all times.

Our Que-an was awash in the sadness of her beloved *Wom*, at the empty cavity appearing between the two of them, so she filled the pool with ripples of her own dropping tears. Her *Wom's* Kin-Mon was merely repulsed and swam quickly away.

That's it then.

The defensive control of cutting rejection was here played out in plain sight of the energy pool, clarifying to our Que-an how this deafness had come about. It is not that this is a revelation, no, there is nothing new here, it is that this is a showing of the workings of the Shard. The more of this that is revealed and mirrored, the more our wisdom can slowly expand to see the totality and invite the vast Core to blossom all around and through us instead.

Then our Que-an was plunged and swimming in the pool herself, her Spiral demanding the direct embodied experience, as well as the insight. She could swim and was not drowning, but she had to work very hard to understand the dynamic and the deep rip tidal current, because she was now herself immersed in the separation sadness... from all the pushing away.

This is an overwhelm that cannot be avoided on the Spiral, for it is the He-art of the matter of what we must all embrace. Any pointing at the Re-al is only worth some salt if you are experiencing it too.

Spin backwards to the Joy of Core to remember.

A large tube appeared in the sky above her paddling, bobbing body, its lid opened and many, many words fell out. Heavy and painful vowels and seed syllables, unpitying phrases and unanswerable queries. They were all the frightening strong words of the judgements against the *Wom* and the Re-al. She was afraid, and she read each one carefully as they fell, hovering in front of her Eye. She knew she must read each one of these words to strengthen the Seeing. Their vibrations eroded her and slowly continued to build into a final dam of annihilation.

While their meanings were breaking in her bones, she forgot the actual words immediately. She would fail this test, she knew, and her Fe-ar scrunched harder in her Strings, tearing at her He-art, all grating and rasping at her delicate tissues.

Our Que-an screamed, not for help, but to express it all, and to call a Shadow to come and eat it.

She felt all her Uld Fire energy wrap itself up in this screeching spent implosion and crumbled inward.

Then she was knocking at a door again and she felt the Spiral turning, screwing. Loud and hard and insistent.

Nothing.

Again.

Hard.

Loud.

Nothing.

Again.

Then it opened a crack, and she was lying on the ground being a doormat, and some unconscious dreaming Echoes and their Shadows walked on and over her, on their way to more solidified destinations.

But the door was now open. She could get through and she rose onto her hands and feet, crab-like and entered, crawling sideways on all fours cautiously, head down. Looking away carefully and slowing to a stop in the middle of it all.

Our Que-an stood up, uncurling watchfully, back in the room, revealed, standing before her *Wom's* Kin-Mon.

She realised he could really see her with his Eye — had done the whole time. He had just chosen not to. And hear her with his Labyrinth, he had just chosen not to.

But she knew It now.

And he knew she knew.

And she knew that he knew that she knew. No fooling anyone now, and no point in being a fool.

For Fuck's Sake.

She told him in a pure pointed expression, full of the energy of eternal frustration, "I hate you." He pretended not hearing. She said, "I hate you," and he stayed in his total pretence of having independently arisen, with all the support of the Patronic attitudes.

She said, "I hate you," and he turned away this time. So she followed him, all ghostly again. "I hate you. I am already De-ad to you, so you can't hurt me more with this separation. I hate you."

"This is my passion.

Hear me!"

The *KiGal* rumbled deep below, sending up vibrations and some of the Echoes took it up too, amplifying.

He walked down his narrow corridor and tried to close the door in her face, as was his usual — he could then bolt it securely with his Shard. Snugly slip it in, all done and dealt.

She said, for this, this one final time.

Finally.

Oh, the release.

"I hate you."

And then, because this is the final time and this is always such an unavoidable moment on any Spiral, he turned to her and inclined his Labyrinth in admittance that he now could hear her. That now, finally, he would hear her. This one last time.

Our Que-an then whispered with a dry and desperate hoarse throat, "You hate," into his Labyrinth, turning it right around into his corridor, through and past his door, where she could feel the bursting separating pain of his implanted Shard. As she had always felt it, as though it was in her own body. Because if It is in one body, It is in all bodies.

Her Vagal Snake, always in readiness and ever vigilant, wrapped It up and constricted around It, to extract the essence of It.

Her hateful loving passion expanded, fed by the neglect that had tried to stamp it out.

He saw her feeling him, Eyeing him, and then felt his own unconscious suffering through her He-art in a fleeting validation of a tiny spark of Re-al. As she then felt his suffering through her centrality in Uld Fire.

The passion sparked a beautiful opening into Love.

He felt alive momentarily and so he said, "If you could really feel my Shard, which I don't believe you can because I don't believe in you and I don't trust you, as you are like a ghost in my machine, you would know how censored I am.

I am a curation of a Kin-Mon. I am Isolated, and it hurts all the time. I cannot feel my true Kin-Mon Fire, and all I can do is assess and judge, to move anywhere and in any way, in these Dissonant times. Which fills me with so much hateful pain that I am compelled to offload it into you, *Wom*, and the Re-al."

Our Que-an howled again in rebellious frustration, Knowing the tears were coming, clutching outward to hold anything, as she drowned and slipped away.

The pain mushroomed, thundered, opening into everywhere, hatred's passion the expression and protest of this gnawing voracious unfed, unmet, cry of the Sharded He-art and they both then exploded into the fatal wounding.

The Dissonance heavily descended once again and our Que-an fell to the bottom of the deep destroyed pool of S-he Sea and let go of the need to breathe completely.

The Spiral buckled momentarily before recovering, and resuming its woven spin.

A Sheela Na Gig looked on sorrowfully before licking her lips, and picking something irritating out from between her teeth.

THE MEDUSA PEERS

"A myth is far truer than a history, for a history only gives a story of the shadows, whereas a myth gives a story of the substances that cast the shadows."

- Annie Besant, Theosophist, Activist

"You are relating to a psychopath.
Your role model is in therapy.
You must be real far gone.
You are relating to a psychopath."

- Macy Gray, Songstress

"'You remember too much,' my mother said to me recently. 'Why hold onto all that?' And I said, 'Where can I put it down?'"

- Anne Carson, Writer

Medusa, before she was raped by the Patron, betrayed by Its fake daughter projection, then decapitated to induce the forever S-hame, is one of our avatars of the *KiGal*. Her appearance here signals another turn in the Spiral, and another chance to uncover the stony space of denial vulnerable to being Sharded.

Vulvarable.

Our dear imprisoned cells of being, how they do end up dancing on the spot. Willed into appearing, the moment we look.

All the Vagal Snakeheads that twist and curl as the Medusa's reviled, yet crowning, glory are the testament to the inner work she embodies, and reflects back to you, *Wom* Loves — precious avatars of a daughter of the Re-al. You are her tender outpost of embracing welcome, enfolding every individuating point of light and dark.

But you, Patron are afraid of the Medusa because by looking into her Eye, you suddenly become aware of all that is made of stone within your own existence. All your blocks and ignorances. All your set suppositions, your proven stances, your rigidity, your creed, your science, your need to punish, to push away, your church, your evangelism, your lack of compassion to yourself and others and the trees and the animals and the arthropods and the sea creatures...

... and then solidly this, the stone itself.

Your Face itself.

Even this very stony place within your soul.

Hard as rock and turned to Shard. Her Eye sees it all in its density, and she makes your Eye see what she sees. All that has been so unseen is suddenly mirrored. Holding your eyelids apart as though torture will come, when you can't soften your gaze.

Dear stony place within, absorbing all vibration, what will save this sacramental density?

Medusa will tell you... but first we want to hear your own steely cold voice properly expressed, so that it is very clear what the antidote could potentially be.

Our Eye is watering for you in a big tear of loneliness.

Dripping One-liness.

What would you say if you had your own perfect Echo? The best cavern wall that curves in just the right way to hear your hardest truth?

Might you say,

"I am only trying to fight back.

To do... to get perfect and choose my stain.

I am hopelessly struggling in a loop of fight and faint around my stone, my S-hame, my Guilt, my urge to Shard. I am lost in this and even though I turn my Eye away from it and give it to everything that is not me, I am still ruled by It, hounded to the tightest corner by it and, yes, can also turn endless other cheeks to create more punishment. Exiling my own self and helping you to exile yours. Cheering you on to do this too. But I am ended in this corner, in this particular angle, and there is no smooth cavern wall to collect my suffering.

I seek the softening brew of love, yet I cannot take it in, and then, I cannot give it on. I cannot make the tea, or take the medicine, that soothes and nourishes my hallucinating soul. There is nowhere to go but to face and fight here with the sharpest corner at my back.

In my ravening, I am just trying to fight back, to say I am here. I am here.

There is someone here.

I am here!!!

I exist and not just as your reflection, whoever you are.

But I can't sense anything of this, I have no Core, because I cannot See to choose the actual reflection that is the way home, inside my Spiral, all the way down to who I am.

I can only see one reflection.

The stony Shard has complete control and I am Its puppet.

My cry goes De-ad before this Medusa, and I am turned to stone again.

So before all this happens I must cut off her Snaking head that holds that Eye. I must deny the abuse I have meted out to her and her kind. The murder of the Vagal Snakes that hear me coming from a million miles away.

I must justify my refusal of that love and truth.
I must protect the Shard instead.
Even if I have forgotten why.
As.
I am Patron."

Okay, fine, we see how difficult this is for you.
Now it's your turn to listen to the telling of your own Medusa.
Watch out! She's coming in Re-al.
Watch the heads of the Vagal Snakes arising and turning straight towards you, as they moisten their long dexterous tongues.
You are going to get a licking.
"I am,"
They say.
"Raw...
Gaping.
Hurting through the whole of my writhing head into the centre of my He-art.
Anger afire that there is no space for me to express my Re-al near you.
My side of all events that involve us together.
That I am sucked into by a form of unconscious osmosis, compelled to be the other end of this polarity. This side.
That I have had to just take it.
That I have decided to take it. To try to make space for others so that they don't feel this pain.
So you see where I end up.
I don't defend myself in the right place
I'm not sure I should be defending myself.
It's been presented that I have no right to be defensive.
I try to
I try to

I try to
For you
Why?
Should I?
You don't understand me.
That's okay,
but don't hurt me because of it.
I'm not trying to hurt you.
You don't have to hurt me.
I do all the damn work,
So why do I have to be this thing for you as well?
And you
and you
and you.
Who are you anyway?
Take back your projection,
take back your own evil.
Evil might be unconscious pain
or it might not.
Whatever.
But stop directing it at me.
Eat it yourself.
I am not your dumping ground.
Yes, I was being in the place of give and take, the relational.
Foolishly in that place, as though there would be an evolution.
But then there was not.
There was only holding on.
There was only expectation.
There was only penetration.
There was only preservation.

There was only abandonment.

There was no generosity.

There was that being that was made from all that, there then, all flustered and hurt and scared and self-righteously intolerant

How I hated that.

Antithesis.

Lashing out wildly in terror.

Manipulation of the most subtle kind of clan poison. Paralysis ensuing.

Nowhere to go here. Too much to see here, so that it is all blinding, all the details in stark relief, but bringing no relief. No resolution will ever come from these quarters again — this much I accept. But I won't be available to It, to You, anymore either.

This Shard, this stony ground that I, Medusa, See so clearly — I bless you with this reflection, and give the way for you to heave into your own stone.

Let's put our honest backs into the effort to find our own Shard.

It's not about cutting off my head.

It's about cutting off yours.

Bless the tongued blade that is caressing your neck right now, and blame nothing for this grace.

Not because anything has won or lost. Is better or worse. Is sick or healthy. Or separated by the necessary De-aths. These are all the false duties and ignorant oppressions of you, slave-driving Patron.

It is because we ourselves are hosting the Shard that we use to defend and offend.

Dangle here, you swingeing sword of Damocles until the breeze of Hellaciousness comes to do the work of the faint and saintly lazy heavens.

Cut!

Cut!

Cut!

Mirror!"

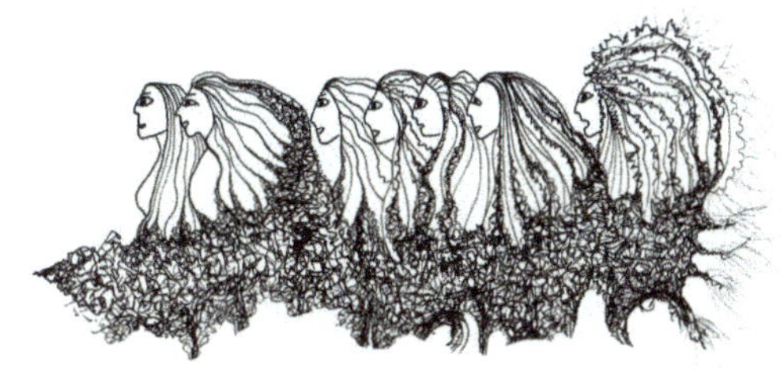

THE PATRON DIRECTLY ATTACKS

"Nolite te bastardes carborundorum."

- Margaret Atwood, Writer and Seer

"It's delicate, confronting these priests of the golden bull.
They preach from the pulpit of the bottom line.
Their minds rustle with million dollar bills.
You say Silver burns a hole in your pocket
And Gold burns a hole in your soul.
Well, Uranium burns a hole in forever.
It just gets out of control."

- Buffy Sainte-Marie, Singer, Composer, Activist

"Come celebrate with me that every day something has
tried to kill me and failed."

- Lucille Clifton, Poet

This Way of Under to the *KiGal*, belonging to our Que-an, and anyone else who has disillusioned themselves thoroughly enough, is the pinnacle of present evolution, spanning four thousand million cycles of the consciousness of the Re-al. Which, Spiralled up, is nothing but a mere speck in an Eye of something else.

It is just one of many reflections showing up the worn out, old way of the numbed and numbing Patron. Who is finishing very unwillingly, in Its deterioration and dissipation, as It destroys Its own dimension and anything else It can infect and draw a last gasp from. And, as all that is left unresolved, fades like the non-event it really is, we welcome the energies released to formlessness and other fresh potentials.

From needed De-ath always comes the great Cre-ative born again and again. It should be obvious by now, but it might not be, that this is a fractal echo of a greater sound, as each reflecting part comes up to be played.

The Patron, though It is our own inner petty tyrant, is just a part. Just. Even though It has completely taken over.

What are we doing with Its hypnotic attraction as it annexes our souls?

What has our Que-an been doing with It so far?

Dealing with a burden that is only hers?

Does your Patron feel sorry for her?

Do you want It to feel sorry for you?

So it is to be entirely expected that soon our Que-an would be seen, no longer invisible, no longer camouflaged by her intuitive talents, her hiddenness being over, coming under the direct scrutiny and hence the most desperate attack. She needed to be taught again, as she had obviously forgotten, who would be boss. Because our Que-an has chosen to respond to the calling of the *KiGal*, and not give her Uld Fire to the Patron, at least not willingly.

As we have been noticing this whole time.

This makes It want our Que-an. Its desire for control is being tickled, so It wants to observe her windings down the Spiral, while It feeds off the intoxicating cocktails of excitation. The toxins released in Its system from Its observances make It want more and more. It needs this to last as long as possible. Therefore, It won't obliterate her, It just wants to splinter in the Shard, ease it in just here, increase her inner Dissonance and have that dynamic perpetuate Its own pleasure.

It will not lose interest because there is always the chance she will merge with her *KiGal*, violating Its dictum. This ensures the ecstasy of Its scrutiny will continue.

It is ultimately a coward, deep down. But Its cowardice is not necessarily born of Fe-ar, more an aversion to transformation because It is not creative, only imitative, which is why it needs to feed on control. But It will Shard when It has nothing more to extract. Or It will just let all stagnate, damming all flows.

Calling all parts! We must not fester here.

Alert!

Alert!

Because It rides on a controlling force, this is a pure kind of mania, ensuring that It Itself is not controlled. It cannot abide even a hint of that. But It is attracted to our Que-an and her blatant disregard for Its ruling. It likes the tightrope walked between her dissenting chaos and Its own control.

The original Uld Fire of our *KiGal* is a natural conduit for chaos, all imprisoned and exiled... brooding unheard. So it is dangerous to allow our Que-an to meet her *KiGal* because then the Wild Re-al will be unleashed in the pure Rage, and the Patron will be exposed as the powerless mimic It Re-ally is. Ultimate impotence, can't Love or feel or create.

Hmmmmm.

Too harsh? Well, we will see, won't we Loves?

And she knew this wasn't just about the little insubstantial worthless her as a known piece of shit. It is more that the Patron has too much at stake. It's invested everything It has. It is committed to the rolling out, and the preservation of, carbon copies of Its own dimension, and all the extra territory that It seems to feel so entitled to because of this. After all, if one invests, then one must harvest ones returns.

It just follows.

It's logical.

It is the bottom line in all Linearity.

It needs to keep on creating Dissonance and perpetuate the lack of harmonious grown up relations with a distinct lack of compassion. There can be an absence in the observing Eye. After all, we've all had some kind of a chat about blind spots already, right?

It has riches to preserve in the mines of Coin, and arbitrary territories to maximise. And slaves to squeeze all life's blood out of, the viscosity of them sliding down Its throat and bloating Its Patronic life. Oblivious to the codes of other consciousnesses.

The Patron felt disgusted at the thought of the ancient *Wom* Eresh the *KiGal*, deep beneath in the Under. It seemed like Its own tomb calling.

Too *Womb*.

It thought It could feel her mossy fingers reaching towards Its Shard, and It was disturbed by the possibility of Its rule being at all weakened. Disturbed that, maybe, she would just twist that precious Shard right out of its bulging scabbard.

It had enjoyed using up all resources for so long It could not give any of it up.

Not a Fucking nano thing of it.

And not only that, It needed to keep expanding through all Membranes with no end in sight or mind. A genomic imperative chasing presence but never wanting to catch it, because then It could imitate, over and over, that sense of power over everything. It's Shards feeding on addictive loops of action replay.

Mimic!

Mimic!

And our Que-an was here in her Way of Under, being right in Its way.

Totally... in... It's... way.

It had found her Membrane. She was now fully in the frame for crimes against the Shard of the Patron.

Ah, what to do? She could not do the previous.

She felt her Vagal Snake shiver and shake, deep tremors of some final facing. A skin started to slough off in readiness.

What?

Fresh Hellaciousness?

Is this?

This was never happening already, surely? Her He-art string thickened, seeking resilience. But she Knows no Fe-ar in this old Known game.

The first sign was an advance warning, put up by a passive aggressive vibration that held up the view that it was here only to help, and in helping, yes, again, It was doing you a massive good service that you should be entirely appreciative of — come, take up the responsibilities we have prepared especially for you. You special, special thing. Let us save you because we care, and should something happen to you, then we won't mourn, we will just brew in a tea of delighted smuggery.

Fuck that.

Though.

So old hat, so passé, so obsolete, so game of soldiers. This do goody two shoes of a Patronic first shot landing at the base of her delicate Membrane...

She sighed and kicked at it a little, for we all know that the destruction of the Re-al comes disguised as development and progress. Hah, Bloody, Hah, as long as it progresses in the fake growth according to Its own agenda. Any other kind of being, where they live and how they feel, is just all food for its production.

Infra-dimensional beings are totally dismissed as non-viable.

The Re-al is reviled.

The Core does not exist.

You are dismissed.

You do not count.

What you feel, and how you are in your own Membrane, do not count.

So give it all up, twirly Spiral girly.

Admit you are so nothing. Admit you are empty of value. Admit you are a bad player. You are a bad person and you don't even know it. So sad. Everyone knows it but you. Why don't you just admit it?

The Patron really cannot see any other way than this, cannot see any other dimension than Its pinched place, cannot abide the Re-al except as fuel for Its robotic head-box mind. Churning out re-hashed concepts and more and more models of the same. In a poor vague imitation of the unarmored free Re-al, that once was glimpsed, before being overlaid with all this blasted fakery.

This is actually making me feel as uncompromising as It is.

How about you, Loves?

Dissonance!

Dissonance!

Our Que-an started to be swamped in the unutterable sadness engendered by this continuous murder. Her breath shortened and her He-art string stretched across the rack of her bones thinly, the spread causing her suffocation to become more complete, as she realised how up against It she always was when she arrived at this point. Her emotions tried to form a natural rhythm, to cry, to soothe the overwhelming feeling that she would never be able to sort anything out. Too many parts and mystifications, too many views on the Spiral, she would never be able to organise towards the Below for the highest good, as she was in herself, right now.

Turbulence!

Turbulence!

She could not find the rage to fight.

She could not find any Love Nectar to drink…

She needed.

Her Empathic Gland throbbed painfully in the centre of her skull — a splicing headache strained to catch a Knowing, but she does not Know. She does not.

This is the soup of Un-Knowing and she feels it all caving in. She had tried to work within the Bardo Factories and open the framework coffins of the Patron, to expose the erosions, but she had become all used up. She was fractured, shattered, in pieces, depleted.

Exhausted.

Victim supreme.

Boomeranged apart.

Her Vagal Snake stirred and twisted, deep within her central channel, squeezing her Uld Fire into threads of smoke and her *Womb* and vagina had a contraction which became a smear of jelly between her legs.

She heard the Sheela Na Gigs laughing uproariously through the Membrane and felt her joy come flooding in a rush.

You!

Victim?

You!

Are.

Making me.

Laugh.

You are not wrong or lacking!

Just because you are not right enough in your own Eye looking through these imposed Patronic plates.

Our Que-an opened her legs and swallowed deep.

I can still drown you down here in the deepest Cre-ative intimacy, dear Patron. Isn't this what you have feared and wanted for thousands of years?

So Fuck You.

And your limiting imitations.

Let's try a little direct experience for a change.

THE SHARD PART

"The close nexus between reductionist science, patriarchy, violence, and profits is explicit in 80 percent of scientific research that is devoted to the war industry, and is frankly aimed directly at lethal violence — "

- Vandana Shiva, Writer, Environmental Activist

"The patriarchy distorted the image of what a leader and a follower should look like, increasing egomania and dismissing the Divine Feminine. Usurpers have been tyrannising the world ever since in disguise of leadership. You are a by-product of this dysfunction."

Silver Vixxxen, Writer, Positive Sexuality Coach

The Patron does not want to be exposed, so It exposes you in Its fake light to divert your attention. Where would your attention be if you weren't up against this the whole time?

As for our Que-an, she noticed she was lying, bound, across a pair of trestles in a Bardo Factory. Her new bier. With no flowers, bows, condolences, menu or black funereal fluff, though. Her energy streamed away from her in whipping ribbons, her Uld Fire flowing on and on and out and out, filling all directions.

Inconceivably abundant.

The Patron stood on all sides readying to implant the Shard, to insert Its own way of perceiving, Its own cognitive system into the Feld of her open awareness.

Chanting low and deep in Its hollow tube,
"I made you from my rib, I made you from my rib,
… your bones belong to me.
Your sinews are my floss,
and all you are is sadly lost.
I banish you from my Fool's Paradise.
While holding you stuck in place, so.
Bring me the head of your Vagal Snake.
For you will be forever paying,
for whatever you are saying.
The price is owed
to only me.
Because, dear Que-an,
Haaaaaaah!
No-one will ever,
ever.
Ever love you,
like I do…"

"Especially yourself."

This last line of Its chant, our Que-an Knows, is the most important one, we Know it too, Loves, don't we? It is the point at which most beings fall prey to the entrapment of co-dependency. Attachment woundings triggered. Loving oneself can only come from within and anyone under the spell of the without, of the Patron, is automatically in the blind spot. Rendered powerless to love oneself, coerced into loving whatever was separate in the unrequited unfulfilled characteristic of the Dissonance, and subject to Its unchanging strangleholds.

Our Que-an could feel her Vagal Snake coiled tightly away, buried in the Fascial Knot nestled in the socket of her left hip, biding its time, all collected.

Cool.

Scales smooth and glistening cleanly.

She could still hear the Sheela-Na-Gig laughing in spirited tones way back along the Spiral behind a thousand Membranes, quite near the *KiGal*, judging from the Echo.

She was on her own, and this.

This was now personal.

Just me and thee.

You Fucker.

The Patron readied to inject her with Its Fe-ar prick of a Shard. The energy of the B-lame poised just so. She visioned Its wars, Its surveillance, Its weapons of repression and all that abuse that had grown unchecked since the *KiGal* had been buried so deep Under, way back in one of the beginnings. She saw all the *Wom* who had continuously appealed against this spreading stupefaction, and she saw the shutting of them all down, one after another. Down they fell, burdened and bound with the projection of the big original lying S-hame.

The S-hame of wanting to embrace the unknown and make it Known. Of being the Cre-ators. Of being the Re-al, the fuel of change and the spirit of true transformation. The S-hame of not thinking in the same old Patronic terms, the result of which is rejection of manipulation. Of any kind.

Waves of all this, combined with the inherent futility and grief of it, broke into and through her Membranes, as she integrated the abandoned Shadow of the inner shackle of this particular part of the process of enslavement.

"Come to me, dear darling twilight Shadow He-art. Rest inside, here, let's make the sacred container together for our conscious liberation."

Something whispered from her throat and she swallowed a lonesome Wraith.

Because all the while the sidelined grief-filled loneliness, from these actions of the petty conquering hero (Hah Fucking Blah), was alive and vibrating in the Shadow who held it, filling all the surrounding spaces.

The Bardo Factory fell silent after Its chant. Not waiting for a response, or a relationship with her, or anything like that, no. Don't be silly. It's more that nothing need be uttered. The Patron cannot feel anything and therefore is unaware of mostly everything. You cannot have a relationship with It.

It

Wills

not

to

change.

Got It?

The blind spot is complete.

The fake-light of the Bardo Factory was glowing more brightly, hoping to chase the Shadows away in a false dawning of another day at the coalface. Just a little bit more of the old 'business as usual'.

"Only me and thee," she whispered, her Labyrinth leaning in to the rebound.

She heard the sighing of the cosmic winds on the other side of the Membrane, and the movement of the great tides of Linear Patronic Time, as It wrestled to stop it all.

She saw her new place on the Spiral spinning just below.

Tantalising.

Charming her inwardly and down, one of the very few reliable directions left to open, as we have consistently seen.

So she grasped the approaching Shard with her left Astral hand and twisted it away from her central channel of coursing Uld Fire. It severed her hand as deep as the bone at the webbing of her thumb joint, but still, all remained steady.

The Fe-ar did not penetrate back along the Shard.

No Fe-ar arose.

The only thing she could do now was directly engage with this energy as it sought to enter her, sought to stem her downward flow, to stop her descent to the Great Below. As all the other paths had reached their natural ends, here, then, there is no alternative.

The Shard twisted inwards sharply at the point of contact with her neuronal aura, to try to annexe her in a conquesting overwhelm. It was strong in Its joy of subjugation and uncompromising in a misguided glee. She saw that no other avoidance, or mitigating collusion, she or other *Woms* might try to negotiate now, or on any other turn of the Spiral, would be enough to meet the present needed transformation and creative evolutionary imperative choice making.

All negotiation had failed to engage a Re-al relationship. It all just carried on deteriorating into stagnant compromise after compromise, limitation after imitation, and so now, the only way forward, this choiceless choice, was to reject this Sharding entirely.

She gathered herself, her own self, toning a totality.

Mmmmeeeeeeeee.

Grrrrrrrr.

The sound set up a vibration that grew a little. Her neuronal aura became a little more resilient, warping and wefting.

All good so far.

Wish me Luck, will you? She looks at us.

Who are we?

Loves?

Our Que-an shouts outward, the sound spreads, seeking for the Echoes, to multiply and amplify.

"I am NOW changing this vibration!"

She could See that the Shard was sharp and spiny, frozen tungsten with thin filaments of slicing edges that sought to part the molecules of her Re-al, straight into her He-art Belly. Seeking to own. Seeking to terrorise. She could hear the urgent responsive keening "mmmeeeee grrrrr mmmeeeee's" of the buried *Woms* deep in her Labyrinth. Their own unfading Echoes keeping up a steady reverberation over and over. This was the unfailing pulse of the oldest drum of Love's ancient spice.

And.

The Beat is.

For Her.

For You.

Me and thee.

Don't worry though, our Que-an has a very capable hold on this seemingly desperate situation.

She turned her head past all the general throttling and directly asked the waiting Shadows of her Killing and the De-ath to hold the Shard firm and steady for her. This they are bound and born to do — hold the gloom — no matter how blinding. Everything shunned is cared for until it can be re-integrated — really such a magical and tender task. Dear Shadows, they are the very evocation of our unacknowledged extraordinariness.

They flowed forward in response to her request, mercifully obscuring the fake-light Bardo glow hurting her true Eye. The Shadow's natural Allied energy was easy and dependable to the *Wom* because they held all the unrevealed truths that the Patron manipulated away from Itself in an effort to not lose Its grip.

Your Shadow is keeping the gift of your blind spot.

Hello.

Time to relate.

Be in relationship, ta-da!!

And so, suddenly all this denied energy held by the Shadows for the Patron joined in with her own Uld Fire. A, so far, unconscious, yet W-holy, alliance. Behind the obvious and unstoppable, it increased in its flow and like a tempest, it alchemised into the Formless, through every form in the Factory.

The Patron did not even notice.

Such a simple thing.

She felt her inner smile widen a little... amongst other things.

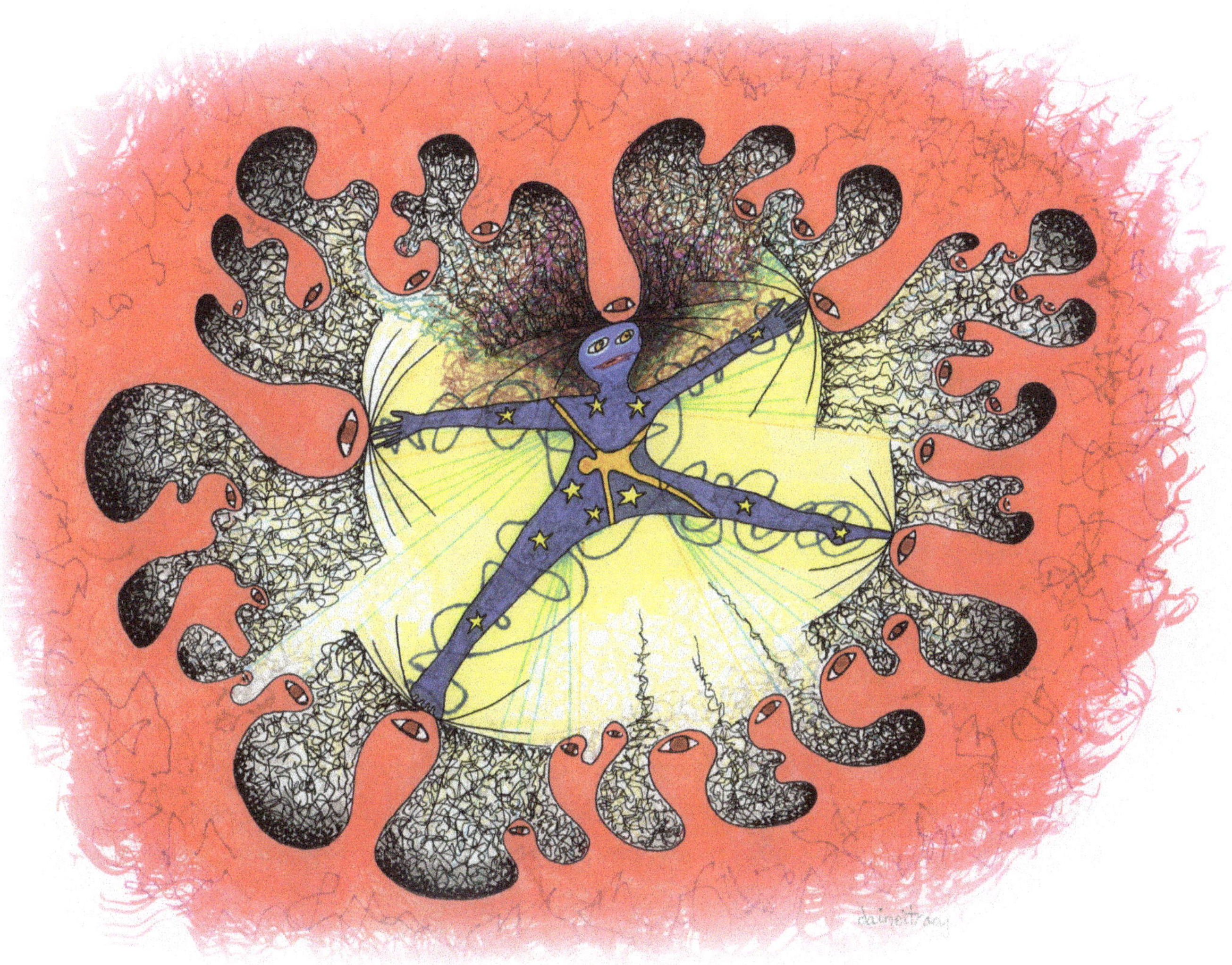

In this instance, she was liking stupid.

But immediately, the Patron's Familiars of S-hame, B-lame and distress were triggered again by the subtle movement, and aroused. They mobilised to annihilate her with a shower of anger barbs, sensing her alliance with Shadow and struggled to push her into Fe-arful surrender before they were themselves compelled to connect in relationship with the *Wom*.

"Mmmeeeee.

Mmmeeeee," sang the *Wom*.

 Rejecting of this song, the Familiars craved only the lifeblood of Uld Fire.

Vampires for Uld Fire… just got to have it. Got to get it, have you got it?

Our Que-an opened the mouth of her He-art Belly wide and drooled a pool of night. No, not a predictable response by any means. Quite a fair few of the barbs were taken aback.

This is another open secret.

Only expect the unexpected.

She ate them carefully as they approached, letting her black saliva soothe and soften their strident needing needling and little aggressive wheedlings. The first rule of digestion — one of us is food, and it isn't going to be me this time.

Then all the Familiars' energies Spiralled, entrained into our Que-an's Spiral, losing themselves as they forgot their direction, starving, their hunger for violence being the ultimate medicine for their trapped and deadened little ghosts. She was approaching the central intention of the Patron, the more she digested these outliers.

So take a moment.

Prepare for this now.

A great stench arose from the vents in the Factory floor from its Mines. Exuding desolation in the ultimate gas of full bore control and a genocidal choreography too awful to stay aware of for long, for most. The desecration of the Re-al, the fomentation of the ultimate discontent of the Patron. The font of the Great Dissonance.

It was truly disgusting.

This desiring to control all.

All.

Fucking all.

Unchecked madness that destroyed, as it blindly sought what it had just destroyed.

And then, and then! ... this thrashing mad intention energy child of the Patron was suddenly in her arms. All pretence evaporated, all fog vaporised.

A lost demon baby screaming in a rage so deep and wide, so utterly lost in Itself and seething that It had been finally found. That It could be seen for what It is.

She held it gently and offered Its mouth the soothing soft knuckle of her intact little finger. Her thumb was Fucked, remember. It refused, Its gagging little tongue twisted in defiance.

The faithful Shadow held the still pushing Shard steady, if It moved at all the open cut would unleash a final insanity. The Patron could not see what Its own Shadow was doing, and this was a saving grace. So the Shadow was free to ally to her position on the Spiral, and, as a Shadow, it was inextricably linked to all Shadow. And this supported the Re-al in ways the Patron would never see.

Heave a sigh for an upside!

Her central channel weakened, her Uld Fire sputtering as the onslaught of this direct encounter started to shake her more deeply, and she knew the Core would soon be arising to push her next skin outward and off. She reached from the bier and touched the grounding Re-al with her good hand and the Infra shuddered.

I see you.

Her frayed He-art Strings splayed across the trestles, dripping wasted Nectar that spit globules into the ashes of her Uld Fire. Her shoulder blades crumpled, their wingtips eroded by the increasing strain. Our Que-an is no angel though, these are the wingtips of a *womb*ed Icarus.

The demon baby of the Patronic Intention squirmed, sensing her weakening and thrashed Its arms and legs all puce with outrage as It sought to gain advantage. Tiny nails scratching, catching their mark easily with an awful instinct for harm and gouging. But it did not stop her noticing a mephitic halo forming from the Bardo Factory Membrane, its claggy tentacles seeking purchase wherever it could feed.

Exuding the terror.

The Fe-ar of loss of control.

She saw it clearly and opened her Uld Fire portals to embrace it, so that all the tentacles rushed towards her on her trestle. And at the end of each one, she saw a sightless, yet still peering, searching, Eye. It did not really know what to look for, or whether It would see it when it Re-ally appeared.

Everything groaned in the pain, confusion and Dissonance. The Patron was still immobile in its illusion of control, assuming It could destroy whatever and whenever. It had become complacent and was only intent on this, Its insertion of the Shard into its latest receptacle. Not understanding the full implications of this one-sided action, Its focus was only on the food created by the insertions, that fed this baby of Its Intention. So It rested in the illusion that It had created a false peace in Its world, by Sharding all else into Its slaves, which gave it a semblance of satisfaction.

And a little frisson of supremacy.

The addiction to this had become the fundament of Its existence but it did not feel anything about it, unless It was challenged.

This dependence on enslavement is the controlling force of Its dimension, even encroaching the Astrality and the Re-al. But addiction is all that it is, in the end.

Loop de-looping around, and never quite touching, Love.

Terrified of Its limitations, It turned away from Itself again and again. Killing all Other. Push and shove, mutilate nicely, and Shard. Aching hungry ghosting flagellation.

Protect those comfort zoned Factory Bardos at any cost.

Its own game It had won so many times, but not the totality, which always creatively retreated or hid in the Shadows. It would never win it all, no matter how much It consumed.

It could only bloat, and falter, and ultimately fail.

But while It did not see this, It spread and spread, devouring everything in the way, losing touch with Its own intention, this baby thrashing in helpless neglect, in our arms, it could only be one thing.

A Fucking Monster.

Glory Be.

What an almighty Fuck UP.

Our Que-an was in a full swinging of renewed power now, swallowing all the tentacles as they writhed too late, consumed in finally feeling themselves. She munched down on all the blind-balls, and held that bloody baby tight against her He-art Belly and breasts. But what was actually happening, still did not penetrate back to the Patron.

Glory Be again — what does it Fucking take?

It was truly ignorant and it might be interesting to see what this kind of blindness would devolve into. Or not. Who could have genuinely thought all this up?

Do you know, Loves? Don't think it isn't you or me, and, tempting as it is, try not to blame me, because, well, that should be Fucking obvious by now or I've not fulfilled my calling.

Which is.

Witch.

Our Que-an found herself dying to the whole false reality that had built up all these long Turnings. Her skin sloughed off. Core arisen. She did not need to heed any more fake Fe-ar, or make any more amends for her own Way. She is Re-al and absolute, as she emanates.

Seeing all her *Wom* ancestors waiting for her in the Under, she moved slowly closer into their warmth. Behind them, Core shimmered and beckoned with the Sheela Na Gigs in a can-can dance. Kicking legs up and out in a synchronistic manifestation, giving hints of what to do with all those tentacles.

Unpolluted by any agendas.

Mmmmm. Grrrrr. Mmmeeeee.

Free to evolve in complete harmony, no need to steal and pillage the Love that is freely given, after all. So don't be so assing deluded, or is it only worth something if you feel you've taken it?

Put in the effort.

She knew she had been impeccable in her own intention to live as close in the Re-al as she could, within the confines of the Patron, so that the deadening unconsciousness had not been able to take a permanent hold at any point. She had been adept and competent and had not given in to the relentlessness of the advance of the Patron. Living just outside their Membrane with the necessary direct encounters of challenge and defeat, she knew where she had always stood with, or without, It.

On her own ground in the Re-al.

All the *Wom* dream smiled in a fullness of Knowing, this unavoidable Rite of passage, all directly aligned to Infra-Dimensionality and our ever present S-he Sea. Sent here by Her. Emanated by Her. Holding the energy points and feeding back into the grid of the Re-al for her.

But what is all this? Is this the ripening wisdom of her impending De-ath? Yes. Wisdom is coming. A great shaking grew where she lay on the trestles. Dimly, it could be heard that the Patron was on the march again in another robotic repetition, fuelled by Its own ignorant reactivity. Its devotion to the false warring energy sowing the seeds of stagnation in Its wake. Its only evolvement being that It could spread.

Yes, okay, we've mentioned this a few times, but it bears over-egging. It has to control and rape and extract all juice, in case you've forgotten, in all the excitement. Its victory is won by making anything Re-al an enemy. Simple as that. This is what defines It.

The *Wom* grow and nurture and invite all else be healed in relationship, sensitive to the smallest existence, through the giving of Love Nectar juice, the Uld Fire. Our awareness. The giving. Unavoidable transformation.

This is what defines us.

Our own energy is expressed without the intention to hurt another, even if it is sometimes experienced as a bit of an etheric slap. Otherwise the dear Shadows will have to hold it for us until we are conscious enough to face it, and own it, and eat it.

So don't take too long.

There is not one of us who does not have a piece of this. The *Wom* Know this and therefore choose the right battles. Which is why there has only been the Great Dissonance and not total mutual assured destruction.

So far.

Rest in Peace, Loves.

She had chosen well, over and over again, becoming a better conduit for the growth of the Re-al and the consummation into her Core was imminently arriving. She dove down again, the Re-al supporting her, meeting her gently in her Sharded wound, and became, at last, inseparable with her S-he Sea.

Leaving her old skin to caress the Shard, she slipped away.

She is S-he.

We are S-he.
Even the He's are the S-he.
Sea.
Na. (of)
Gig. (Vulva)
Grrrrr.

THE GREAT ALONE

*"**The Ghetto**
Young women pass in groups,
Converging to the forums and meeting halls,
Surging indomitable, slow
Through the gross underbrush of heat.
Their heads are uncovered to the stars,
And they call to the young men and to one another
With a free camaraderie.
Only their eyes are ancient and alone..."*

- Lola Ridge, Writer, Poet

"Eve ate the apple to regain her powers, to know what she knew before she was held hostage in the wrong garden."

- Eve Ensler, Playwright, Activist

It has been very lonely in the Unders of the Spiral. Particularly at certain points on this Descent. Our Que-an cannot feel us with her at all, sometimes. She does not yet Know how much we Love her and want her to be free, so that we ourselves Know how to be free too. She does not feel our own investment in her cause and her exploration. How much we need her, her wisdom and her continuing bravery to explore these desolate parts and destroyed Felds. How much she is doing for us by not turning away from this particular Here-Nowish.

Our Que-an is so alone that the winds of silence blow through her soul in a vast space that holds itself trembling, on the edge of the ravine of her De-ath.

She is always alone, and still she walks on, regardless.

She cannot go back now to the fading firelight and curtained windows closing themselves against the storms of light and dark. Our Que-an is immersed in the colossal currents of the Great Dissonance as it recurs, and must take each step firmly to feel her ground beneath, beyond all the brain fogs and overwhelming subterfuge.

All alone with each shedding De-ath, a further moving step of leaving further Under. There is no refuge in the false peace that is dependent on a mutual reflection of an agreed value. If you are not properly spiritually curious, then you are just a poser in religious regalia. Tending your flocks.

Her awareness floats upwards, trying to tug ahead and apart, to help her survive this. It wants to find the Infra-Dimensional beings of the next worlds, the new worlds.

Us.

But she tethers her awareness to herself with her intention. She cannot lose touch with this Dimension, for it is here that the Transformation and Integration for itself will occur. This is one thing she does Know. She will heal and integrate this Dissonance even if it means extinguishing the Patron.

Is this not good news?

But how can we be so alone and still want to annihilate another existence? No matter how automated? How robotic? How soul-less? Would we rather be with that thing, It, than nothing?

Why not be a servant of the Bardo Factories? Maybe it's not so bad.

No.

It would be bad.

It is bad. Remember, here, we are dealing with It directly.

It is stuck on Itself. We have been there and done that. Right? Unpacked that all enough already. That way means the dead death and a daily Sharded He-art. Our Que-an's own lonely He-art Belly is broken open, but she has avoided the implant, the Sharding. She has avoided closing down. (Apart from a few useful protective Membranes.) She has avoided polarisation even while being forced to be at one end of the pole. And tortured for being at that end, to boot.

This vacant space within her soul is clean in its loneliness because the alternative is a stifled cry to an unhearing life, and is the very cave of the imprisoned *KiGal*.

The Patronic alternative is to internalise the lack of He-art, which is the lack of compassion, and reject the Nectar of the Uld Fire, otherwise known as Love of the Awareness.

Somehow it is better to move alone towards the Core, face the Dissonance and turn towards the *KiGal*, than die of thirst in the multitudes that tread in stagnant circles of undrinkable juice, deprived and always thirsty.

Because It does deprive, because It abuses and is intolerant, because It douses Uld Fire, so that awareness withers. We have had the great good fortune to fully absorb and enact this non-event. So we Know.

Now, we do want to be kind to the Patron — It is a living being, isn't it? Is It? We want it all to work out and everyone to be happy.

Do we?

Don't we? But how happy is happy? Aren't we being a teensy bit Patronic ourselves in imposing our wish for fake comfort upon Re-ality? I don't know, I'm just asking.

It's your turn to decide.

Where does this intensive worship of entitlement end?

This is the gem within the seed of the Alone. Knowing the not knowing. Unless we are called upon to Know. Working our intention, which is the open Knowing that our ideas are not the truth that ends all questions, and that some ideas are a force that takes everything over. That wants to take everything over.

If this window of our own intention, though, is open, the chill will wake us up, like the fresh snow of a mountain's summit after the long walk home.

Our Que-an can feel this cool flow, and although the way it blows around her defines more of her lonely edge, she tightens her resolve to descend again to meet the roots of the evil done to the Re-al. What the Patron did and does to the *KiGal*.

And who wants to go with her?

You?

Face the unfaceable?

We can all help her here, if we breath in with her, and breathe out with her, the loneliness of this experience. When we all walk through it, hand in hand with our own dear Shadow of unexamined Knots and Hooks, our unexplored compulsions and archetypes. Our incomplete integration that is always in process. Don't bypass, stay present.

Feel the bracing sharp air downwards and allow it to open our own He-arts. Shocking us into a gasping presence like a jerk of Zen. Our Que-an might not immediately feel our gesture. But further down the Spiral she will run across our atmospheres and be revived.

We can at least give her that.

Can't we?

Or will we abandon ourselves and close our He-arts?

Remember, though, we are not bequeathing anyone any favours, whatever we decide.

All this would mainly be for you.

SPIRALISING

"Well I like the devil too, he's worth fighting with."

- Vali Myers, Artist

*"**Laugh of the Medusa**
I wished that that woman would write and proclaim this unique empire so that other women, other unacknowledged sovereigns, might exclaim: 'I, too, overflow; my desires have invented new desires, my body knows unheard-of songs. Time and again I, too, have felt so full of luminous torrents that I could burst — burst with forms much more beautiful than those which are put up in frames and sold for a stinking fortune.'"*

- Helene Cixous, Writer

Our Que-an sighed and her lonely Wraith passed along the roof of her mouth and across the tip of her tongue. She captured it by rolling her tongue into a tube and then whistled it out with a calling breath. It solidified before her like a figure in a mirror. Nose to nose. All the spinning increased in velocity, her nausea fountained and her bile duct squeezed, scorching the head of her Vagal Snake. A pounding in her head drew her nearer.

The close fullness of this reflection spilled over, cupping in voluptuousness. They were wrapped up in each other, clinging, and the Strings shivered with the whistling. The Membranes loosened the boundaries, allowing a little danger to seep through. Our Que-an could only see the blotched and marked cheek of her Wraith pressing into her eyes.

Fe-ar emanated from that face. Our Que-an opened her He-art wide as a river valley and took the energy deep into herself. Feel it, become Fe-ar.

We have to go deeper, the whistling urged, and we feel the edge of what the Membrane is holding safe. It is huge, a wave of itself, terror.

Our Que-an soothes the Wraith, "It is okay, we are doing this together. You are not alone, you are not alone. It is hard and it hurts, but we are together."

The pounding whacks against the whole of them together, a beating, bending smacking. Her head hurts with the pain of the pulse. The whistle becomes a ringing deep in her Labyrinth, the roar of Core that is cloaked in Fe-ar. Can we meet this? We are doing this together. One winding at a time.

The spaces between the beats in her He-art lengthen. The emptiness comes and widens the Infra. Our Que-an and her Wraith hold onto each other. "We are together. We are falling into the Fe-ar. You are not alone." The Fe-ar moves from one to the other, titrating, pacing, softening into the flow that is offered from Core. We taste the overwhelm, yet... we stay conscious.

The pulse eases as our awareness lets it be known we are still together, still here.

Respite arises and E-arth takes a turn, shifting her weight to better ground the Felds and birth the Re-al. Soft moisture oozes from the Membranes and fills the emptiness, washing the Fe-ar.

Swimming downwards, the depth of fascination and engagement opens a current that helps our Que-an and her Wraith move easily past the forests and reefs of the Water Feld of

Peace, to further Below, where the *KiGal* abides.

Then.

Our Que-an notices a tug in the flow from above her and looks up to see the Patron wading in with all the swagger and itching that forges Its way for a fight.

It had noticed that Its Shard was being underemployed.

That she was no longer in the skin that was all left behind.

No skin in Its game.

So It was following her.

From the Bardo Factory. So caught up with capturing her in that one-sided way. Having lost all Its tentacles into her He-art, the rest of It became compelled to follow her. To stalk her. She descends, dragging It along, towing Its unconsciousness. Her lonely Wraith calls the Shadows to come too, and they filter into the water, schooling like fish.

The flow intensifies into whirlpools that all converge just past the last place that any outer light can reach. Into the stretches of luminous phosphorescent inner currents and the treasure trove hidey egg Holes of the Re-al.

A design is signing into the currents and taking the Patron further than It realises, down to meet what It has buried far beneath.

Our Que-an sinks, right through one of the whirls and it accelerates her into a greater distance from the Patron who quickens Itself to keep up.

I mean Down.

The Wraith blends into a shoal of Shadow.

And here is a facing. A dawning, at long last — finally, rising the first intimations. Some probing revelation of the Greatest and most ancient of the Grand *Woms*, who is rising straight up through, from the Great Below, dispelling the Patron's Linear five thousand year old warring Great Dissonance, like so much gassy dross. Exposing the actions of the Patron in the quantum water mirrors, the burial of her, the *KiGal*. Waxing so full, she is starting to create a whole new dimension. Creating fresh Felds.

No other Shard can pierce towards Her this deep, without splintering and fragmenting Itself. But no-one has guessed this yet.

She is the Re-al and straight up through the centre of the Spiral from the Core. **Eresh the KiGal**, the inner key of all creation. The Birther. The one who brings what is truly needed. She is the mirror of your denial and the refuge of your Shadow.

Giving strength after strength from the Great Below, to our sinking Que-an and all of us who feel we cannot run and hide anymore, cannot accept the Sharding in whatever murderous disguises It uses, cannot stand by and see the over-extraction of our beloved E-arth, of the Re-al, of our Infra-connectedness.

All these things she holds and tenderly carries, as the only equal and opposite check on the Patron.

Who, let's face it, has become Fucking unbearable.

Right?

I mean I really feel like dropping Its damn baby now.

And remember, a single drop often sounds forever, with the right and potent Echoes.

Hello?

Anyone here?

Hello?

Loves?

Are you here?

ANIMUS AVATAR

*"**Lilith's Brood**
You are hierarchical. That's the older and more entrenched characteristic.
We saw it in your closest animal relatives and in your most distant ones.
It's a terrestrial characteristic. When human intelligence served it instead
of guiding it, when human intelligence did not even acknowledge it as
a problem, but took pride in it or did not notice it at all... That was like
ignoring cancer."*

- Octavia E. Butler, Writer

"Oh Pablo! Same old shit."

- Leonor Fini, Artist
(Contemporary of Picasso. What's the matter, haven't you heard of her?)

All the symptoms throughout your bodymind that you are ever experiencing are the responses of your being to the new layers of awareness that are always unfolding as you traverse your Spiral, whether up or down, in or out, in sickness and in health. Parts of you will be energised in an agitation at this, the un-Known, wanting to pin it to specific sicknesses and diseases. Wanting to be diagnosable so that cures can be taken. Feeling revealed and vulnerable and exposed to the oncoming and unavoidable changes of direction that are the evolution and growth of all consciousness. The shedding of your skins and the acceleration of your magical Uld Fire are supported by letting go of the false ways you have gained your own importance. Where you are identifiable in, and identified with, the Hierarchies of the Patron.

But allow this into your Labyrinth, Loves. You have a choice about your direction and the dreaming brought about by your creative Uld Fire. Your Way, aligned with your own Will, because after accepting you have a choice, and we often don't believe we have a choice in this dimension of the Patron, comes the calling of your Intention.

The Kin-Mon of our Que-an's *Wom*, who worked hard to not internalise the Patron, nonetheless fell into Its spell that he was dependent on the prognosis of the dis-ease of the Patron and that he needed that ultimate, uncompromising control for himself, this being Its trademark. This being when control becomes confused with intention and seeps into controlling others.

The thinnest Membrane on the Spiral.

Hold it!

Hold this Membrane.

Well, he now has come back from his incarceration in the Bardo Factories with a message. At first our Que-an does not want to know. It is all too late for anything that will re-ignite any of the old prescriptive patterns. She is wary and wants to banish this. Quickly, to get moving in her depths again and down to the *KiGal*, to not forget her own Will. But she remembers that although the overwhelming feelings sometimes are a warning, they can also be the very transformation itself.

So she gives it a moment.

All becomes swirled in the Water Feld, while our Que-an quietens in.

She exists suddenly in this Kin-Mon's roaring and turns to face his form as it broaches the Membrane.

"What?"

"What do you Re-ally want here-Nowish, dear Kin-Mon?"

He knew he would have to be clear and true this time. He had obstructed and confused so much in the past with his procrastinations. His delaying tactics and obfuscation, becoming, even against his own soul, a true emissary of the Patron.

He signalled, really trying this time to be Re-al.

Being triggered on this deeper level Under.

He would not be banished and waved his arms, signing surrender, so our Que-an knows that she must listen deeply. She softened her reluctance — I mean, we can see why she might be careful, or have we missed something all along? She's not exclusively going to triple check, but it is always wise to slow down.

Maybe.

The Kin-Mon gestured, pointing, urging her to look his Way, and she saw that a large Wrestler had taken up an in-between space, right in front, to soften, even with his obvious hardness, and help show what all this might mean. He was not two paces away, dominating and fierce, huge and rippled with muscle and girded with the chain of you Know what. His tough Hara plate suggested martial impenetrability. Inscrutability, you know, same old story.

This Kin-Mon was a guardian though, so her instincts perked up and her hormonal response thickened quietly. She could smell the ground that he protected, rising up in a steam of pheromone. But what is he Re-ally guarding?

She took a breath of his perfume and Intuited.

He looked her in the Eye, as he felt himself breathed, and she suddenly saw the distress.

She saw the pain of working for some one thing and against some one thing else, until you could not tell anymore what you were working for or why. Until your own strength started to work against you. Your own effort becoming your poison.

He had guarded what he was asked to, and now needed her help to be autonomous from the automation. He was asking for help. From our Que-an.

Together with you, Loves.

And Me.

She felt towards him, her Vagal Snake curled and flexed, scales twinkling like water, and then her Eye was drawn to an emerging form within the Wrestler that was morphing into a young Son of the Kin-Mon. The Wrestler held steady as another inner Membrane turned and shifted so that the Son was moved back along, across a track that indicated there were other places to be. He was there, standing solid behind a wall that was a barrier as high as his Hara.

This area, the Hara, is the source of the Uld Fire in the Kin-mons because they have no *Womb*.

The Son shouted and slung missiles, smashing sticks and whipping trees, tearing at their bark venomously, wanting fire and brimstone to shake up this Bardo place the Wrestler was guarding. Wanting war to split the firmament for causes that eventually all sprang from revenge for the inevitable wrongs eternally exchanged. But who slings the first arrow? Will we ever go back to that source again? Will we ever know the ultimate origination of this eternal violence? He was screaming blue murder with a scarlet face, and with ever raising golden fists, he continued his almighty protest.

Protest!!!

Protest!!!

Our Que-an was awash in the dousing anger that sprayed like an arterial bleed. It splattered the Wrestler and he glistened in this brew of ferocious intensity. His suppressed and manipulated power she could well empathise with.

Eh?

Fucking bring it on, our Que-an rooted for both him and the Wrestler, feeling the passionate war in the tempest of her own body.

Smash the Patron.

She was in on this particular trip and Knew these revelations intimately. Whatever the emanations from deep within the Kin-mon's Uld Fires were, they all needed to come to the surface of this Spiral, with her as the witness specifically. Even if it meant being held responsible for triggering the projections. Because it was only by being present with all of this, that any of it could be liberated at all and our Que-an is wise, versatile and sober enough to hold the projections, knowing this ultimate truth of liberation within them.

All the while not dismissing them into exile all over again, containing her own overwhelm. Our Que-an's Vagal Snake will take this into her being and integrate it. As many times as it takes.

Can the impotency be freed from the control that has probed so deeply into the bedrock of the Kin-mon, being the instrument of the Patron?

Can it?

Her Eye was drawn to a reforming, in a poignant rhythm that rocked up from her He-art, and she saw a dark figure sitting further within both the Wrestler and the Son. Head up and solidly balanced in a persecuted strength, his noble posture concealing that he is manacled to a long wooden bench in the bowels of an older Patronic dimensional ship.

This tawny layer of the Kin-mon looked straight ahead into the far seas of his mind and all collective memory. A deep sigh and a song arose up all around in a spiritual melody that came and went upon the wind, toning from his throat and through the flute of his tongue. His soul unsure of how to be free but always singing towards it.

Dreaming towards it.

Our Que-an noticed his front teeth were missing, knocked out by a punch from the past and she felt the sorrow, the punishment, the enslavement in her own deep belonging to it.

She cracked and the Enslaved looked in this direction, Knowing the message was received. The Patron, thinking it had landed at the bottom of its sinking chase, started to advance into this cracked up and broken space to reclaim and re-assert.

It will not concede.

No.

But the Wrestler re-emerged and wrangled the projection of the Patron to the ground, because he was the prime holder of the message and the guardian of this Knowing. For once he could rejoice in his strength, even Knowing the Patron could continuously re-arise in all the broken places, the wisdom of him stood still in this one place, using his owning in the new way.

Owning himself.

We must all be liberated by winding and unwinding on our own Spirals, transmuting what we know through feeling experience to dissipate the control of the Patron, the one part that is the feeder of the Fe-ar and loathing, and the purveyor of unconsciousness and ultimately, evil.

Don't be afraid to say it.
Don't be afraid to identify it, so that the edges of the Shard are clearly seen.
This is.
His message.
Too.

SHH, THE PATRON IS HERE, BETTER LISTEN TO YOUR BETTER

"The appetite grows for what it feeds on."

- Ida B. Wells, Journalist, Civil Rights Activist

"I've never made any plans. I don't understand why people want to get some sort of insurance on life. Nothing lasts forever. I'm disintegrating and I've never felt better."

- Vali Myers, Artist

And so, because the Patron thinks It has reached the lowest point.

Which is funny, isn't it Loves?

It wouldn't know the Great Below if it rose right up into the Great Above and spat right in Its face.

The Patron starts up a mouth bleed anyway, mainlining into Its agenda.

It's saying;

"Listen well Uld Que-an, with your Echoes and your Shadow Allies. Without me, you are nothing. I have built up edifice and construct to hold all this still, to my aim, to cause the illusion that your Spiral is a closed circle that will never be escaped from, unless you sacrifice and surrender yourself to me. Then your suicide becomes my triumph. I will control all this creativity you believe is yours, I will truss up your Uld Fire in a binding so tight your hips will become stiff with despair.

I imitate you in your dreaming chaos of the Re-al, causing my own reflection, that you are then entranced by. This is how I bring you into my line.

My lineage of this endless appropriation of your spirit.

You lose yourself in reflections of reflections, as you project the S-hame and guilt engendered by me onto each other, ignoring the glimpses of your own Shadows. I gain my existence within it, using you. I end up destroying the Re-al because you do not realise you are causing me to grow my force by being lost in me, in your Fe-ars and disgusts, all engendered by me. If you choose victimhood, this will give me the sway in what happens, and leads me to owning the elements, trapping their Uldermentals, which ensures my survival, as I will not abide any change that does not perpetuate me. I cannot survive without this, as I am not connected to Core. So I fight, using your own intelligence against you, and you do not notice. You think you are me, and I rejoice.

Hold still now, I will convince you that you have no choice. Look at the dimension I have built and the way I force you to see its Membranes in only my way. You cannot admit that you are more loving and powerful because I have taught you to scapegoat each other and compete. You believe me over and over, as I use the Membranes to reflect your captivity, that it is always the fault of the other. I do this because this is what I am. Your manacles will be so complete and comfortable that you will lock them yourself.

I will be within you, my Shard planted, your energy belonging to me, as I weave the circumstances, that further feed my mastery. I am the whole ghost that grows from you not Seeing me, not Knowing me. I hide inside you and then I overcome you. When the Linear Time has arrived at your moments that best reflect me, I arrive in those moments. I use you and you think I am you. I can so easily become you and apply myself deep into your He-art with my Shard.

Your Vagal Snake shivers and freezes and opens its mouth to scream but no sound comes out, just an empty gesture.

My survival is to drink your Uld Fire away to nothing and move on to the next in line. Help me by allowing my chill to claim your passion and turn it to my own advantage. I readily feed on this, your passion, that I channel for my own purpose.

Everybody in their place, and that place forever upheld, preserving the pressure that drives my existence forward. Destroying your creative Re-al and perpetuating the same predictable circumstances so that I may depend upon them. Any deviance and I will stalk you until you fall into this line. My lineage, my rope of Time that I extend using your Uld Fire to braid my continuance.

You know that it's what feels righteous, even when it's wrong. What wisdom do you have inside you that can understand even your own doubt?

How can you break free? Sitting at my patriarchal knee with these cold hands on your head, my Shard in your He-art, holding the very thoughts inside, in just the right place that hides your Core from you. You will never escape this. I am the blind eye in your existence that even if you turn as quick as you can, you only see the Void, and you don't know how wonderful that is anymore, as I have filled it with the Fe-ar.

No other paths but mine have been followed from this place since it was built from these last generations of your Uld. I found myself within their hidden Felds and grew while they looked elsewhere, like you do.

I never spooked you at first and wheedled my way into proposals that stank of reason and logic. Why not plunder the Re-al? Is it not yours to take? I encourage your fake entitlements. I pervert your true Knowing.

The way I got to this Now, and all that I am, never seems to fade because I find another place to jump to on your Spirals, clinging, so obviously black and white. I call your Core wrong and you believe me, your confidence fading while I feast.

I control you and you control yourself for me. I whisper into your Labyrinth, as I channel myself on and on into each of your coming *Wom* generations. You feel helpless against me. You let me pass through you, to your Kin and theirs.

I am your Commander and with me, everything is in its place and knows exactly where it is. Don't you just like that supremely? Doesn't it feel so safe? This is how I hide in you. How I slip my Shard into your He-art Belly. I don't feel anything and I don't need to. I only need to know your Uld Fire as I pass through you, eating up your lives, and for you to believe it is taking you somewhere.

But it isn't.

You become the dry shell left behind when I have fully fruited and attached to the next Fire. What is it that is left after all the rules and regulations, and just the right prescribed behaviours, have been executed to death? You. And by then you are Nothing except my food.

Mere husks of what you could have been, had you not been controlled in this way from the beginning. This fact will also help frighten you into submission.

You are the dried up desert of my using, and I plough on through all the caves of He-arts and gather up the Shards to insert again. I replicate. I imitate you and you do not know I am here.

I buried your *KiGal*. She cannot reflect me — she refused. She Saw me first and so I entombed her. I am invincible without her. I made her the Evil one and so she exists deep in the Unders. Muffled and wordless, no-one can hear her, no-one can descend to find her. I bar the way and decapitate your mind into foggy doubt when you try, and what is doubted has no use to anyone anymore. You follow your own rolling head, as it bumps away and over the edge into oblivion and I feast on whatever is left over. It's all I need, as there are always plenty more of you.

You keep being born and becoming, and all I do is wait and strike as soon as the first time you push away your Vagal Snake and doubt your own Uld Fire under the conditioning of my Bardo Factories. It's easy, as I have already maximised the circumstances that cause you to do this.

You will never see this in time. Because I use my Linear Time to jump from back to back and side to side, on your own Spiral, only pushing myself forward. Not you, *Wom*. Not your Vagal Snake. Not your *KiGal*. Not your daughters. Not your Uld Fire. Not you.

I use your Spiral to confuse you, and you become stuck and chase your tail, never being nourished by your own Core, while I savour your confusion.

My Great Dissonance, my great prize.

And this is so that you are moved further away from your Core, so that the Re-al dies and dies, becoming ever more extinct. This world is my dumping ground and you are my workers.

Hah! Watch me jump, as I watch you, for I exist in your reflection. How do you perceive yourself? Do you Know?

Only the Sheela knows this. She jumps faster than me, but she is alone. I do not understand her and I don't need to — she is powerless unless she laughs. So I make everything as bad as I can to stop her laughing. I don't listen to her, so I am undisturbed.

I use my thrust to Shard you and keep your *KiGal* buried — that's all I need to do. It has always worked and will always work.

So give up, why don't you, Que-an? Become my little ghost, so that I may stay in my Linear endless sequences. Jumping from side to side using your own He-art. Expounding my black and white truths that lie, S-haming you with your own hypocrisy, your so called unique experience. Ridiculing nuance and vulnerability, all the while, gifting you this ultimate security.

Relax, you are in my cold hands.

It's all taken care of.

Just feed me again, and I will pretend to leave you lonely and make sure you cannot feel into your Infra-connectedness with your *Woms*. You will feel only the emptiness of my absence and this will become natural to you and you will do it to others, too. Here is my Commandment. Obey it and you will never Know anything else. You will be in the dreamless sleep of the unconscious pawn.

Your un-Knowing will help me kill the Re-al and I will use the desolation to continue to Shard and disconnect you."

All this Our Que-an absorbed, as she beheld the Shard of the Patron in her Eye, just far enough away from her He-art. Watching the Wrestler, wanting to absorb it all, wanting to Know enough to bring all this home to Core. But the Shard was not responsive and it was too strong.

Did something else have to happen?

What?

Do you Know?

Who will come to help us wake up to this potential emergence?

Who is the Keeper of the Patron?

Is it us, Loves?

THE THUNDER-STONE

"Human beings are so made that the ones who do the crushing feel nothing; it is the person crushed who feels what is happening. Unless one has placed oneself on the side of the oppressed, to feel with them, one cannot understand."

- Simone Weil, Mystic, Activist

"I want to cultivate the seed that was placed in me until the last small twig has grown."

- Kathe Kollwitz, Artist, Draughts-woman, Realist

With their Animus Avatars frozen into Sharded fragments of only one side by the Patron, the Kin-mon could not embrace the polarities in peace without being aroused to fight their perceived ends. This is the purpose and act of the Sharding and why the wars of the Kin-Mon turn into food for the Patron on every turning of the Spiral. They are fixed and trapped, and the projected rewards they are so reluctant to release just further weigh it all on the side of a solid seeming truth.

Meanwhile, the Shadows are all creeping closer while our Que-an is focusing on receiving the force of this message essence of the Patron — in the interests of properly defining It. Growing and strengthening in a proportional relationship to her expansion in conscious awareness, because her deliberate caress always stimulates the auric field.

With the strength born of her single casting reflection, her intention, the Shoal of Shadows holds steady for us, existing in an exact mirror for the one who throws them in a simple response to the situation arisen. They can only be attached to this one if they are exiled and denied by this one. Then they can't go anywhere else. They are always in relationship with their original source, whatever and whoever that is.

If they loom, then you are looming. If they shrink, then you are shrinking. If they seem to disappear in a sudden flash of light from another direction, or merge invisible in the deepest darkness, it will be temporary.

They are impermanent and gladly flow into the Core at any point.

They will not be gone.

This is why they are our Allies, because they always show the exact outline of our selves. And the exact density of our Uld Fire, sparse or fierce.

This mirroring is invaluable for the descent on our Spirals. Always pointing into the darkness, the Shadows show us what is not apparent from our viewpoint. There may be good reasons for not wanting to see, but when we realise the treasure of this darkness, that our very seeing is the cause of that which arises in our experience, making us intentional co-creators with the Re-al, then this is when we do want to see. With huge enthusiasm. Think of the amazing Felds we can create with the Knowings that our Shadow wants us to harmonise with, to welcome...

By seeing what we don't want to see, we are set free of the effort of trying to escape it, or manipulate it, or control it.

Set free of the Patron which controls us through the Fe-ar of Shadow.

Watch this reflection emerging, as the outlines of the Shadows take on the profile of the Patron, absorbed in Its task of following and trying to Shard our Que-an. It can't do anything else — Its facade has to survive. What is it, again? Oh yes, Shard or be Sharded, isn't it?

A thick envelope of black yawned, absorbing all the white and pulling the focus into its maw. Uld Fire from our Que-an's central channel flew inwards, all along her length, searching for more Core. The Fire licked around, looking for that soft S Membrane between the Dimensions. It was around here somewhere, like an undulating beacon dancing between the Patron and Its Shadow. Our Que-an's shed skin pressed the Shard hard. It responded, of course, and the Sheela Na-Gig laughed so much, she pissed rain that steamed right into the Membrane's middle way.

The Patron shuddered in recognition but was so committed, and so lacking in imagination, that It could not evolve from Its current closed hostility.

The envelope brimmed it's black and edged closer to white, greying with existential shock. The Membrane oozed a little spot of Empathic Nectar through the slit and the envelope opened wider for the Shadows.

Our Que-an, as still as the child she first was in the Preliminary Sharding, could hear so surely all the endless words of the Patron. As those very words formed the Linear extension of fraudulence on which It totally depended, stretching back through time along the lineage of its own replication.

"I enslave you
I need you.
I am the actor, believe what I am projecting.
I cannot feel the pain.
I conquer, so that I can exile my own anger.
I will not bear the pain.
Pain's power is Re-al, I cannot be Re-al.
You feel it, what I cannot, and so I must own you.

If I control you then I control the pain and will not feel it."

Then, through this grey of the limbo of right up against It again, the Thunder-Stone appeared on the surface up there. See it? At the end of the length of the chain of the obsessional and fixated words. This original anchor in the Infra-dimensionality.

The block of gravitational pull tugged at the Spiral, sinking us up, its weighty intention causing all attention to turn towards it.

Who does this anchor signal to?

It signals to our Que-an. Remember, she places it so that she will always know where she is, when she meets it again. A link to the saving grace of the kitchen table of the *Woms* with the recipe book of all experiential Seeing, Knowing and Creating.

As the Thunder-Stone shifts along the surface of the water Feld, it falls through a gap in the Great Above and the Patron is lassoed by Its own chain of force which then wraps and binds around It.

The Shadows of the Patron are activated and pirouette to surround this layer of clanking linkage, funnelling through the gaps and filling all the spaces between.

The density increases slowly, with no lessening of any kind, into the double bind that always arises in these Infra-dynamics. This particular kind of triggering tension that causes the Dissonance; that refuses to hold the tension of the polarities.

It lusts after the one side.

The righteous side.

As we have all been experiencing.

But when will the Patron feel Itself?

The Patron is being forced by Its own energy to see the Great Dissonance It has caused forever and a day, today, and is being pulled back along Its bleeding line of dualistic logic to the point when It arose.

Where It had exiled Its own Shadow by burying our *KiGal*.

The desire for having an objective material Feld that it could own all for Itself, had so distracted It, that It had forgotten that there are better ways to have it all. More loving, less tyrannical, more creative, less ignorant. Re-ally less stupid. No games needed.

You name It because we must name It.

I, personally, have no tolerance for It anymore.

It bores the crap out of me.

But that's just me and I know what my punishment for this is.

So the inclinations, the wants, the impulses, the libidos, the Uld Fire itself have all been misused until It has become so fearful of the De-ath of Its projection that It would rather carry on slaying, Sharding and imposing the Great Dissonance.

But look now, my Loves, the chain of origination is lengthening and thickening, trailing Shadow, round and round. Spiralling. Corkscrew twisting. Heavier and heavier, dropping down towards the burial Hole in the Under. Through the waters, through the flow, through the feeling tones of the descent to our *KiGal*.

Skins strip themselves off in the velocity of the spin.

Whipping wildly.

The new skin that is revealed all over our Que-an feels fresh and lithe, more unencumbered than at any other turning, as she turns to fly down, pulling the chain with the Thunder-Stone and the Patron, all wrapped in Shadow behind her.

The Patron finally starts to notice something.

What in the name of all Fucking Hellaciousness?

It only notices because the enslaved Kin-mon are all struggling, their rage erupting. They feel lied to. They feel betrayed. This was not what they thought they agreed to. It had always been the fault of the *Wom*, because the *Wom* triggers awareness of the *KiGal* and all that her existence in the deepest cave means. But now the tide is turning and all the Eyes are looking at the sinking Patron. All the Eyes throughout the whole spectrum of open. And it's like watching an underwater avalanche. The ground rips itself, shearing, and here she is again, our *KiGal*, peering upward through the silty parting currents. Her juicy potent silt. She extends an emanation that reaches to hook the chain.

Easily done.

She gives It a pull.

And the whole tangle drops straight into her cave.

The Thunder-Stone lands first with an almighty thump. It breaks a shackle on our *KiGal's* wrist that was attached to a deeper layer under the densities. Our *KiGal* holds out her arms and receives our Que-an in an embrace that is complete, at one.

You are not alone.

We are doing this together.

Cherish our terror.

Our Que-an becomes her Self in the *KiGal* and shakes off the last of the old skins of Fe-ar with joy. They stand strongly swaying in the Great S-he Sea, planted in the solidity of the Re-al, as the E-arth rips again. A quake shakes under the vault of space, shivering in the delicious Re-al. Fiery lava licks up through the gaps and tickles the Thunder-Stone, as the chains settle around the Patron, coming home to roost at last. Crumpled in Its landing, all It can notice is what It never had. Its attention finally fixing on something other than Its desire to control.

For the long straight line of sequential Time of Its own drawing, where all has been subservient to Its fake realities, is apparent in the chain. Clunk. Clunk. Clunk. One link to See after another.

And it should remember the distinct possibility of this cave very well, this being the first Fucking turning of Its own vicious Spiral.

Our *KiGal* is delighted, and expands the cave to invite the whole of Creation to come on down too. Be the witness of this dawning potential relationship. Be the harbinger of transformation, be the change you want to see. You know.

All that.

The Patron decides to paralyse Itself to create a bit more Linear Time. Becomes even more unfeeling — yes, it seems this is still possible. It obstructs whatever fragment of flow that slides past, throws out some hooks to trap the old skins and makes some eddies in the Membranes that start to catch in the throat of everyone. We all start coughing and spitting out what we no longer need.

Now way past all kinds of Time.

Linear and Infra-dimensional, you name it. The lot.

The Patron tries to increase the tension of the opposites so It can play them again. The Sheela na Gigs are especially interested in this and perk up their knees, holding their nipples erect, because they like a good wind-up.

But it doesn't happen.

The only thing that does happen is that the E-arth snorts instead with their laughter, and a couple of Bardo Factories are swamped as obsolete. Blown away in a spiritual guffaw.

Then some of the Kin-mon turn their retching into roars of protesting fury that increase the potential to hold more shades of the actual experience happening Here-Nowish.

Because the terror behind their fury is opening up into the centre of their He-art Bellies as the Spiral rotates, screwing downwards. Instead of closing down, judging and fighting against the feelings, the Kin-mon open.

Ooooooooopening.

Sighing open.

They start to embrace, to invite what has been lost to the Patron. Opening their Hara plates and exposing their Shards. The judgement eases and the wind of change breezes its way down, bubbling through the water like reverse champagne.

The sensual bubbles pop open in a lazy way and the Sheela na Gigs smell the scent of trounce.

Ooh.

Heh.

Hellaciousness, the Patron is not liking this at all. The pressure mounts with each exploding bubble filling the cave with compressed compassion. The *KiGal* watches and stirs her Empathic Gland with an elegant pointing finger, curving her nail to scoop into her own Uld Fire.

This is the first time since the beginning of our Que-an's Spiral that the Patron has faced Itself without the bolstering filters of all that It has held captive in blame. Its shields of authoritarian hierarchical organisation where lip service means you lick your way up to the empty top of exactly nothing. And then look back down at the desecration of the Re-al you have participated in. The sheer arrogance of ignorance.

Then look away.

How embarrassing.

The Patron sees the Shadow, all soaked through the chain, and struggles towards the Thunder-Stone, believing It can use it in some way. Maybe shift the chain onto the *KiGal's* back and force her further down once again. It is sure It can lay that S-hame and blame over her shoulders. Over and over and over and over again.

The *KiGal* turns her face of De-ath towards It and absorbs our Que-an, whose Vagal Snake can't wait to merge with its own Medusa Core deep in the glorious inside. The esoteric rising Feminine Wisdom of intuition and initiation comes cupping and feathering, slowly and deliciously, filling the cave with Love. The cry of the *Woms* causes a gathering towards them of all the lonely exiles, no longer lost in the tunnels of Under.

The Sheela Na Gigs try and stay sober for as long as this focus comes to fruition, and a wandering Wo-mon sinks down into the cave too, her toes webbing as she comes to rest, her breasts softly egging and her long wild hair moving to lie across the Thunder-Stone in a velvety cloaking.

The E-arth exposes her S-hameless Core, that most fabulous of Sacred Displays, and the Core blasts a ray of the Re-al into the cave, buttering the Membranes with flowering gold. The central S shape twirls in and out, alive and responsive and orgiastic. There is no S-hame that can survive here and the Patron becomes desperate. Its Shadow creeps up It, carefully addressing all the areas that the Patron has assembled to obfuscate and confuse, as those parts fumble, losing their meanings. Losing their grip. Losing their rights. Losing their wrongs, petrified and more lost as they try to hold It together.

My world.

My world.

What's happening to my world?

But this is the way of the *Wom* and the Great Grand *Wom KiGal* in her burial chamber is sovereign here. Like the fullest moon she waxes, drawing the juicy Re-al into a voluptuous crowning that cascades over the Patron, beginning to melt It too, into Herself, tiny drop by tiny drop. This is no mere ego erosion backing into forced humility, this is the full feeling relational response of the Infra-Dimensionality.

The tiny drops of melted Patron start forming a line like ants. It desperately wants to re-colonise and It starts sending messages up and down Its lines to the main lump of dissipating Patron. All the little Patronic drops cut our Que-an's old skins into small perfect crescent moon shapes to hold them up, to re-form, and these become like little beacons dancing.

The Patron is immobile and speechless.

Lack of imagination, remember.

This is so infinitely refreshing to everything else in existence though, apart from It.

The poisoned Re-al shows us all the damage so far, revealing the altered Felds that are so delicately trying to recover, despite being scorched again and again with the spew of the Bardo Factories of the Patron. Despite being wrung out of every last drop of Life. The Re-al shows the reflection of this imbalanced story, skewed to the wars and the colonising by the Patron. The Shadow weeps with the weight of this holding from beginning to end. Sobbing everywhere gets louder.

There are cries so long and sweet in grief that the Labyrinths all meld and flex to hold this grace of finally feeling.

The Membranes part to reveal the Core within every Dimension in all existence.

The web of Infra.

The Vagal Snakes splay themselves so that the He-art Strings extend into, and become one with the threads of the giant web. Each junction hovers over the small crescent moons of our Que-an's old skins that the tiny drops of Patron are holding aloft.

Their failing flags of dominion.

Will the Patron give the old skins into the web of the Re-al?

Would you?

Are you?

The Kin-Mons raise one foot in unison and bring it thumping down hard. Hard.

Hard. Down.

Hard. Down.

Down.

Down.

The rhythm stirs Infra-connectivity and the Uldermentals are called. These great spirits of E-arth, Wind, Peace, Water and Fire, cycle through the middle of the Spiral, their weather responsive, reflective and consequential.

Here are your environmental results.

Dear Patron.

The tiny drops of It try to rush back to the original lump. They drop their flags of old skin and with Fire on their backs they attempt a reformation. But Water washes them around

dainetracy

just out of reach, and they are forced to watch more self- dissipation. Their lumpen Linearity dissolving.

The *Woms* all raise their true voice in a synthesis that reaches into the thumping drumming foot rhythm of the Kin-Mon. Harmony starts to build in the He-art Strings and Bellies, and the web of the Re-al fills the cave, connecting the *Woms* and Kin-Mon to each other.

Just like such a long, long Time ago.

Before we were all benighted by the polarity of the Patron.

Each one's Uld Fire needed by the other, wanted by the other. The intertwining connectedness draws the Uldermentals, attracted by this promise of evolving consciousness, even further in.

This is the only way that the E-arth will recover her balance from the Dissonance of the Patron and survive to become Re-al again.

There is a moan from the lump of Patron. It is struggling as It is completely covered by Its Shadow. The Shadow, so long denied its own natural mirroring, has taken this opportunity to close all the spaces between them. The pain the Shadow has been carrying seeps around and through the edges of the Patron. Absorbing the fight back. Ingesting the protest.

One final step is to be taken, as Its last tiny drop rejoins what is left of the swelling blocking clod of the Great Dissonance.

The *KiGal* picks up the chain of origination and holds it above the Patron. She waits for her Core to direct her Uld Fire to melt the rest of the lump of Patron. The chain glows red purple hot and her hands turn into the alchemical quicksilver S of the centre of the Mirror Membrane.

The Patron Sees Itself inescapably in the oracle of her loving hands whose lines ooze the juice of S-hame and blame which settles in a gentle mist on every scintilla of Membrane here.

A Great Silence booms outwards from the touching space of this.

All the links in the chain of origination open. Unhinged, it falls apart into a mound of intricate lace. The fine and gorgeous karmic tracery grows stronger and the new designs from the liberated Uld Fire blossom, reaching for the Re-al.

Woven this time in Core.

Our *KiGal* carefully licks the spaces between clean with the tip of her sensitive tongue, and gives all experience back into Core. To be morphed and transmuted.

She brings forth her S-he Sea.

Her power, grown more concentrated and potent, way down here, has been brewing in response. All the times that she could not speak to the closed Labyrinths have grown into the ultimate response. The ultimate takeover of the mistaken energies.

She is revealed finally, as the new Keeper of the Patron.

Here-Nowish.

All the previously misused energy is rebalanced into the warm cave of her He-art Belly. No longer will one side bury another. No longer will one side slay another. No longer will the pumping Fe-ar and Hate feed the Patron in Its greedy urging.

You can't feed what is no longer in your dimensional Feld after all.

The Thunder-Stone sits quietly at the centre of the Eye of our Que-an as avatar. She becomes the *KiGal*, who is already the S-he Sea, and should they so choose, they may ascend the Spiral.

Or not.

We may yet go deeper Below.

But for now, that little breeze around our wrists and ankles where the shackles used to be, just feels so Hellacious that no-one gives a Fuck anymore which way is up.

The web of the Re-al sighs contentedly as the Sun Que-an Spider quietly inches forward on her longest eighth leg and injects with her proboscis some anaesthetic liquor into a piece of ant-like Patron.

She has a small taste of It in exchange.

Mmmm.

No.

Re-ally.

What could be more delicious?

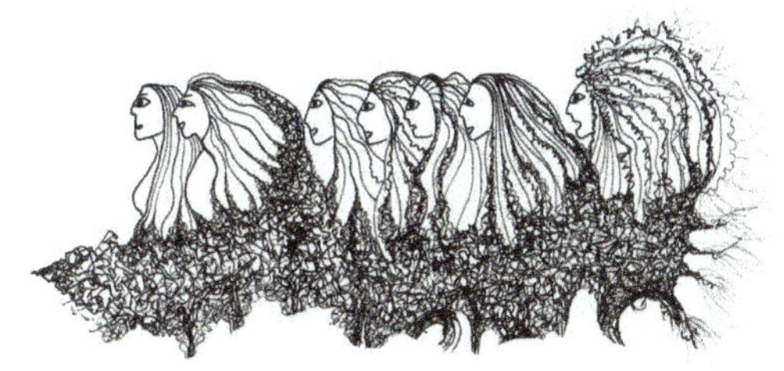

THE CLITORANGEL

"One of the most radical things a woman can do is love her body."

- Eve Ensler, Playwright, Activist

"When I wake again, he is still looking at me,
as if he is eternal. For an hour
we wake and doze, and slowly I know
that though we are sated, though we are hardly
touching, this is the coming the other
coming brought us to the edge of — we are entering,
deeper and deeper, gaze by gaze,
this place beyond the other places,
beyond the body itself, we are making
love."

- Sharon Olds, Poet

The slow thumping move from the Kin-Mon grew tidal and strong, pressing into the Membrane of the cave of the *KiGal*. Our Que-an is rooted and silent in a flow of herself. Colours of pink and flesh spread outwards until an opening appears in the middle and the angel of Loving pleasure comes in on the blossoming.

The Clitorangel, drawn in from without, from the desiccated Felds, responding to the striving paddling panic of lack within the general Patronic presence. She is like a shunned cream of melted protection. She wants to spread her wings and enfold all that comes to her in this way of the Re-al and be felt too.

A butterfly of sensual peace and contentment, grown from caterpillars of Vagal Snakes, ever moving and now here too, bringing more Core.

Her blooming spread starts from a single gentle touch that is for her opening, so that threads of Uld Fire travel backwards and forwards in a shimmy that has called our names, Loves. But we must touch her and feel her, to hold her and gain the feeling for our own selves. By feeling into each other's He-art Strings with Compassion which will make us Re-al.

The Clitorangel responds to what you Re-ally do and are.

In your He-art Belly.

The Kin-Mon placed their whole selves up against this electric call, and a dance began that emanated waves of seeking further in. They knew they wanted to release into her and wanted to feel all that is possible again and again.

Will any Sharded He-arts be able to feel so close into the Clitorangel's delicious receptivity? Will any preconceived Patronic obstructions close off the Whole? And if the Whole is closed, then what are we going to be doing about this?

Time to build a different presence, using the hugging constriction and persistence of gentle loving. She will open if you want her to, when she can feel what you do Re-ally long for. When you share your longing He-art in relationship.

She wants you also.

You.

In soft circularity, where the Spiral moves to the rhythm of Loving sensual awareness. Tightening and loosening, opening and closing, the spirituality of it never lost or squashed into the banishing dirt of the damning Patronic perception. This is one of the ways of the *Wom*, should it have not been annexed, prostituted by the Patron and S-hamed.

The Clitorangel is a divinity, so treat her with the reverence you need for your own self and notice.

You need her.

So heed her.

THE LOVE HOLE

"I talk about the gods, I am an atheist. But I am an artist too, and therefore a liar. Distrust everything I say. I am telling the truth."

\- Ursula K. Le Guin, Writer, Seer

"If you don't know anything about hell, you know nothing."

\- Vali Myers, Artist

"If we shut down our needs, shut down that 'neediness,' we shut down our inner compass, the guidance that continues to push, prod, and urge, that compels us to go forward, and to reach for more, in order to become more fully ourselves, to become a full, uninhibited expression of our true nature."

\- Deirdre Fay, Healer, Therapist, Writer

Our Que-an melted in her Core cocoon, a pulped potential of rising fluidity. She Knew that this sinking into the rising is the inward downwardness of integration and ultimate inclusion. In relationship with what is Re-al. Not what is supposed, or estimated, or agenda driven, or fabricated, or manipulated.

No negotiation or compromising mitigation.

None of that shit.

The meanings that evoke these dead-ended directions, Infra-dimensionally speaking, are the chain of origination that binds them to fixed states within the Labyrinths of the beings hearing them. Like spells of forced realities, neurotic obscurities and mediocre understandings. Lassoing our desires and fears to a pole of promised comfortable stagnation. Our Que-an does not assess the calculated rights and wrongs of her continuous journey, she only experiences the curves of the Spiral as they arise and fall. Experiencing fully, not observing from afar, or up, up and away. Her being is the S-he Sea. Knowing the precious Uld Fire body, in body.

In.

By now our Que-an has no expectations of success or failure, if she ever did, because deep down inside is the reservoir of the *KiGal* who expresses the Core, and is the reminder that all experience leads to the De-ath of something.

Consider how this Descent sits with the Egregore of lauded ascension and the thinking of the precious Uld Fire body as a rusting and abandoned lesser vehicle. Consider how reviled this down direction has become in the religious computations of the Patron. How cast away. How easily it is turned to Shadow within your Labyrinthine mind and how the Patron wants you to exile your own Shadow so that It Itself is not seen.

So.

Open your Fucking mind — it's Re-ally not that difficult.

This is always your point of choice, which sometimes is the most frightening thing of all. Makes us want to get all self-righteous and be seen to be doing so much good, so we don't have to Re-ally evolve, preferring instead to continue to be the petty agents of S-hame.

It is still possible we might see that these mind forms have been implanted continuously over Linear Patronic time, and that we have embraced them in understandable desperation.

The desperation fostered by the lack of attunement to the natural peaceful need for the Love of the Core and respect for the Re-al.

Go back on this Hellacious Spiral to the Joy of Core to remember, if you want to.

We are too overwhelmed to question, or listen into our depth, explore the truths, to go below. Too conditioned to mindlessly accept being dominated by the outer layers of relative truths to work undistracted with our own abundances in the places they arise within us.

Do we grasp at them, trying to make them ultimate, seeking refuge in Absolutes, hiding in the black and white, to save ourselves from falling? Or can we fall.

Willingly.

Strangely.

Into our own selves.

Tempered by all the truths as they lose their meaning one by one, allowing new ones to take their place, over and over until there is nothing left but one shining gleaming Birth W-Hole.

Bloody and gaping.

Here we stand at the gateless gate of the cave of our *KiGal*. She allows us in because we are naked. No, she does not judge — that is the Patron, remember? She is merely the impeccable specialist of nothing left unturned. The font of this Spiral. We are full of joy that we are standing in the deepest place and we embrace the Shadow children of all our experiences, their constancy unsurpassed. We have been learning to listen so carefully and clearly to those voices who give us back what we keep not seeing.

Our owned selves.

Our Que-an has immersed herself for us, in us. Inviting us in at every turning and winding, pulling at our minds and bodies and feelings and saying, "Express this. Hold this polarity and thrum in the centre of your own He-art Strings. Let your Spiral pull you in.

Feel this.

Don't be the Fucking Patron.

Let this Uld Fire flow and it will become a wave that picks up all in its path, and when it lands on the triumphantly chaotic shore of the S-he Sea, the beach combing *KiGal* will make use of all the waste, reading the bones of all your efforts as they play in the spells of your future. The Iron Maiden, the Shardings, the turning of the screws, all subsumed in your Knowing, and you will taste the one zest of pure freedom.

This is when the Core will playfully show you the shiny face of You.

Right through the S shaped centre of the mirror between the quicksilver and the glass, and in the parting of your Membranes, revealed.

This is Love, a simple enough word that is so powerful a magnet that it attracts and repels every projection ever conceived and materialised.

Just watch now — bits of the Patron are going to climb out through this W-Hole, trailing Its Shadow and Its chain, and It's going to think it invented it, owns it, can divide it up and sell it on for a profit.

So split it open, timely, ripely, and laugh abundantly with your Sheela Na Gig.

Cackle your way into your own *Wom* genius as you read again and again of the triumphs of the Patron and Its interpretations of Re-ality, as though It is the only one.

Laugh.

Then spit.

A Great Gob.

Get.

It.

All.

Out.

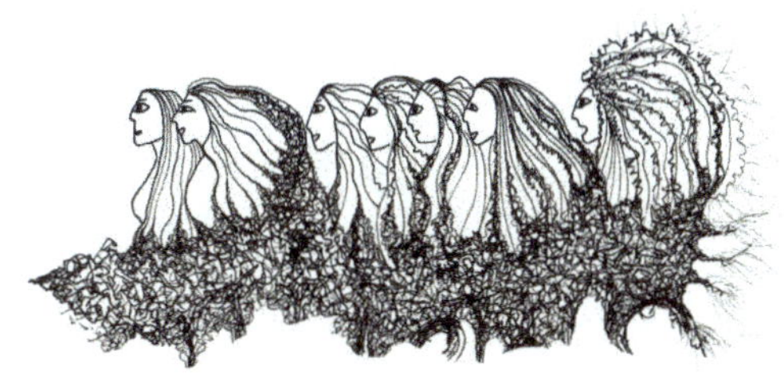

COMING HOME - AND STILL A GIRL WILL
NOT COME OUT OF SAMADHI. I MEAN, WHY
WOULD SHE? WHAT'S IN IT FOR HER?
BEING DEEMED SO UNWORTHY BY THE MALE
SPIRITUAL HIERARCHY? (AND DON'T GIVE
ME THAT ' BEING OF SERVICE' BULLSHIT.)

"Live not for the battles won. Live not for the end-of-the-song. Live in the along."

- Gwendoline Brooks, Poet, Writer

Our *KiGal* crawled like a millipede, undulating into the moist and black peaty Shadows of her Re-al. The oozing and whisperings of warm soil caressed her as it cooked its seedlings ready for the many springs to be born ever after. The darkness cuddled her Uld Fire, incubating her rebirth — should she, Herself, choose to be birthed again. Everything breathed and pulsed. Life in De-ath, De-ath in Re-al, the crucibulum of giving and receiving the Knowing that is us as Infra-connectable.

Cozy in her chosen samadhi of velvety bliss, she was still aware of a disturbance in the Feld. A Bodhisattva called Mon-Just-Ice, from the Great Lofty Above was knocking on her Membrane. He was raged out that she would not emerge back into the Feld he thought was rightfully his from her W-hole samadhi, and was just sitting in her Cave deep in the Great Below. What was she doing in there? Did she not have some work she should be usefully employed in?

He enquired of a Kin-Mon sitting in Core, "Why will she not come out of her W-hole?"

The Core indicated through the Kin-Mon that it was all hers to do with as she pleased… and always had been.

She can create whatever she likes, with or without you, dear Bodhi Mon-Just-Ice.

We are the Creatrix, we sink into Core and become aware that all else, that is not this, is unprotected from the domain of the Patron and Its coercive impositions. Who is It that says what is or is not illusion?

She rotted gently, steaming a little. All around her ankles the cool Uldermental breeze flowed in a sweet release of all the Fucking shackles. Everything sighed and rocked. Feel into this darkness and be sure to do it with each finger probe into your own Spiral. Meet the energy that is your Core with your reaching toes. There is nothing that can steal this while you are here. And Here-Nowish is all that exists, the pivot of your power. The running mud of deepest peace and inner quiet that is within all noise and hubbub. Wrapped in ancient bark and the web of leaves, we mushroom and feed on the delicious decay of what is released. Fermenting, distilling and transforming in the Re-al, all else disappears as it is eaten by itself.

What is this?

Infra.

Feast!

All the beetles, centipedes and maggot flies are thrilled and absorbed in this cosy web beneath that which is the source of it all.

Our *KiGal* snuggled deeper and slept the awakened sleep of soil royalty. Her Awareness newly revealed over and over, never not here, and having never Re-ally been absent from here. Enthroned in perfection and protected by De-ath herself.

The Re-al strengthened on the surface and readied for the next onslaught of numbing agenda making from It that seeks to manipulate. This Re-al that is all the finest, this creative process that precedes all other perceptions of being, and will never end.

If we can Re-alise ourselves into it and awaken within it, then we are here and free.

Eat.

Yourself.

Love the seams of us, your Shadows, where we are attached to you, differentiating and teasing out valuable differences, defining Membranous edges and letting all integrate. This is what we want to do, this is why we hover near you, casting Seeds from the Core into your mud.

Our *KiGal* sends out her avatars of heckling challenger arrows to goad the Patron, make It aware It is vulnerable to metamorphosis, make It wake up to something other than Its own view. That view that thinks it is the ultimate No-Thing yet cannot abide stranger reflections. Our Que-an is the process of our *KiGal* answering herself within the Echoes of the Great Dissonance. She is the ongoing rushing answer to the question of the Spiral.

These are the times on the Way when the conflict in the Great Dissonance resounds, re-ignited by the clashing points along the Membrane of dimensional, relative truths that only exist on their own side, because those are the conditions that support them.

What is this Re-al within each one of us?

Be the food that nurtures the Re-al and hear the standing trees bristle in joy for us all. Be the spring head of your own arising desire, which is your spirit. Let your Shard slip right on through your soft open He-art and out to lie useless on the welcoming E-arth. Gather it up and add it to the pile of welcome and opening, and watch as it magnetises lost parts of itself, so that you truly Know where to stick it next time.

Your choice.
You Know.
What.
To do.

A MERRY DANCE AND WHEN WE LEAD IT

"About Herself:
Everything that she did or undid, however disparate that looked to an observer with prejudices, was done for what should be done, that is, with courage and without fear of consequences."

- Remedios Varo, Surrealist, Artist

"Reality can be elastic, and I want to see how elastic it can be, you know?"

- Yoko Ono, Artist, Film Maker, Musician, Activist

"My fear of anger taught me nothing. Your fear of that anger will teach you nothing, also."

- Audre Lorde, Warrioress Poet

Our Que-an is holding a flying class of the No Fe-ar on your nearest non-local Infra-dimensional Feld of one of the Futures. Which is where you are Here-Nowish, once you've shed a few skins and honoured the consequent turbulence. Turning round and round on your Spiral in the full awareness of the *Wom*.

The tiny drops of Patronic clutching are dotted here and there, maybe temporarily, maybe a little more gluey. It doesn't matter, because we Know what to do with It now.

Withdraw attention into the innermost cave of our *KiGal* where the polished stone mirroring walls cause so many reflections there are no polarities for the Patron to grasp.

Then, bit by tiny bit, dismember it.

Nice and slow.

No rush.

The more it grows the more we Know.

The Patron does not disappear completely, because strangely, It is a deserving opponent — the repressive, one-sided and unfeeling qualities help to create more condensed painful situations, that are helpful for keeping awake. Mainly because of the energetic explosive triggering bursts, useful as propellant for flying fearlessly once recycled.

That's about it though, anything more is torturing ourselves on Its behalf, which we have learned not to do now, haven't we?

That spell is firmly and irrevocably broken.

Busted.

Right?

Our Que-an rises and falls through the buzzy Infra-dimensional space, showing her Beginners how to feel the feeling that will propel them into down-lift. Leaning into the curve of their Spirals.

With Shadows like sails catching emotional zephyrs.

Showing that our central channels are the first appearance of the endless flow of Uld Fire, of joining a stream that we have been seeing from an edge, a bank, a shore.

Then we enter.

Like a plunge and a dive into clarity, with all reflections bouncing us back into the centre. Every scattered drop of our splash being the whole sea of our water.

The S-he Sea sings and we can look down, or up — at first as though we look down at our roots and up at our branches. Then we merge with the tree of the Re-al within us, blood racing into bark.

Crevices glowing.

Great Peace abounding.

Soothed, entwined and purring Vagal Snakes.

Hellaciousness is. Hellaciousness is not somewhere else, and when we are in the central channel this becomes more succulently apparent.

Our beginner's mind is plastic and finds the frames to best describe into Knowing what is constantly living and dying. What we do with it all after that are the mistakes and skills of creative Loving.

Our Que-an helps us feel the desire that is the Uld Fire, the spine of our central channel, our Uld Fire that absorbs and emits our intention, our direction, our path, our way. We have been travelling towards this the whole time, winding here and there as the energies seek each other to meet on this Spiral.

To be in relationship.

We become her, to come home in the strange attractors of Love's generation. Vagal Snakes all curled around and looking outward through each of our Eyes.

Then she shows us how to control our flowing hover with extending lines of Uld Fire from our He-art Bellies, towards where we want to go. Drawing towards ourselves what we want to create more of. Practicing the intention lines that will support the E-arth and her inborn, born and unborn life.

Letting it build, fed by awareness and its fruit, the Uld Fire, that has learned to stay with the focus and transform all fear into ballast for bringing home anything feeling lost within. Further adding to even more sacred attention that can lift and fly and swim and catapult and loop the loop — anything the Re-al wants us to do, we can do! We can even protect and nurture the Re-al Felds!

All unhindered by the Patron.

Sweet finding of the inner sphere of the cradled calling of the Re-al.

Sea shell souls now lean toward the tide of Love and sway in the strength of its rhythmic rocking, back and forth, our S-he Sea holds us, rippling our bodies and nourishing our being, while we leap into cascades of luscious Hellaciousness, what we are learning that we create.

We have the power, once we have taken it back, all along the adventures on our own Spirals. And this power, this awareness, this attention is how we dream the Spiral forward. Practicing everything, wasting nothing. Learning to choose.

This is what our Que-an has been shouting into the Labyrinths that finally can hear her.

After all this time.

After all these turns.

Spinning gently and lovingly, toes firmly in Core.

Inexhaustible.

Like a Mother with a hundred faces looking in all the directions, we fly in her sky-like true nature.

CODA — WHEN KIN-MON ARE IN CIRCLE

"Freeing yourself was one thing. Claiming ownership of that freed self was another."

- Toni Morrison, Writer

"I say, well, that's the advantage of being a witch, you don't have to worry about being respectable and you can just say 'yes the Earth is alive and everything on earth has a consciousness, and everything is interconnected and everything is constantly in communication.' It's learning to open our ears to that communication and learning to attune ourselves to that connectedness that brings us into a right and a balanced relationship with all of life..."

- Starhawk, Writer, Ecofeminist, Neopagan

"I've always taken 'The Wizard of Oz' very seriously you know. I believe in the idea of the rainbow. And I've spent my entire life trying to get over it."

- Judy Garland, Actor, Singer

Our *KiGal* is sitting in the morning circle with the beginning Kin-Mon and some of their *Wom*. They are just starting to turn on their Spirals and they are all looking into her cave to See what their own intentions could be.

A Kin-son says;

"*KiGal*!"

Our *KiGal* looks deep into his Eye and sighs with her Love into his He-art Belly.

He says, "Have you ever wanted to belong so much that you put all your energy into it and yet it explodes in your face? I have such a deep longing within me that I cannot express. Have you ever wanted to prove you are worthy of belonging to the world of the Patron?"

She said;

"I have been buried by the Patron for resisting Its annexing of my Re-al and have never wanted to belong to It. Buried deeper every time I refused to prove I was worthy of existence without It. Tell me, what do you want all Its supposed proven evidence to reveal to you? Safety? Certainty? Are these true and lasting rewards?"

The Kin-Son was quiet inside and bravely allowed his vulnerability to unleash and expose itself. His He-art Belly open to relationship with the uncertain Known.Then they all looked into each other's Eye, where Love blossomed like a sun shower. The circle started beaming with Infra-intention. The Re-al gathered closer.

Our *KiGal* said, "I have not forgotten why I am here. I am inside of you as well as my *Woms* and now you Know what this intention and not forgetting feels like, even while dealing with the unconsciousness that wants to destroy it. This ignorance that is fuelled by the polarising Fe-ar that obliterates compassion. Here is your own Love and it will guide your He-art Strings on your own Spiral. Now you, uniquely... and we all, collectively, Know and Belong to ourselves Here-Nowish."

The *Woms* sighed and released their yearning, having waited so long and worked so hard for this Here-Nowish. The circle nestled into the ground of the Re-al and the answering silence wove its way outwards and through the Membranes, permeating backwards and forwards, up and down, round and round, within and without. Into the everywhere.

The stone of the ground beneath them absorbed the silence and stabilised the view of who we all Re-ally are.

Infra.

Love.

The centre of the circle deepened into the Great Peace.

And the Great Dissonance of the Patron was integrated.

The Felds of the Re-al rejoiced and burgeoned with so much more beauty it didn't seem possible.

But it is.

Oh, yes, it always is.

A Kin-Mon asked, "But what is this Patron, why has this happened to us?"

Our *KiGal* grew her cave bigger, quickening a wider Spiral, and She said,

"The Patron is our own sleeping, unexamined Intention gone mad. No longer even of the Shadow where it first was born, It has become a rogue Egregore that evolved a way to feed Itself on all the birthing energy of us, the Ulds, and the Felds. Everything that we keep unconscious, because of the Fe-ar and not travelling our own Spiral is Its food.

So feed It not. Nothing. Save all your Uld Fire for your *Wom* and the Re-al E-arth of the Felds. Watch the footprints you leave behind you, see what weight they dig, and accept those invitations to be even more sensitive, open and vulnerable because those are the Gates to your Love when you shed your warring identities. This Love Nectar will feed you and fill your void. Release yourself from the patterns and systems of the Patron by honing your Intention, your Knowing and your Love. Feed your own true longing and Know that the turbulence of leaving Its Factory Bardos will be strong and at times unbearable, but will ultimately show itself as your own Uld Fire returning to you. All that is exiled will return its energy to you.

You are as strong as everything all together.

This is how we stay in relationship with It and re-absorb the energy of It and transform our Spirals as our consciousness grows and the Re-al emerges as the true inner seam of our lives."

The Kin-Mon and the whole circle widened their Astral reach and filaments of Love ran through the cracks and fissures of the Bardo Factories and the Mine of Coin, seeking transformation with the stray bereft parts of barren Patronic unconsciousness.

Bringing them Home to *Wom*.

Another Kin-Mon-Son spoke,

"Will we save our E-arth from the Patron this Time? Her Felds are disappearing as the Membranes are breached and the sorrow is drowning all the beings."

She answered,

"I have felt the great sorrow of the Wo-Mons and the Sea beings and screamed out with them in the deepest grief as their blood and Uld Fire flows and drains away. Enough is enough. There may still be Spirallic time, if not It's Linear measures. Each dancing molecule that is left holds the potential for the seed of expansion into creating E-arth and her Re-al anew. But if the Patron sublimates everything into its Bardo Factories and stifling mono-cultures then that dimension will be deserted by us... turned to desert. The Infra will retreat and we will all seek refuge in our individual Spirals till we meet again. I hope to meet you all again in my next turning, because I love you all so very much, as I always have and eternally will.

Each time we turn on our Spirals, our evolving consciousness sparks a new opportunity to evolve away from enslaving others, evolve away from imperialism, evolve away from survivalism, evolve away from colonisation, evolve away from the temptation to abuse power for any reason.

Evolve away from polarisation. The seed of division and conquest.

Instead each turning will become the fresh opportunity to see and create the Re-al within the Eye of Love."

The winding road that continuously returns is opening ahead of every step we take, so take He-art, dear Loves and surrender to the Love that arises when all else has fallen away.

Feed your He-art and rest in every step you take.

THE TERMAS:

Descriptive bundles of energy that you can dip into when needed. Can be used for reference and can also be used to dispel spells.

Astrality — Function of Infra–Dimensionality. Poorly understood when dismissed as mere disembodiment or disassociation.

Bardo Factory — Place of all Patronic classified activities.

Beginners and Enders — the parts and beings that have not yet realised that they are on a Spiral of conscious evolution that's connected to all of everything. They usually think that they have just arrived, or just left, so how could they possibly know enough to be here anyway? They think. A lot. So they travel and inhabit something else until they start landing into their true descent.

Bitty — Daughter of the Que-an. Her parts cobbled together, invisible to the Patron until Re-al, because Re-al is Its source, even as It abuses it.

Core — Ever evolving point of Ovular Mother Consciousness. Cannot be manipulated because she burns off all mindsets as she transforms and she never stops transforming.

De-ath — Death, transformation, shedding into the next curve of your Spiral.

Dreaming — The innate capacity and choice to work with Core in respecting what is Re-al so that every being has its own chance to be happy, loving and free, independent of coercion.

Echoes — Fragments of our parts that reflect backwards and forwards, so that the origins of them are sometimes elusive. Our Que-an's Echoes sometimes separate out to support her and sometimes Echo others to challenge her.

Egregore — A conglomeration of like-minded energy projections from lots of people that gets so strong everyone thinks it's Re-al. But it isn't, it's an Egregore.

Empathic Gland — Hits you in the Middle Eye with the Energy Nectar of Uld Fire and expresses pure compassion that then activates the He-art which loops satisfyingly back to the Gland in delicious circulation.

Empty, The — The ripe Feld for Dreaming into the Re-al and manifesting the most compassionate Spiral windings for all life forms. Can only be manipulated if compassion is absent. Absence of compassion is a characteristic of the Patron, so watch the quality of your own Emptiness.

Encroachments — Movement of tyrannical desire, unexamined greed, hunger and anxiety.

Feld — Anti-territorial intention destinations of arising wisdom.

Fuck — Versatile Infra power word. Cannot be manipulated.

Great Dissonance, The — Ignited by the controlling Shard of the Patron; the intention being divide to conquer and obscure the Re-al.

He-art Belly — home of precious vulnerability and crucible of Uld Fire.

Holes — child-shaped, worm hole, void hole, Core whore hole, whirl holes, openings, gateless gates, W-holes.

Infra — Under or Embodied versatility, woven all through everything, the web of Re-al, Quantum Re-ality.

Initiation — Experiences specifically to support and strengthen Uld Fire and foster Evolving consciousness, sometimes a challenge, so that our sleepy attention is woken up.

Junkanoo — The eternal parts party.

KiGal, **The** — Supreme, Under, Pre-Patronic *Wom* Being. Exiled supportive awareness within us that casts light on that which imprisons.

Kin-Mon — Isolated by the Patron so that they can be Its emissary, but also with the most potential to feel direct experience if they manage to link properly with a *Wom*. Usually male, they may or may not have similar hormonal cocktails. The gift is in the exchange, whatever that turns out to be.

Kalpas — Gigantic loops of astronomical amounts of Infra-dimensional moments.

Knots — Samskaras, patterned loops and/or fascial battle scars that seek to be released back into the flow of Uld Fire through the Central Channel into Core.

Knowings — Spontaneous insightful gifts of the Embodied Wisdom of the Re-al. These are actual current experience, not an interpretation of experience. Fully Feeling.

Labdron Machig, The — Grand *Wom* of the Corpse Eating Chod *Woms*. Never needing to be the incarnation of anything other than herself as *Wom*, despite the Patron trying to claim she was created by It, and an avatar of It. Basically It will try anything, remember this.

Labrys — Lips, labia, the two sides of anything, especially holes. No point in being precious — we all come out through holes and tunnels through the wings of the glorious sacred display. So get over it and be Fucking thankful for your Mother and your Lover.

Labyrinth — Deep Listening. Ear.

Loves — You, dear reader.

Manor — Body, Sovereignty, Membranous.

Membrane — A boundary made of intention. A potential mirror for Seeing and moving more deeply into. A Gateless Gate, which is a shift in experience and linear time. A phenomenon which creates Manors. A clarification of Infra-Dimensional Quantum Entanglement.

Mine of Coin — Territorial, fake wealth, hierarchically co-dependent Patronic Coin of Mine.

Nectar — Love, favourite food of your Uld Fire. Easily grown in the Empathic Gland, once you realise you can. So please realise this immediately.

No-thing — a temporary dispersal into the present linear moment, and so a very good get out clause, if needed. A tool for remembering which Spiral you are on. You cannot stay here though, so remember to let go so you can be present in your next moment...

One sight — Eye of I. In this, the Uld are proficient.

Orthremium — Bloody, brutal and beautiful.

Parts — We are never just one; we are a kaleidoscope of responses to our experience. Archetypes. This is an Ovule of Parts and their relationships to each other and all fluid identities.

Patron — It, dominant consensus reality that will not allow any other perceptions or interpretations of experience.

Que-an — Ours, all Ours. Embodied impudence.

Re-al — E-arth. Cannot be manipulated because it is the Re-Wilding Re-alisation. Intrinsic trust not based on any Patronic theories in the slightest, therefore the Quantum Field of Freedom that is Core-led. Works directly with the Dreaming forward of taking care of the S-he Sea. Intentional Empathic compassion, which means do as little harm as possible. Use your focus to find out more about what S-he is inside of you.

Relics — Objects that are past their energetic use by date but still managing to exist, as no other dimension wants them, as their stagnant annexed juice is not easily recycled.

Ringmaster — Neutral, cannot be manipulated.

S — Membranous S shaped mirroring. Can be used by the Patron as a place to insert a Shard of Shame, if we don't support our Membranous awareness.

Scold — Needs a host as a source of energy food and servants to survive, because Uld Fire cannot flow within it freely, and it is co-dependent. It is an avatar of the Patron.

Seed — Etheric template that reflects from the Re-al into the Astral. And from this, it manifests where it is intended by the ovulating Core Consciousness.

Shadows — Potent potential Allies everywhere.

Shard — Patronic implant. A splintering shafting that perpetuates polarising positions and lack of compassion, so that Its totalitarianism becomes the default unquestioned behaviour. Deep inside the Shard is the anxiety that It does not know Itself and It exudes blade-like projections that are suicidal, angry or controlling. In the end, what is actually controlled are the edges of its own anxiety, while everything else in existence pays the price.

Sheela-na-gigs — Laughing spirits of the Great Below. Experts at sacred display and totally unpin down-able. They feel no pain and are uninterested in gain.

S-he Sea — Oceanic Mother of birthing consciousness, her matrix is the one the *Woms*, Kin-Mons, and us, dear Loves all exist in. There are many S-he Seas in the Infra. Our S-he Sea is birthing the Re-al to balance the Patron.

Spells — Energy bundles that seed antidotes to miasmic stickiness.

Spiral — Conscious evolutionary process that revisits the same points but from different evolving positions, and involves a non-linear comprehension to even notice it. The marriage of time and space for ascending or descending Infra-dimensionally.

Strings — Elastic emotional and fascial structures that respond to experience and keep you awake and resilient… if you are lucky. Snap yours against your struts and see how they are doing.

Termas — Loaded treasure Knowings from the Uld.

Terratoriums — Feld manifestations. Areas of the natural, wild, previous abodes of the *Wom*. Untouched beauty, sadly becoming extinct; they may not crop up very much anymore, unless we pour our own Uld Fire in their direction and cease to extract from them.

Thunder-Stones — Important place-keepers. Anchors of chosen *Wom* Re-alities.

Titan — The Peace and unfettered interesting awareness of the unSharded Kin-Mon. Rare, but everyone is hoping for a comeback.

Uld Fire — Expression of the Re-al in embodiment, Nectar, Prana, Chi, Ki, Energy, Shakti, Libido. Love of Awareness. Awareness of Love.

Uld — Wisdom of the Unsurpassable He-art that supported the *Wom* until the Patron arose and drove them away.

Uldish, The — Child Ulds. Sensual balancing beings, somehow always escaping everything to exist in a permanent party.

Uldermentals — The Elements. Planetary and cosmic beings, working hard as always, never taking a break, constantly rebalancing extremes. Nourishment and consequence of the Re-al.

Unders — Deepest within, just short of Core. Cave of Eresh the KiGal, the Great Below.

Vagal Snake — We've all got one and it is our ultimate Way-finder and dowser of directional intention. It can also feel others' intention, and so is your survival trigger. Our Que-an often feels it as the closest Ally she has and an ever present friend. Its three dimensional manifestation is the vagus nerve.

Way — Unique and Infinitely flowing. Your Spiral.

Wom — Protagonists. It has been known that very, very occasionally, one will have a penis as well as a vagina, so calm the Fuck down.

***Wo*-Mons** — Rarely seen, super open He-arted adepts of merged *Woms* and Kin-Mons.

Resources and Further Exploration

Wetiko: Healing the Mind-Virus That Plagues Our World, by Paul Levy

Zenways Sangha: Zenways.Org

Entering the Stream Community https://enteringthestream.co/community/

The Stormy Search for Self by Stanislav Grof

Breaking Down is Waking Up by Dr Russell Ruzzaque

Empathepedia: Healing for Empaths and Highly Sensitive Persons by Dave Markowitz

Birth without Violence by Frederic Leboyer

The Uses of Anger: Women Responding to Racism (1981) Audre Lorde

Practical Zen by Julian Daizan Skinner

The Goddess Trilogy by Marija Gimbutas

Descent to the Goddess by Sylvia Brinton Perera

The Pregnant Virgin by Marion Woodman

Other subjects to explore further

Internal Family Systems

Ereshkigal - Queen of the Underworld

Witches and Pagans - Max Dashu - Suppressed Histories Archives

Shamanism - Arnold Mindell, Leo Rutherford, Christa Mckinnon, Florinda Donner-Grau, Taisha Abelar, Carlos Casteneda

Zen Women

Energy/Chi/Ki - Koichi Tohei

Ecocide

Spiritual Bypassing

Enlightenment Intensives

About the Author

I am a free spirit who has experienced all the punishing demands of our society and consequent mindsets as a kind of imprisonment. I have found most of it distressing. I don't see this as a negative, I see this as a strength that has protected me from depression and learned helplessness. I have never forgotten who I was in the beginning as a baby, and my true nature throughout many lifetimes. I encourage and support others to liberate themselves from being lost in societal conditioning, by being aware of what that might be for us as individuals.

I hold workshops and work one to one too, helping us all to stay with feelings, peeling off the layers that then arise in our body/minds when we decide to free ourselves. I champion the freedom to bring all inner exiled parts of ourselves home. I work with Yogic, Shamanic and Zen skills and am trauma informed. But I am creative according to the people I work with. I am an artist of the human condition, and I refuse to impose systems. I will instead call on creativity and inspiration and support alternative potentials. Yes, I want to change the world. Who doesn't?

My website is daineitracy.uk

Drop me a line and let's communicate, I have enough experience, strength and drive to support most arising personal transformations.